The Alukam

The Alukam

Jacob Thomson

Riverdale Electronic Books
Riverdale, Georgia

The Alukam
All Rights Reserved © 2001, 2004 by Jacob Thomson
Cover design by Eva Willaert

Permissions Department
Riverdale Electronic Books
PO Box 962085
Riverdale, Georgia 30296
http://riverdaleebooks.com

ISBN: 1-932606-02-5

Library of Congress Control Number: 2004092576

Originally published by:
Writer's Club Press
Original ISBN: 0-595-20804-5

Printed in the United States of America

For beautiful naked women everywhere—
But especially the ones close to me.

"*The* alukam *hath two daughters that say: Bring!Bring!*" (Prov. 30:15)

The familiar King James translation of the *Bible* translates the Hebrew word "*alukam*" as a "horseleech," a type of aquatic parasite that attaches itself to a horse's muzzle when it drinks from a stream or pond. But mystical commentaries suggest that the word actually refers to a type of blood-sucking demon. That is, to a vampire.

Prologue
Sunday, April 2, 1684

Kapelskof, Poland

Standing at the graveside of his son, Nosson Sh'muel ben Reb Pinchas Chayim wasn't quite sure what he should be feeling. Grief, obviously. His eldest son was dead at 24. Yet there was tradition to consider, and tradition said that he shouldn't mourn Itzak's death.

Even under more normal circumstances, he would not have begun formal mourning for several more days, for this was the second day of *Chol Ha'Moed Pesach*. Burials were permitted on the intermediate days of festivals, but one did not begin to formally mourn the deceased until the festival was over.

In this case, there would never be any mourning. For Itzak ben Reb Nosson Sh'muel had killed himself that morning by jumping from the roof of the synagogue into the street. A suicide. And the law was that there should be no mourning for a suicide. You simply buried him and went on as if nothing had happened.

Of course, it was never quite as simple as that. How could you not mourn a dead child? The law said that, for a suicide, he could not observe the normal mourning practices. But the law could not compel a parent to simply forget his child had ever existed. It could not prevent him from missing him.

There was no real precedent to follow in such a case. The markers on the other two graves in this tiny section of the cemetery dated to the previous century. If those two had left parents —or even children—they would be long dead by now. So who could you talk to for guidance in such a case. The Rabbi?

The Rabbi had ruled that it *was* a suicide, which was actually very unusual. Jewish Law was quite specific about what was suicide, and what was merely an unfortunate death. If someone couldn't control his own actions, if he couldn't recognize that what he was doing was going to kill him, that it was *wrong* then it was obvious that he wasn't responsible for the result. A person had to know that what he was doing was wrong in order for it to be considered a sin. For it to be called a suicide.

So an insane person could not commit an act that would be considered suicide under Jewish law. And, in a lovely piece of circular logic derived by the Sages many centuries earlier, because suicide was an inherently irrational act, someone who committed suicide was obviously insane.

This left a very large loophole in the law, and the rabbis usually tried to take advantage of it. Self destruction normally carried a terrible stigma, for willful suicide implied a defiance of God, who had given each person his life, and who, alone, could properly decide when that life was to be taken away. In general, suicide was considered permissible only when the alternative was to accept baptism, and so be forced into an act that was perfectly proper for a gentile, but constituted idolatry for a Jew.

The *Talmud* defined a suicide as one who declared, in front of witnesses, that he was going to kill himself in defiance of God's law, and then proceeded to do exactly that. And Itzak had stormed into the Shul during morning prayers, cursing God, and invoking the Divine Name, and loudly declared that he was going to kill himself.

Then, before anyone had sufficiently recovered from the shock of his blasphemy to do anything about it, Itzak had climbed to the roof of the synagogue and dived off, plummeting headfirst the 50 feet to the pavement.

So now they were standing here, beside a hastilydug grave in the back corner of the cemetery, where despite the usual congestion that came from having to crowd a thousand years of burials into a halfacre plot, there were only two other graves in the tiny section, which was carefully set apart behind a low stone wall.

In the rest of the cemetery, the markers were thickly packed together. Knowing that the gentile rulers of the city would never permit the Jewish cemetery to be expanded—just as they would never allow the ghetto itself to expand beyond its walls—the earliest residents of the Kapelskof ghetto had dug the first graves as deeply as possible. Most now contained at least four bodies, buried one atop the other. With care, and by assuring that each individual burial was separated from the one beneath it by a minimum of three tefachim of earth, this was permitted if there was no alternative.

As required by Jewish law, the section where the suicides were buried was set apart from the regular graves. True suicides had publicly defied God, and the law emphasized their outcast status by refusing them burial amongst decent men and women. By now the suicide section was actually sunken behind its wall, for the main part of the cemetery had been built up with earth to allow another layer of burials. In a curious irony, only the true outcasts of the community were afforded the dignity of a private grave.

There was no ceremony. The normal practice was first to wash the body, in an ancient purification ritual, then to dress the deceased in white linen shrouds. But Itzak had naturally bled when he hit the pavement, and the blood had soaked into his clothing. In such cases there was no washing, and shrouds were not used. Instead, his fullyclothed body was wrapped in a sheet, placed into its coffin—which like all Jewish coffins was made of plain, flat boards held together with wooden pegs—and simply buried.

Reb Nosson Sh'muel put a shovelful of dirt into the grave, using the back of the shovel, as tradition decreed, then stood back while the grave diggers completed filling it in. At this point, had this had been a normal burial, the Rabbi would have read the traditional passages over the grave. Were it not the middle of a festival, the Cantor would also have participated by chanting the *El Moleh Rachamim* prayer, which asked God to take the soul of the departed under the wings of His presence. And someone might have said a few words about the deceased. (Eulogies are not delivered, nor is *El Moleh* said, on festivals.) Then Reb Nosson, as the father of the deceased, along with all of his immediate relatives, would have gone back to their home and remained there, in formal mourning, for a week.

But, because Itzak had killed himself, as soon as they were finished, Reb Nosson would return to his normal life, opening his little tailor shop as if nothing had happened. It would be difficult, but this was what his faith dictated, and he would not defy God, as his son had been willing to do.

How could he have done it? Reb Nosson wondered. To throw away his life, and to curse God at the same time! Granted, life in the Kapelskof ghetto was difficult, but the holy Torah taught that the Jewish exile amidst the *goyim*—the gentiles—was a punishment for their lack of faith, and for their sins. For their tendency to wander off after strange gods.

Reb Nosson also recognized that any exile must eventually end. Hadn't the prophets promised that God, at the appropriate time, would send His Messiah to redeem His people, restore the dead to life, and lead them back to the land of Israel?

"It's a pity, Reb Nosson," said Reb Mendel, the head grave digger, as they walked away through the cemetery. Like Reb Nosson, who was his friend, Reb Mendel couldn't understand why anyone would kill himself in such a blasphemous manner. It was true that Itzak had been acting crazy over that girl. But surely that wasn't enough to cause him to kill himself? He was young, and would have got over her and found another girl—a more appropriate girl—before long.

"The Rabbi made his ruling," Reb Nosson said. "That's why he's the Rabbi, because he knows about these things."

"True enough."

"So, I will accept the ruling, and I will go on with my life, right?"

"What else can one do?"

"What else indeed?"

• • •

Rabbi Shimon ben Rabbi Velvel was concerned. Had he made the right decision when he declared young Itzak a suicide? True, he had absolutely and totally fit the legal description of such a death. But there had been his strange obsession, which had prompted his blasphemy, and no doubt kindled the fury that had made him curse God and kill himself. If he hadn't so precisely fit the Talmudic definition of a suicide, the rabbi could have declared Itzak insane, and so permitted a normal burial. And there was also the matter of his red hair. There were stories about such people.

He decided that he would have to look into it more closely. If he thought there was any danger, then he would go quietly to the cemetery and say the proper prayers himself. Just as a precaution.

There would be nothing on this matter in the *Talmud*. Nor would the Codes address it, for it was beyond the ken of normal life and death. The *Talmud* and Codes addressed the question of how to conduct a funeral, how to wash a body, and even when a death was truly a suicide, or when it was merely an insane act committed by an irrational person.

But not the matter of the color of a man's hair, nor of the things he had said before he killed himself. He vaguely remembered a reference to such a situation in the Kabala. Just a passing mention, in a rare and obscure text. With a sigh, he took down the large manuscript volume and began reading.

•   •   •

Prince Yusef Kapelski watched them from the tower of his palace. You could see over the ghetto wall from there, and it was a good place to watch. It was all Father Istvan's fault, of course. Every Easter it was the same thing. The peasants would troop into the church, as they did every other Sunday, to worship in the manner of their ancestors, as they had done through all the centuries of Roman Catholic Poland.

And there they would hear the wonderful story of the Risen Son of God, and of the marvelous thing he had done by taking the sins of the whole world onto his shoulders. But the damned priest always insisted on not only repeating the Passion story, as the Church demanded on this day, but on adding his own lurid embellishments, and always putting his strongest emphasis on the passages which condemned the Jews for deicide.

Kapelski considered himself an enlightened ruler. As such, he suspected that it was probably wrong to kill people today for the crimes of their distant ancestors. The prince didn't particularly like Jews—he was a typical Pole in that respect—but he also didn't like the idea of killing people who were useful to his city, and these damned Easter riots always seemed to kill a few of the useful ones.

It wouldn't be so bad, he thought, if they just killed the old people. They were of no real value to him, since they produced nothing and consumed as much food as the younger, more valuable, ghetto residents. But the old people were usually in their houses, and his peasants seemed to lack the ambition to break down the doors and drag them out. Instead, they went after the shopkeepers. They were easier to get to, for the very fact of their being in business meant that their doors were generally open. The most useful Jews in the entire ghetto, Kapelski thought.

Last year they'd killed the only man in Kapelskof, Jew *or* Christian, who was capable of making a comfortable pair of boots!

•   •   •

Rabbi Shimon finally located the passage he'd been searching for. The text was an obscure one, rarely encountered by even the most ardent student of Kabala. And the passage was actually in a *commentary* on that text, written in miniscule on the right-hand margin of the page. A manuscript text at that, of which fewer than a hundred copies had ever existed.

And it had confirmed his fears. There was a terrible danger when *any* man killed himself under those particular circumstances. And the danger was magnified if he also had red hair. This danger could only be averted if special prayers were read over his grave. Not the usual burial prayers, but special kabalistic formulae, which were to be found in yet another obscure text. The Rabbi wasn't even sure that he owned a copy. He might have to write to a colleague in Krakow, and hope that the reply came in time.

Still, at least he knew that he could do *something*. And there was a special amulet that would provide protection in the interim, until the danger could be permanently averted. He could write it out in only a few minutes, seal it in a tube, and place it in the freshly turned earth of the grave.

The Rabbi looked up from his studies at the sudden noise in the street, realizing with horror that in the excitement ensuing from Itzak's spectacular death everyone had completely forgotten what day this was on the *goyishe* calendar.

The Alukam

It was their Easter holy day; the day when the *goyim* preached love, and then *expressed* their love by killing Jews. It was a day when every sensible Jew should be carefully bolted behind as many doors as possible.

In some cities even thick doors and stout bolts hadn't helped. There, the "pious" rioters had simply burned down the houses with their owners trapped inside. But in Kapelskof there was little danger of that happening. The gentiles' homes were pressed up tight against the ghetto wall, so to burn the ghetto would almost certainly result in burning the rest of the town as well.

And, perhaps more to the point, the Prince's palace also shared a wall with the ghetto. Their 'benevolent' ruler might tolerate a few dead Jews each year, but he wasn't likely to allow his subjects to burn down his own home in the process.

So the rioters always settled for grabbing anyone who was foolish enough to let himself be seen. Or rushed into open shops, before the owners could realize what was happening and lock their doors.

But he had forgotten. Itzak's suicide had shocked him so completely that everything else had slipped his mind.

The suicide, and Itzak's red hair. There was a horrible danger to the community. Worse, even, than the *goyim* who were now pouring through the streets of the ghetto.

But Rabbi Shimon had no time left to concern himself with the dead man's hair, or with writing to his friend for the special prayers, or even to write out the amulet that would give interim protection, for at that moment five men burst into the room and began to beat him with heavy clubs.

•   •   •

Reb Mendel, the grave digger, was exhausted. In the aftermath of the riot, eight people had been left dead, and all of them required burial as quickly as possible.

Worse, one of them had been their beloved Rabbi, who had been clubbed to death in his own study hall. Reb Nosson, the tailor, had already written to a cousin in Warsaw, where there were many rabbis. But it would require time, and probably a certain amount of pleading, to entice another to fill the post of a murdered man, so for now the community was without a leader.

It would also require obtaining special permission from the prince, who had the final say on the settlement of any outsider in their ghetto. Special permission that would probably involve a heavy payment for the prince's assent.

•   •   •

Two weeks after the Easter riot, the strange deaths began. The first was a pig butcher, found hanging from a meat-hook in the back of his own shop. His throat had been cut, but there was no blood on the floor beneath him, nor anywhere in his shop.

Chapter One
Thursday, July 8, 1993

Benjamin County Medical Examiner's Office, Port Morrow, Florida

Detective Sergeant David Schneider sat quietly in the tiled corridor outside the autopsy room. There were windows in the doors, and he could have watched what was happening. Many detectives would. But he had never cared to observe that particular procedure. Heredity and upbringing, he thought. Schneider was an Orthodox Jew, and Jewish law actually *prohibited* autopsies, unless performing one might help save the life of someone who was dying of the same thing. Something, he knew perfectly well, was not the case here.

But Schneider was also a police officer, and he had to balance the strictures of his faith with the requirements of Florida law. That law mandated an autopsy in all cases when the deceased had not been under a physician's care, or when there were suspicious circumstances surrounding the death. The State had a vested interest in preventing murder when it could, and punishing it when it couldn't.

Schneider was curious about this particular case, which was why he was waiting in a hallway in the Medical Examiner's Office, and not at home in bed, at 2:00 o'clock on a Thursday morning.

The girl on the table had been found on the beach just before nightfall. That particular section of beach wasn't normally very crowded, and no one who had been there remembered seeing her alive. No one, at least, that they'd been able to find up to this point.

On the other hand, no one really remembered seeing her dead, either. One of the realities of life in Florida was that most people who saw a young woman stretched out on a towel on the beach would simply presume she was asleep, or sunbathing. There had been nothing about her appearance to suggest otherwise. The only reason she'd even been noticed was that a ten-year-old kid playing Frisbee had thought it odd that she didn't wake up and start yelling at him when he tripped over her in making a catch.

The boy's father had then approached her and realized that she was dead. He had stayed, sending the boy back to their hotel to call the Sheriff's Department. (Port Morrow Beach was an unincorporated section of Benjamin County; only incorporated towns and cities had police departments. The sheriff provided all law enforcement services for the rest of the county)

The girl had been dressed in a tiny, black bikini, and even in death there was a rather stark aura of extreme physical fitness about her. She looked like someone who worked out every day. An absolutely gorgeous brunette, with a good tan, though now much paler in death.

And that was what had been so odd. Though many people—particularly murderers—are unaware of the fact, it is almost always possible to tell if a body has been moved after death. When the body is naked, or, as in this case, very nearly so, the indications are even more obvious. These indications develop from entirely normal physical processes.

As long as a person remains alive, and their heart continues to beat, no matter how feebly, blood circulates through the body. This is why Caucasians tend to look slightly pinkish, their sparsely-pigmented skin taking on some of the color of the blood circulating beneath it. This is also why embalming fluid is a bright pink color.

But at the moment of death, the heart stops and a different set of natural forces take over. Gravity quickly exerts its influence, and the still liquid blood, no longer being forcibly moved around the body, acts like any other liquid and begins to collect in the lowest parts of the body. The technical term is post mortem lividity. The parts of the body where the blood collects turn a reddish purple color from their overload of blood. After a relatively short time, the collected blood leaks from the capillaries and permeates the flesh, and after a few hours the discoloration becomes permanent.

When she was discovered, the girl's body, which had been shaded by a huge live oak tree, was cool. The Deputy Medical Examiner who did the initial examination at the site had pulled aside the scrap of cloth that made up her bikini bottom and shoved a thermometer up her rear.

Schneider's faith taught that the dead were always to be treated with the utmost respect, and the doctor's action always struck him as particularly undignified. But he also knew there was a good reason for it. Dead bodies cooled at a fairly regular rate, and temperature was used to estimate the time of death.

The doctor had removed the thermometer after a couple of minutes and compared the reading with a chart in his notebook. "She's been dead about five hours," he had announced. "Might be longer, though— this spot was in the sun for some of that time and that may have slowed the cooling process." He didn't need to say that extra solar heating could have thrown off the dead girl's internal temperature reading by several degrees, which would in turn throw off his calculation of the time of death.

Any time someone has been dead for five or more hours, lividity is generally starting to become obvious. Except that, in this case, there seemed to be none at all. They had turned her over in the process of examining the scene, and had been unable to find any marks on her body.

●　　　●　　　●

Dr. Robert Edgars, the Chief Medical Examiner for Benjamin County, came out of the autopsy room. "Weird case," he said.

"How do you explain the lack of lividity?" Schneider asked.

"No blood, Dave. We found maybe 100 milliliters in her body. And that was in the heart. That's all. I can't really explain it yet, but I'm damned sure going to try to figure it out."

The detective shook his head. "I can understand how someone without any blood in them would be dead," he said. "But how did anyone get the blood out of her?"

"If I believed in such things, I'd guess a vampire," the doctor laughed. "But I'm a scientist, so I tend *not* to believe." He smiled. "On the other hand, I get the feeling that someone wants us to *think* we're dealing with a vampire."

"How so?"

"There are two marks directly over the external carotid artery on the left side of the neck, with penetration into the artery. There even seems to be a hint of what look like tooth marks at the site, as if someone had bitten into her neck with a set of fangs and then sucked the blood out orally. Not possible, though. To extract that much blood you'd need a machine of some sort."

Schneider nodded. "So what are we looking for?"

"Damned if I know. Maybe a crazy undertaker—I think you might be able to do the blood extraction with an embalming machine." He shook his head. "But, then again, maybe not."

"Anything you know for sure?"

"She was moved after she was dead."

"How can you tell?"

"Even without the usual post mortem lividity, there are other indications. She was found on her back, but there are tissue indications that she was on her side for some time after she died. And the time of death was probably in the early afternoon. Stomach contents are indicative of someone who had just eaten lunch. Specifically, a couple of hot dogs, with the digestion process barely started."

"Official cause of death?"

"Pending some lab results, exsanguination through unknown means. And no matter how much someone would like us to think we're dealing with some sort of supernatural creature, the time of death rules out any possibility of a vampire. She was definitely killed during *daylight* hours."

Chapter Two
Sunday, July 11, 1993

Port Morrow Beach, Florida

One of the first things Schneider had discovered after joining the Benjamin County Sheriff's Department in 1978 was that police work is mostly boring. It was also, frequently, more than a little frustrating. The dead girl's body was still being held in the morgue after four days. So far she hadn't been identified, which meant that there was no one who would know to claim her body.

She had been found on the beach, dressed in a bikini, and there was no sign of a purse, a wallet, or even of street clothes. The closest thing to a clue to her identity was an ankle bracelet with a tiny heart, engraved with the initials "S.B." But whether "S.B." was the girl, or the person who had given it to her, remained to be seen.

Schneider merely took this as a sign that Bob Edgars had been correct in his preliminary findings. The girl had been killed elsewhere, and her body was then taken to where it was found.

He wondered about the ankle bracelet. The killer had eliminated every other normal clue that would be used to identify a murder victim. The bikini still had its labels intact, but they were of no help, since it was a major national brand, and could have been purchased in any one of a hundred stores in Benjamin County alone. The ankle bracelet was obviously something that was personal to the victim. There was actually a light mark in her tan, indicating that she habitually wore it. He thought it might be possible that the killer had simply missed it in his efforts to hinder the investigation. But it was more likely that the killer knew that the bracelet wouldn't provide a real clue. Unless *he* had given it to her, it would just be a simple piece of jewelry.

For that matter, there was nothing to indicate that the killer was even interested in doing any more than slowing down the identification process. Or it was entirely possible that the way she was found had nothing at all to do with keeping them from figuring out who she was. After all, if you were going to leave a dead girl on a beach, it would be perfectly logical to dress her in a bathing suit.

The towel was no help, either. It had come from the Ramada Inn, but they'd already determined that the girl hadn't been a guest. And anyone could have picked up the towel just by walking past a maid's cart while the maid was inside cleaning a room.   There wasn't even a clear indication that anyone had recently been where she was found. That was the trouble with sand. It didn't take decent footprints unless it was wet, and it hadn't rained in a week.

Simple logic argued that *someone* had killed the girl. A continuation of that logic argued that the same person had then taken her to a relatively secluded stretch of beach and left her body there. But there was no way of proving who it had been.

Just to complicate things, Port Morrow Beach was a popular tourist destination. If the girl had been a local, someone would probably have been looking for her by now. A tourist, on the other hand, was unlikely to be missed until she failed to return home at the expected time. Which meant, Schneider thought, that the Medical Examiner was probably going to be stuck with an unclaimed body for an indeterminate length of time.

It never seemed right. Schneider's personal beliefs included burial as soon as possible; preferably on the day of death. It was an ancient tradition, based, curiously enough, on a Torah passage that prohibited leaving the body of an executed criminal unburied overnight. If it was important to bury a criminal on the day he was executed, the tradition argued, how much more so was it important to bury an *honest* person on the day of his death?

There were exceptions, but only when the delay was necessary to give honor to the deceased by allowing time for relatives to gather for the funeral, or if the death was on the Sabbath or the first day of a festival, when funerals were forbidden except in times of a plague. But, in general, Orthodox Jews continued to bury their dead as soon as practical.

And none of that, he thought, was going to help the dead girl. She was going to remain laid out in a drawer in the Medical Examiner's cold room until someone either figured out who she was, so that her relatives could be notified and claim her body, or until the courts decided that she was likely to remain forever unknown and turned her over to the county for disposal.

Disposal, he thought, was the proper term. The county no longer buried paupers and unclaimed bodies. They were taken to a local crematory and the ground up bone fragments that most people called "ashes" were put in a shallow hole in the old city cemetery on Wisconsin Avenue. It lacked dignity, he thought.

Cremation, of course, was also forbidden by Jewish law. It always amazed Schneider that any modern Jew could choose to have his body incinerated—particularly after Auschwitz, where the Nazis had treated Jewish dead as so much rubbish to be burned. He had no evidence to conclude that the dead girl was Jewish, but he had none to preclude the possibility, either. And if there was even the slightest possibility he naturally preferred to see her buried properly.

Even, he thought, if she's a gentile, a proper burial would still be better.

In the meantime, Schneider himself was following up with the normal investigative procedures. Even a few abnormal ones, such as a new laser process that had shown promise in being able to reveal fingerprints on human skin. In this case it had revealed nothing.

So Schneider was spending his time canvassing the hotels and condominiums on the beach, hoping someone would recognize the girl from a photograph they'd taken at the morgue. It was a long, slow process, but it was necessary. If you didn't know who someone was, then you had to ask around and hope you could find someone who did.

Chapter Three
Tuesday, July 13, 1993

Port Morrow Beach

Schneider finally hit a winner on his fourth day of knocking on doors. The resident manager of the Hawaiian Haven, one of the oldest time-share resorts on the Beach, recognized the photo as the owner of Unit 7 for the first three weeks in July.

"I haven't actually seen her in several days," the manager said, still looking at the photo. Like all morgue ID photographs, they'd done their best, but it was all too obvious that the girl was dead.

"But around here," he went on, "you don't pay that much attention when someone's not around. Here's a good-looking young woman in a resort community. If she's on the lookout for a little romance, and she meets someone, there's nothing at all unusual if she shacks up somewhere else for a few days."

"This one is dead," Schneider said.

The manager looked at the picture again. "I could tell. When?"

"Sometime Wednesday. Late morning, early afternoon."

"That fits," the Manager said. "The last time I remember seeing her was Tuesday evening, out by the pool." He smiled. The girl had been exercising to some high-energy music. It was a pleasant way to remember her. Much better than a morgue photo.

"Do you also happen to remember her name?" Schneider asked.

The manager shrugged. "Most of these units have a couple *hundred* owners. And I've been married to the same woman for 32 years, so I really don't pay much attention to the female guests." He was lying. He paid a lot of attention to them, though only with his eyes. He would never have dared to try to start anything. His wife would have killed him. "I'd have to look it up," he said.

"You mind?"

"Sure. In the office."

They went inside and the manager sat down in front of a desktop computer. It was the latest addition to the "resort"—which had actually been a failing motel when the timeshare concept came in during the early 1970s and saved the place. The manager had resisted computerizing the place for years, but the parent company had finally insisted, and installed this system. It was the best available, with a 386 processor, and a huge 130 megabyte hard drive.

After six months, he wondered how he'd ever managed to get along without it. A few mouse clicks later, he'd pulled up the appropriate unit records and found the right weeks.

"Sandra Baring," he said. "Lives in New York City. Lived, I guess I should say. I've got a New York phone number and address here for contact purposes, if you want that."

"Please."

The manager wrote down the number, along with Baring's permanent mailing address. Schneider would have the NYPD make the actual contacts. If it turned out to be a husband or parent at that address—and not just an empty apartment—it was probably better not to tell them over the phone.

Besides, he wanted a trained observer there to see how they took the news. The most likely suspect in any murder case was a relative or close associate. They had more reason to dislike someone than a stranger. And there had been more than enough time since she was killed for her killer to run to anywhere in the world. Including back to the girl's own home.

Chapter Four
Thursday, July 29, 1993

Benjamin County Sheriff's Department

While he now knew who the girl was, Schneider was no closer to finding her killer than he had been three weeks ago. The address in New York had been the girl's apartment. Her roommate had been willing to cooperate, once she got over the sudden shock of realizing her best friend was dead, but the New York detective who had interviewed her was pretty sure that she really didn't know anything.

According to the roommate, Sandra Baring's usual practice had been to go off on vacation and stay entirely out of touch until she got home again. Since Sandra hadn't been due back in New York until the 24th, her roommate hadn't been worried about her yet.

And that was it as far as the New York detective could tell. He'd done some background checks, but there was nothing to indicate any threat to her life.

She had been 23-years-old, and a graduate of City College. Since leaving high school, she'd had five different roommates, which he considered pretty normal. The apartment was in her name, and the first four roommates had all left after getting married, or, in one case, simply moving in with her boyfriend. All in all, a typical progression that would probably have ended when the Baring girl herself found the right young man and settled down to raise a family.

She had worked as an aerobics instructor in a big health club in the garment district, where many of her "students" were fashion models. This explained her superb physical conditioning. But, yet again, it provided no clues as to what might have happened to her.

There had also been a couple of casual boyfriends. Nothing there, either; both had been at their jobs in New York on the day she was killed. Neither of them, the detective had told Schneider, seemed to have been serious about the girl in any case.

After being notified by the New York authorities, her mother had come down to claim her body, taking her back to New York for burial. Schneider had the mother's phone number, and would call her if he learned anything. But he had a suspicion that this might be one of those cases that sat in the "open" file for years.

There was simply nothing to go on. If the case was cleared, it would probably be when someone they'd arrested for an entirely different offense had an attack of conscience and admitted to the Baring Murder as well. Or let on that he knew something, and tried to make a deal with the State's Attorney by fingering the killer.

Port Morrow Beach

He had discovered that supermarkets were a wonderful place to meet women. Everyone had to eat, and, if they cooked their own food, they had to buy it. So now he was pushing a shopping cart around the WinnDixie on Port Morrow Beach, studying the other shoppers.

He knew that he was attractive to women. He always had been. Even when he still lived in his father's home. That was what had got him into trouble in the first place. That Polish bitch he'd fallen in love with, precipitating the confrontation with his father and all that had followed.

There was a likely one now, he thought. A tall brunette, bending over the meat case inspecting a Styrofoam tray of steaks. She was dressed in a sleeveless top, at the moment hanging slightly at the armholes, and exposing the side of her right breast. Her shorts were a dark tan color, cut very high, and revealing long, firm legs and the outline of a solid derriere. It was an advantage to doing his hunting at the beach. The women tended to dress rather casually, and so showed off their figures to best advantage.

He had certain criteria. He was quite tall, five inches over six feet, which had been considered gigantic in his birthplace, and was taller than average even here. So he naturally preferred taller women. He also liked them to be fit, with good figures.

He allowed himself a slight smile. It hadn't always been so. Once he had preferred his women to be plumper. But most men had in those days. Today the standard was for a more athletic look, and he had come to prefer it as well.

Putting on a puzzled look, he pushed his cart up beside the woman. "You know anything about meat?" he asked.

"It's supposed to be red," she answered. "Except for pork, which those people on TV keep saying should be white."

"I'm a lousy shopper. Ever since my wife died, I have a hard time feeding myself." In fact, he had never been married, but a young widower was somehow very appealing to women. Perhaps because it made him seem vulnerable, or brought out their natural maternal instincts. They always seemed to want to comfort him.

"Well," she said, "these steaks look pretty good."

"I'm not sure. The grill's out of gas, and I wouldn't know how to cook a steak indoors." He had also discovered that many women liked a man who seemed a little helpless. Even if it was only in a so-called "feminine" domain like cooking. It was a stereotype, obviously—men only cooked outdoors over a grill—but it seemed to work. And it was a lot more sporting than compulsion.

"Maybe," she said, "I could help?"

He allowed himself a weak smile. "Do you think so?"

"Why not? You look like a nice enough guy."

"I hope I am."

"Do you live near here?"

"About a mile down the beach." He shook his head. "You'd really help me cook?"

"Sure."

•   •   •

They left her car in the parking lot and drove to his house in his. The sun was still high in the western sky, out over the Gulf, and he left the top of the red Mustang down as he drove. Women, he had noticed, seemed to like convertibles. He had learned to arrange his lifestyle in ways that would appeal to beautiful young women. It made the hunting more like a sport.

His house was one of the older places, built in the years before Florida had passed a spate of laws designed to reduce the potential for damage in a hurricane. The first floor was raised on short, brick piers, only about three feet above the ground, with a broad porch surrounding the first floor on two sides. It kept the sun out, and the big windows and high ceilings helped to keep the place cool even when the air conditioning was off. Combined with the thick plantings, it also made it very difficult for anyone to see under the house, which was important to him.

"I like this," she said. "Kind of old fashioned, but nice."

He laughed. "I prefer old fashioned."

"Where's the kitchen?"

"Through there. You want a drink?"

"Just some sparkling water, if you've got it."

"I think so."

He walked over to the bar and found a bottle of Perrier in the refrigerator, taking a second for himself.

The woman, her name was Elaine, had found a skillet and was starting to unwrap the steaks when he came into the kitchen. "How do you like yours?" she asked.

"Rare. Nice and bloody."

"They say you shouldn't eat rare meat any more. Something to do with bacteria."

"I never get sick," he said, honestly. He never did.

"I'll cook mine a bit longer, if you don't mind."

"Sure. It's your steak, after all." In fact, it really was. They were having the two steaks she'd been looking at in the store, and *she* had paid for them.

He sat at the table and watched her as she cooked. His steak was done in a few minutes, but he said he'd wait until hers was finished before he started. He enjoyed watching her as she worked at the stove.

When she sat down, he excused himself for a moment. "The steak knives are in the other room," he said.

It was curious. Elaine found herself fantasizing about the tall, redhaired young man. After knowing him less than two hours, she was already wondering what he would be like in bed. Wondering, even, what it would be like to be with him for the rest of her life.

She thought that it had to be, at least in part, his house. Old-fashioned, except for the kitchen, which only looked so, with its turn-of-the-century appliances that, on closer inspection, turned out to be of the most modern design in old-appearing guise. Which, she thought, meant that they were probably *very* expensive, like most things meant to fit into the décor of restored homes. The whole place seemed almost like something out of another century. There had been tall, built-in bookshelves, filled with what looked to be hundreds of volumes, many of them in old style leather bindings, and in several languages. The furnishings all seemed to be antiques.

The look of the place suggested the touch of a decorator, and that meant he probably also had money.

She wouldn't object to getting to know a wealthy young man. It would certainly appeal to her mother, who was always bitching that she kept dating worthless bums with no futures. This was something Elaine had never understood. The men she dated actually tended to be a lot like her father, who had worked hard for a living his entire life.

Most of them, to be sure, lacked her father's absolute certainty about the value of religion—that is, they didn't think you had to be married to have sex—but they all had good jobs. Not executives—her last boyfriend worked in a cabinet shop, and the one before repaired air conditioners—but good, secure jobs. Her own father, after all, had worked as a mechanic in a gas station, and made a decent living for his family in the process.

But her father was gone now, taken by a sudden heart attack at 57. And maybe, she thought, that was the problem. He had left some insurance, and her mother's house was paid for, but there was no pension. So maybe, to her mother, a "future" meant someone whose pay package included stock options, and a hefty, company-funded pension plan with survivor's benefits.

On the other hand, she would probably be just as happy if her daughter brought home someone with a large enough bank account. And everything about this young man—his car, his clothes, his house—said there was money there.

Elaine smiled at her reflection in the window. Dark clouds had covered the sun, throwing that side of the house, which was shaded by several large trees, into shadow, and darkening the window, so that she could see herself, and the room behind her, reflected in the spotlessly-clean glass.

She started as his hand touched her shoulder. How had he got behind her without her seeing him in the window? She turned to smile up at him. "You startled me," she said.

"Sorry."

"I mean, I can see myself in the window, but I didn't see you behind me."

He shrugged. "Some trick of the light, I suppose," he said. His hand was still resting on her shoulder, and she reached up and gently stroked it. He kept his hand where it was, reaching around her on the other side and placing the steak knives on the table. In the process he had to bend over her, and it seemed perfectly natural for her to kiss his cheek.

He walked around the table and sat down. "You live on the Beach?" he asked, cutting into his steak.

"At the north end. I've got my own place." She smiled. "No roommates; just Herman and I."

"Herman?"

"My cocker spaniel."

"Sounds nice."

"You live alone, too, right?"

"Right."

They consumed the steaks, along with a salad and half a bottle of what she suspected was a fairly expensive red wine. She wasn't an expert on the subject, but the label was French, and it had a smooth quality, and a delightful taste, she had never experienced before.

When they had finished eating, he offered his hand, leading her into the living room, where they sat down on the big sofa.

"You're an excellent cook," he said. "That was the best steak I've had in months."

"Thank you." She moved closer to him, turning her upper body to face him. His arm went around her quite naturally, and she lifted her face, her lips slightly parted.

He bent and kissed her. She responded eagerly, turning more fully toward him. The tip of her tongue probed between his teeth. His left hand moved across her body, lifting her right breast, kneading it through the thin cloth of her top.

After a time they stood, hands working hastily at buttons and zippers, clothing dropping to the floor, forming two heaps on the antique area rug. She pushed him down onto the sofa again, kneeling on the floor beside him, her lips leaving a trail of kisses from the middle of his chest down to his groin. Her soft hands took him up, her mouth closing over him, working on him.

Strong hands lifted her, swinging her legs over his head so that the moist center of her womanliness was offered to his eager tongue. She trembled as he probed at her, his fingers spreading her open, his darting tongue licking and searching.

All the while, as her breathing grew ragged, and waves of pleasure swept through her perfect, athletic body, her mouth was rising and falling, her hands caressing, in a futile effort to bring him to a usable hardness.

She gasped and stiffened, the powerful spasms of her orgasm coursing through her. Her body acknowledging the skill of his lips and tongue.

Subsiding, she rolled off of him. He sat up, lifting her onto his lap. Her right hand continued to caress him, yet he remained adamantly soft.

"I've had problems with that lately," he said. "It doesn't seem to work any more. I just hope you're not too disappointed."

She kissed him, her left hand moving to her own crotch, her fingers drawing across the heated portal, then lifting, to be held out before him. "You see that?" she said. "You see how wet you've got me? How could I be disappointed? I think I'm in love with your tongue!"

He took her hand, brought the fingers to his mouth, licking the juices from them. "You taste good," he said. "My favorite flavor."

She kissed him again, tasting herself on his lips and tongue, the sweet muskiness entering her nostrils. "I don't *smell* that good, though," she commented.

"You're straight, right?"

"Of course. Did you doubt it?"

"No. But that's why you don't think you smell or taste good down there. If you were a lesbian you'd like it—just like any normal man loves the smell of a woman."

She laughed. "I never thought of it that way."

He bent and kissed her, pulling her close to him, her breasts hard against his chest. His head dropped, his lips encircling her left nipple, sucking it into his mouth. She sighed, running her finger through his dark red hair, pulling him into her. His lips moved up her breast, kissing her throat.

She gave a sudden gasp of surprise at a sharp pain in her neck. But after a moment the pain faded, and a strange warmth spread through her body.

When he lifted his head, his lips seemed redder than before. But the truth was slow in coming.

It was blood. Her blood.

She wanted to say something, but found that she couldn't talk. He had obviously bit her in the neck, and sucked out some of her blood. She knew it should hurt, yet there had been no pain after the moment of the bite itself. Only a curious feeling of contentment and pleasure that tried, with a considerable degree of success, to overpower the natural revulsion she felt at this sudden attack.

She felt as if she had somehow wandered into a cheap horror movie. Yet that couldn't be it. She was wearing a tiny silver cross around her neck, and he had touched it a number of times during their lovemaking. It obviously had no effect on him. So he couldn't be one of those. But if he wasn't, why had he bit her in the throat? Was that why she hadn't been able to see him reflected in the kitchen window?

His head bent again, and she could actually feel the blood being drawn out of the tiny puncture wounds. How had she failed to notice the length of his upper canine teeth? Was she dreaming all of this? And at that moment it became clear. This wasn't a dream, and it certainly wasn't a movie. And crosses were clearly not a preventive.

Her ideal lover, who had brought her to such heights of ecstasy, was a vampire. Not a mythical creature from a Hollywood special effects shop, or the erotic creation of a novelist. A real vampire.

But it no longer mattered. Her blood, and her life was draining out of her, and she was utterly unable to move.

Chapter Five
Friday, July 30, 1993

Port Morrow Beach

He had taken all night, and most of the morning, to drain her. After the initial attack, when he had taken perhaps a pint of blood from her, he had lifted her off his lap and placed her, supine, on the sofa. The wounds wouldn't bleed unless he applied suction to them, so there was no danger of blood being left on the furniture.

Nor was there any danger she would try to escape. He hadn't taken that much blood at the beginning, so she could easily have walked, or even run, from the house. But one effect of the first bite was that it had placed her under his mental control. She could no more leave now, he thought, than a parakeet could open the door of a padlocked cage.

He left her nude, though he had soon gone into his bedroom and returned properly dressed. He found that he enjoyed looking at her; that beautiful women were a great source of æsthetic pleasure for him.

Compliant, she allowed him to pose her on the sofa. The part of her mind that was still under her own control was oddly pleased that he placed her with her legs straight, and her ankles crossed, so that her genitals weren't spread open like the centerfold in a cheap men's magazine. He placed her left hand in her lap, covering the triangular patch of black hair, as if in a curious gesture to modesty. Her right arm was raised over her head, her hand hanging over the arm of the sofa, lifting her right breast.

Every few minutes he would return to her side, kneeling by the sofa and pressing his mouth to her throat, sucking out more blood.

That was important. *The blood is the life*, the Torah declared. *You shall not eat the blood.* That was an essential element in the kosher diet he had so carefully adhered to when he lived in his father's house. You didn't eat the blood.

But now he did eat the blood—had eaten nothing else for a very long time. And with the blood he absorbed the physical strength, the lifeforce, of his victim. The blood contained the essence of the person. Their vitality. The blood of a healthy, athletic young woman was particularly invigorating.

Of course, it didn't really matter. Blood was blood, when you came right down to it, and it wasn't that important who it came from. As long as it was human. He'd tried subsisting on animal blood for a time—even in his condition, there was something inside him that had objected to taking human life—but there was something lacking in the blood of animals, and before long he had been compelled to revert to people.

As for his preference for the blood of beautiful young women —it was simply that he had always been a thoroughly heterosexual male, with a healthy appreciation of beauty, and so was naturally attracted to beautiful women. His impotence was an effect of what he was; male vampires were incapable of an erection with a mortal female, no matter how much they might desire the simpler pleasures of the flesh.

He needed the blood of young women to live, but there was more. It was the sensuality of the taking. The feeling of ultimate power. He could prolong their lives, stretching a death out over a number of days. or he could take all of the blood at once, in a few minutes, when he was particularly hungry.

Still, there was something lacking in that. To kill quickly was the result of extreme hunger, or of a special need, and not of the passion that normally predominated in his character. For in a curious way, he actually loved all of his victims. He was not a predator by choice. He knew, better than most, that true predation was not a part of the human character. People killed for food, but there could be no true pleasure in the act of killing. In the ghetto, the *shochet*—the ritual slaughterman— had been one of the gentlest of individuals; and one with a great love of animals. He took their lives because it was his job, and in order to feed the people who depended upon him, but he did so as painlessly as possible. If an animal showed any sign of having felt pain as it was slaughtered, or if there was even the tiniest defect in the knife, which might have cause a twinge as it was drawn across the throat, the animal was no longer kosher, and could not be eaten by observant Jews.

As for himself, while he took a degree of sensual pleasure in the killing, and in the consumption of the blood, it was, he thought, more like the action of the *shochet*. He did it because it was *necessary*. And he was aware that there was actually little pain involved. Were it possible, he would eliminate event that.

During the time he had been traveling, he had purposely fasted, not killing at all while on the road. It was safer that way. If he was to eat at regular times, it was important to have a secure base of operations. A place where he could take his time in finding appropriate victims, without the threat of discovery.

Elaine had remained conscious through most of it. Conscious, but lacking the will to resist. Somehow, she knew that she could if she really tried. She worked out regularly, and was stronger than the average woman from the weight training. Not muscular, but extremely fit.

But her body was ignoring her commands. She had tried to tell herself to fight back, but her arms and legs wouldn't obey. She had let him pose her as if she were a limp doll. He watched her, clearly taking pleasure in observing her naked body.

Once, sometime in the very early morning, he had held out his hand to her, and then she found that she could rise and walk into the bathroom. She sat on the toilet, for some reason mounting it more like a horse, her legs well apart, and he watched with a calm smile on his face as she urinated into the white porcelain bowl.

It was curious, she had thought. She could sit on the toilet and control her normal bodily functions. Overcontrol them, really. It had never occurred to her that she would be able to urinate with a man watching her. She expected that some degree of modesty would have prevailed. But she had, and she had even positioned herself so that he would have a clear view.

But when it came to something really important—to fighting back, and perhaps to saving her life—her body refused to cooperate.

At one point he removed her neck chain, with its little silver cross. Her father had given it to her when she was baptized, accepting Jesus at the age of 14. Back in a time when religion still meant something to her. Now she wondered if that was her mistake. If she had stayed in the church, continued attending services, would this have happened? Wouldn't faith have given her the power to resist this man?

No, she thought, it probably would not. If he was sitting calmly in his chair, watching her, holding the little silver cross, spinning it around his finger on its chain, he couldn't be a *real* vampire, could he? Just a crazy person who thought he was Dracula—but not to such an extent that religious objects repelled him. And, besides, he'd encountered her in the afternoon, and driven her to his house with the top down on a convertible in full daylight. Sunlight would destroy a vampire. Everyone knew that.

That was logic and knowledge speaking. But logic and knowledge couldn't explain why she hadn't seen a reflection. All the books and movies said vampires couldn't be seen in mirrors, and he had come up behind her without reflecting in the window. And vampires could influence their victims through the force of their will, couldn't they. Had he exerted some sort of hypnotic power over her, when he so casually approached her at the supermarket?

Deep in her mind, she knew better. She had seen a good looking young man, and her libido had got the best of her common sense. He'd picked her up, pure and simple. And right up to the moment of the attack, she had been *happy* that he'd picked her up. He was a skilled lover, who had brought her more pleasure than any of her recent boyfriends.

And now he was kneeling beside the sofa, his head bending toward her neck. She could feel his lips on her skin, and the powerful suction that was drawing the blood from her veins. It was still the most curious sensation. The life was being sucked out of her, and she felt a sensation that was precisely like the feeling of really good sex. The fingers of her left hand were moving involuntarily, spreading her nether lips, probing and caressing herself.

And, she thought, Yes, if I'd stayed in the church this would not have happened. But only because I'd never have let a strange man pick me up in a supermarket!

This time he didn't stop after a few minutes. Her body tingled, trembled, her hips moving involuntarily in a slow, sensual rhythm. She was dying, and she was going to come! And as her muscles quivered with the intensity of a sexless orgasm, the world went dark, and there was no more feeling at all.

After Elaine was dead, and the last drop of blood drained from her body, he went into his bedroom and took down a cardboard file box from the top shelf of the closet. It was filled with women's bathing suits. They had all been purchased in several shops in Charleston. He had never killed in that city, and it was very unlikely that Florida police would ever check shops in South Carolina for the purchase of national brand swimsuits that were commonly sold in the local area. In fact, the only reason he had bought them where he had was so that no one in a Port Morrow Beach swimwear shop would remember seeing him.

Rummaging through the box, he picked out a skimpy bikini bottom and bra and carried them into the living room. Not black this time, but pure white. Elaine had a dark tan, and the white suit would emphasize that, making her look more alive, and giving him more time to get away.

It took only a minute to dress her body in the bikini. That was why he liked them. Putting them on a limp body was just a matter of tying a few knots. Then he picked her up and carried her out to the car, now parked inside the semiattached garage. He placed her body in the passenger's seat, sitting her up and fastening the seat belt around her. Her head lolled to one side. With her eyes closed, she looked as if she was asleep.

The garage had been built in the first years of the century, when horses were still common, and had been designed to accommodate carriages, which were much taller than his Mustang. He turned on the engine and put the top up before opening the garage door and backing out. The windows went up at the touch of a switch, and with the dark tint on the glass all that could be seen from outside the car were vague, blurry images.

Backing out of the driveway he passed the mailbox. He got out of the car and slipped several envelopes into the box. It was now after 2:00 in the afternoon, but the carrier was never there before 4:00 pm. There were bills that needed paying, and he was always scrupulous in making utility payments on time. When you moved every few months, it was important to be able to refer utility companies to the last place you'd lived. They always wanted credit references.

He smiled. It was probably his most obvious point of vulnerability, but no one, as far as he was aware, had ever bothered to follow that particular paper trail. If they had, they would have been more than a little surprised to discover that a man in his mid 20s seemed to have been a customer of one electric company or another since 1903, though not always with the same name. (And the "him" who had opened that 1903 account would, of course, be claimed by the current version as his grandfather.)

He closed the box and put up the flag to alert the carrier to make the collection. His name—he hadn't really changed it in all the years since he'd adopted it, though he had taken occasional vacations from it—was written on the box.

Isaac Nathanson.

• • •

The drop was simplicity itself. He pulled her out of the car, draped her left arm over his shoulder, and put his right arm around her waist. People always saw what they expected to see, like those two fools in the movie who'd walked a dead man around a resort community all week-end without anyone noticing.

Like all of his kind, his physical strength was far out of proportion to his appearance. Elaine was 5' 10", and weighed an athletic 130 pounds, very little of it fat. But he carried her so lightly, with just an arm around her waist, that anyone who saw them would think she was moving under her own power. He didn't have any of the powers Hollywood invested his sort with; he couldn't cause a dead woman to walk under her own power. But he could create that *illusion,* and the illusion was sufficient.

He took her down the beach access path and spread out a towel on the sand at the upper edge of the beach, under a tree. He had stolen the towel from the Holiday Inn late last night, while Elaine lay helpless on his sofa. When he sat her down on the towel, her back resting against the trunk of the tree, her head nodded forward, as if she was sleeping.

Then he simply walked away. The closest person on the beach had been over a hundred yards away, and would have seen nothing out of the ordinary. Just a man, coming onto the beach with a young woman, kissing her, and departing. A young husband, leaving his wife at the beach while he went to work, perhaps.

The key to not being noticed, he had discovered over the years, was simply to do nothing that looked out of the ordinary, even if it really was.

Now, he thought, as he drove back to his house, he must prepare for his rest. It wouldn't be dark until 8:16, so he had a few hours. He would spend them studying; his house was filled with books on hundreds of subjects, in several languages. It was an advantage of this existence, he thought. You had plenty of time to learn things. He had, after all, been around, living and otherwise, since 1660.

Cape Marl

Schneider always left a little early on Fridays. When he was first hired, the old Sheriff, John Reilly, had agreed that he would be scheduled off from Friday sundown until Saturday night, unless there was a genuine emergency. An emergency being something Reilly had tended to think of as a shootout with a bank robber, or a hurricane. Exactly the sort of life-threatening emergency when Schneider would willingly work on the Sabbath in any case. Reilly had been a Pentecostal Christian, and Schneider had never had any doubts about his old boss's genuine concern for the welfare of Israel and the Jewish people. Even if he suspected that Reilly's concern had been more than a little tinged with missionary tendencies.

But Reilly had retired in 1992, and there was a new Sheriff now. The old policy had been continued, but only after Schneider had invoked a piece of Federal civil rights legislation that had been passed to protect the rights of employees to practice their religion as long as it didn't create an undue hardship on their employer. Since Schneider had been taking the Sabbath off since 1978, the new Sheriff had found it difficult to argue that continuing to let him do so was going to cause any major problems. Naturally, the new Sheriff, Bill Mitchell, was also a Jew. It had been Schneider's experience that the worst persecutors of observant Jews were rarely gentiles. They were usually nonobservant Jews. In their desire to "fit in" with the majority culture, they had taken on some of that culture's worst traits, including a tendency to dislike anyone who reminded them too much of what they really were. Such as a Jew who insisted on wearing a *yarmulke* all the time, and thus making himself identifiably Jewish to anyone who saw him.

Schneider was also aware that Mitchell had originally been named Garfinkle. Name changes were another manifestation of the desire to assimilate.

Schneider arrived home at 5:00 o'clock, and went immediately into his study to recite *Shir Ha'Shirim*—The *Song of Songs*—as was customary on the eve of the Sabbath. In the kitchen, his 17-year-old daughter, Chayah, was taking the four loaves of challah out of the oven. There would be three meals on the Sabbath, and two whole loaves of the rich, twisted egg bread were needed for each. At every meal, one of the two loaves would be eaten. In his family, the second would be left untouched, and so could be used at the next meal. Jewish tradition required two whole loaves at each meal on the Sabbath, in memory of the double measure of *manna* that bad been gathered every Friday, so that the Israelites in the wilderness with Moses would have enough for the Sabbath, when none would be found. In larger families, it was necessary to bake two loaves for each meal, as both might be eaten. But Schneider's wife had died when Chayah was four, and he had never remarried, so there were just the two of them.

It wasn't that Schneider was one of those men who had been so much in love with his first wife that he couldn't bear the idea of every marrying another—though he had, indeed, loved her very much. It was just that he hadn't been able to find anyone else who was willing to do all of the things demanded of an Orthodox Jewish wife. In Benjamin County, the Orthodox community consisted of thirteen families, all of them residents of the same condominium building.

There were another 5,000 Jews living in the county, but they were either members of one of the two Reform and three Conservative synagogues, or else—and this was the majority—their only connection with their faith was an annual donation to the United Jewish Appeal. And that, he thought, only because the local Federation had a particularly effective fundraising department.

Schneider had looked, but where he lived it was hard to find a woman who would keep a strictly kosher home, refrain from the temptation to eat out in non-kosher restaurants, and—and this actually seemed to be the biggest stumbling block—be willing to sleep in separate beds for about half the month, during the time when Jewish law said that physical contact between husband and wife was forbidden.

Finishing his prayers, Schneider took a shower and dressed in a grey suit, with a white shirt and striped tie. He carefully patted down his pockets, making sure that he hadn't accidentally left anything in them. There was always the danger that you might do that, and so inadvertently violate the law against carrying anything in a public domain on the Sabbath. The key to his unit was gold plated, fitted with a clasp, and served as a tie clip. In this way he could "wear" the key, which was allowed. The building had an *eruv*, an enclosure around it that merged the "private" domains of the individual units into a single, all-enclosing "private" space where carrying was permitted, but Schneider had always felt it was better to act as if the *eruv* didn't exist. That way, if he happened to step across the line by accident, he wouldn't find himself involved in an inadvertent violation.

He kept out a pair of dollar bills, which he placed on the sideboard where Chayah had already set up the as yet unlit Sabbath candles. She would put the two bills in the charity box before lighting the candles. (The money in the box was periodically sent to a Yeshiva in Cleveland.)

At 7:35, he left his apartment and walked down the stairs to the community room, where the other men were also gathered. The builder had, himself, been an observant Jew, and had consequently designed the building with observant families in mind. There were 15 units, 13 of them occupied by Orthodox families. The community room had been fitted out for use as a sanctuary from the beginning.

• • •

They began promptly at 7:45 pm, when Sam Heilman, who operated a hardware store in Cape Marl, walked up to the small lectern at the front of the room and began to chant the opening words of the afternoon service. The Benjamin County Orthodox community had never been in a financial position to hire a fulltime rabbi, but any of the men were capable of leading the prayers, and Heilman and Schneider both knew how to read from the Torah, so they got by.

Upstairs, Chayah had finished setting the table, and would soon light the Sabbath candles. Sabbath was a special time for her, as it was for her father.

Port Morrow Beach

As the sun began to set over the Gulf of Mexico, a naked Isaac Nathanson slid the kitchen's central island to one side on hidden wheels and dropped down under the house, sliding the island back into place from beneath. His body seemed to melt into a grey mist, flowing into the sand beneath the house until he had reformed, dressed in his burial shrouds, inside the coffin he had buried three feet under the sand. The Sabbath was about to begin, and he would be able—be compelled, really—to rest for the next 24 hours.

Unlike the vampires of legend, Nathanson was entirely unaffected by sunlight, crosses, or holy water. Not only did he not retreat to his coffin each day at dawn, he couldn't. He could rest only on the Sabbath. But when the Sabbath came, that rest was unavoidable.

Cape Marl

Schneider lifted the silver goblet and chanted the Kiddush prayer, sanctifying both the wine that was customary at all festive occasions, and also the Sabbath itself. Then he washed his hands from a two-handled silver cup, waiting silently while his daughter did the same. Drying his hands, he recited the special blessing for the washing ritual. Then, returning to the table, he uncovered the two loaves, held them one above the other, chanted the blessing, and broke a piece off the end of the bottom one.

This piece he broke in half, giving one part to his daughter. He dipped the bread into a small bowl of salt and took a bite.

"Delicious," he said. "As always."

Chayah smiled.

Port Morrow Beach

Eric Craft hadn't paid much attention to the girl who had been sitting in the shade of a big tree at the upper end of the beach. But now it was getting dark, and she was still just sitting there. He decided to walk over and try talking to her. No one else had been around her, after all, so there probably wasn't a boyfriend or husband to worry about. And even from where he was standing, he could see that she was beautiful, with the kind of figure you usually saw only in men's magazines.

She seemed to be asleep. Deciding that it wasn't a good idea to let anyone sleep on the beach once it was dark, Eric touched her shoulder gently, trying to rouse her. Her skin was cold, and at his light shake she simply fell over onto her side.

Eric stood there for several minutes, not quite able to make himself move. When he had first seen her, his only thought had been of her beauty and her figure. He had delayed approaching her at least partly because of the fantasies that had suggested themselves to him. Fantasies he was afraid could never be, though they had been sufficient to produce a noticeable bulge in his trunks.

Now he felt almost unclean. He'd been fantasizing about fucking a dead woman! What the hell was the matter with him?

Finally, after standing around like a fool for several minutes, he walked back to his car and punched in 9-1-1 on his cellular phone.

Chapter Six
Saturday, July 31, 1993

Benjamin County Medical Examiner's Office

Dr. Robert Edgars began the autopsy at 6:30 in the morning. It was already hot outside, but for obvious reasons the autopsy room was kept quite cool. Edgars habitually wore long underwear beneath his surgical greens and gown. The "Quincy" days, when forensic pathologists performed autopsies in shortsleeved greens, and frequently without a mask, were gone. He now wore a mask, full surgical gown and cap, and two pairs of gloves.

Even the protocol for handling body fluids had changed since AIDS came on the scene. Before, blood was simply flushed down the drain. Now it was collected and treated as infectious waste. This had even affected funeral homes, with the blood forced out of the body during embalming now collected in plastic milk jugs and placed in the lower end of the casket, so that it could be buried with the body. The alternative was contracting with a licensed disposer—burial was cheaper.

The girl's body was laid out, face up, on the stainless steel table. He began by taking measurements. Height, 177 centimeters; weight, 58.7 kilograms. The subject was female, obviously. Black hair, dark brown eyes.

His first thought on seeing the body was that they had a repeat performance by the beach killer. The physical location of the body hinted at it. This victim had been seated, while the first had been supine, but that wasn't particularly important. The location of the body, under a tree at the upper edge of the beach, was. The killer, he thought, seemed to be a "poser"—someone who thought of himself as an artist, with his victims as his sculpture. In this case, he liked to place them so that they appeared to be sleeping, or sunbathing. Postures that would tend to delay the likelihood of anyone noticing that they weren't moving.

Secondly, the physical description of this victim was similar. She was an inch taller than Sandra Baring, a few pounds heavier, but both had been in nearly perfect physical condition. Hair and eyes were the same color in both victims. And both had a certain facial similarity—each had been a very lovely young woman in life.

Then there was the same curious lack of lividity even several hours post mortem. He examined her neck, again finding the two puncture marks, this time on the left side of the throat. And there were the same faint indications of tooth marks surrounding the wounds.

Edgars put down these findings by speaking into a microphone suspended over the autopsy table. They were recorded on a cassette tape, which would be transcribed later in the day. The Medical Examiner's office was busy enough that they employed three fulltime transcriptionists. It was a much more practical system than having to write everything down as the autopsy progressed. Particularly once the body was opened, and you had internal fluids to contend with. He'd never had to write out his findings himself—the current system had been in effect since the early 1970s—but he'd seen copies of the old reports during training in Los Angeles. The clean copies that were delivered to everyone were redone by a medical transcriptionist; the originals, handwritten by the pathologists, were gruesome, with the writing frequently obscured by bloodstains and other fluids.

The overwhelming majority of the bodies that came through his office, however, were routine cases. Murders had become more common in the last decade, but still averaged less than ten a year—until now, mostly drug related.

He took a scalpel and incised around the punctures in the neck. As before, they were directly over the carotid artery, which was also punctured. It seemed odd that there appeared to be no leakage of blood into the neck itself. That would have been normal in any case where an artery was punctured.

It was the same when he opened the body, using the standard "Y" incision. No blood. The heart contained a few milliliters; enough for the basic serology tests. But it was beyond him how the blood had been extracted.

He had talked to a friend after the last case. His guess had been correct. A mortician's equipment was incapable of extracting all of the blood in a human body. And, in any case, the method of extraction was by pumping embalming fluid *into* the arteries, forcing the blood out through a separate puncture in the groin. It was a technique that had been developed by a Yankee doctor during the War Between the States, to make it more practical to bring the battle dead back to their home towns for burial. Seemingly a humanitarian gesture to the families, though also a calculated stunt to inflame everyone who saw the corpse and help recruiting.

What he had determined was that an undertaker might have been able to get rid of nearly all the blood in a body, if he was extremely thorough, but it would have been replaced with embalming fluids, and neither body had been filled with pink formalin.

It took three hours to complete the autopsy. Edgars was certain this was a murder, and he liked to be extremely thorough in any suspicious case. Too often, killers had gone free at their trial because a pathologist missed something. There had been plenty of cases, for that matter, where a hospital pathologist had completely missed the evidence of crime, and signed off a murder as a natural death.

It took several years of additional training to qualify as a forensic pathologist, which meant that too many autopsies were still being performed by the clinical types. Their training was mostly concerned with detecting *medical* causes of death. Or, for that matter, with *preventing* death —a clinical pathologist's primary job was the interpretation of tissue samples removed during surgery, as well as analyzing blood and other fluids for signs of disease.

It had even been suggested that much of the controversy over the Kennedy assassination might have been avoided if the Secret Service hadn't stolen the president's body from the hospital in Dallas, and the

Dallas Medical Examiner—who had a great deal of experience in violent death, and actual legal jurisdiction over the case, the assassination of a President not being a Federal crime in 1963—had performed the autopsy, instead of a Navy pathologist at Bethesda, who was no doubt quite competent to diagnose a sclerotic liver, or a malignant melanoma, but had no experience in the complexities of legal—which is what "forensic" means—pathology. The mechanics of wound pathology were far more complex than they seemed at first glance, which was why an inexperienced man could easily confuse an entrance wound with an exit wound.

So Dr. Edgars, who did not wish to be accused of missing *anything*, always took his time with the suspicious cases. If you had to hurry, he thought, better to do it on the 83-year-old men who were found by their wives on the bathroom floor in the morning. Those cases were almost always exactly what they appeared to be—heart failure. It was amazing to anyone but a cop or a medical examiner—or an undertaker—how many elderly corpses were found in the bathroom; when you started to die, the muscles that controlled elimination failed rapidly, and the natural instinct was to try to get to the toilet.

After sewing the girl up, he put down his preliminary findings. Pending serology and toxicology results supportive of another diagnosis, he was listing the cause of death as exsanguination by unknown means. Exactly the same as the Baring girl.

Port Morrow Beach

In his coffin, beneath the secret access in the floor of his kitchen, Isaac Nathanson lay utterly inert. The stasis that had come upon his body as the sun dropped below the horizon, bringing in the Sabbath, was so complete that someone could have torn the house down around him and, while he would certainly have noticed such an action, he would have been unable to move or respond.

On the Sabbath, only his mind remained semiactive. Curiously, most of his thoughts hearkened back to his living days, when he sat in Rabbi Shimon's study hall in the Kapelskof ghetto. The words of the Torah marched across the back of his eyelids, and the complex discussions of the *Talmud.*

It was the same for him as it was for those undergoing punishment in *Gehinnom* for the sins committed during their lives. No matter how great their torment might be during the six working days—and that torment was not the fire that Christians pictured, but an enforced separation from God, which was far more difficult to endure once the spirit had shed its fleshly shell—on the Sabbath all punishment was remitted, and they were given a foretaste of their life in the World to Come. A life consisting not only of learning in Torah, but of finally coming to a full understanding of the meaning of the words they had studied—or neglected—for so many years.

But for those sinners in *Gehinnom*, there was an end to punishment. No more than a year, and generally less. *His* punishment had so far lasted 309 years, and would not end until the coming of the Messiah. Or until the proper ritual was performed over his remains to release his soul, which no matter how desirable this might be to him while he was *in* his coffin, he would do his utmost to prevent while he was awake.

It was curious, he thought. He recognized in his condition a divine punishment, inflicted upon him for self-destruction in defiance of God. When he was alive he had noted, in the abstract, the idea that God gave life to all who live, and therefore only God could take that life away from them. But that was only an abstract principle. It had simply not occurred to him that to kill oneself was to declare that you were more important than the Creator of the world, and that such arrogance would naturally be severely punished.

But only *after* he had done so, and come awake in his coffin with a terrible desire to drink the blood of the living, had he recognized the sort of punishment it could bring.

Cape Marl

David Schneider sat at his dining room table, a volume of the *Talmud* open before him. He always turned off the ringers on his phones on the Sabbath, which meant that he was unaware that another victim had been found. A victim who would make the case officially a serial murder. His Sabbath was an island in a sea of time, when he could forget all the concerns of the working week.

The Sabbath is central in the life of any observant Jew. In Hebrew, it is the only day of the week that actually has a name—*Shabbos*, which comes from a verb meaning to cease working, and is derived from the fact that God ceased all of his work of creation on that first Sabbath. The rest of the days—the working days—are simply numbered according to their position following the Sabbath—the first day, the second day, and so on.

On the Sabbath, he could put aside all of the cares that filled the working days of the week, and concentrate on drawing closer to God. Jewish tradition taught that the world was created only in order that the Torah could be revealed through Moses at Sinai, and the peoples of the world taught to live in eternal peace and harmony under the kingship of God. Observed properly, the Sabbath gave a foretaste of that world to come.

Behind him, Chayah was busying herself with the preparation of the Third Meal. This would be a simple repast: two more loaves of the twisted *challah,* a few pieces of herring and *gefilte* fish, and some pastries. It was important that three meals be eaten on the Sabbath, and a meal was defined as the eating of bread, with the appropriate blessings before and after.

Two of the meals would always include hot food. The Sabbath eve meal was, of course, prepared before Sabbath began, and was the most elaborate. It generally began with chilled *gefilte* fish, served with a topping of wickedlyhot ground horseradish. This would be followed by chicken soup, sometimes with *matzoh* balls, and sometimes with noodles. The main course was usually chicken. Often there would be a noodle kugel, and there was always a choice of pastries for desert, all of them made without any dairy ingredients, since Jewish law forbade eating meat and dairy foods together, and chicken was classified as meat. In the European ghetto, the Sabbath eve meal was often the only substantial meal of the week. In America, while people generally ate better than their ancestors, it still retained the same special atmosphere in observant homes.

The noon meal, which was also supposed to be hot, was likewise prepared beforehand and then kept hot over a low flame. Usually a *cholent*, a type of stew, made with onions, potatoes, barley, and meat. Chayah's personal variant included garlic, carrots, and half a dozen assorted spices. To keep it from boiling, a *blech*—a flat piece of sheet metal—was placed over the burners and the flame adjusted as low as possible. The *blech* diffused the heat sufficiently to keep the *cholent* simmering, without raising it to the boiling point.

The stove was left on for the full 24 hours of the Sabbath. Actually, closer to 25 hours, since the day was always brought in a little early and lingered over at its conclusion. It was forbidden to light a flame, or to extinguish one, on the Sabbath. This even applied to turning electric lights on and off, and for this reason all of the lights in Schneider's apartment, except the one in the bathroom, were connected to timers that would operate them automatically. The bathroom light was simply left on; some things were beyond scheduling.

It was also forbidden to cook anything, which was why the *cholent* was put on the back burners before sunset. It *was* permitted to finish cooking something that had been started before Sabbath.

The *Talmud* page Schneider was studying was the *Daf HaYomi*, which literally meant the "daily page." This was a system whereby observant Jews throughout the world learned the same page of the *Talmud* each day, and resulted in learning—which in the Jewish tradition meant "studying," not "memorizing"—the entire *Talmud* every seven and a half years. On this particular day, he was studying page 11 of the tractate *Sotah*, a relatively short work whose major subject matter was the law concerning a woman suspected of adultery.

But, like all Talmudic tractates, the discussion often wandered well afield from the putative subject matter. The tractate *Gittin*, for instance, whose title referred to divorce documents, was mainly concerned with agency law. Not so much with the content of the divorce document itself, but with who was authorized to deliver it, how it was to be authenticated, what the witnesses had to say if it was to be valid, and so forth.

"It's going to be time, soon," Chayah said. They would eat the third meal, then go downstairs for the afternoon service. This was customarily recited late in the afternoon, so that it would be sundown shortly after they had finished, and the evening prayers could be said. Even the daily prayers were arranged in this way, and for the same reason.

In larger synagogues, where there was a rabbi, it was customary for him to deliver a short discourse between the services. Also, in those larger synagogues, arrangements were usually made to serve the Third Meal immediately following the afternoon service, in the synagogue's social hall. The same thing was done here about once a month, but most of the time the members ate in their own apartments.

And the men took turns preparing a brief talk on the Torah portion of the week. It would be Mort Cohen this week.

"I'm nearly done," Schneider said.

A few minutes later Schneider closed the book and returned it to the shelf. His daughter quickly set the table with fresh dishes and silver. The plates they'd used at the first two meals were out of sight, in a special cupboard Schneider had installed when they first moved into the apartment. You were allowed to wash dishes if you needed them again during the Sabbath, but the family had more than enough, so they simply put the dirty dishes out of sight until the Sabbath was over. The Codes decreed that this was, in any case, preferable.

Schneider took the wine from the refrigerator and filled the goblet. The complexity of the *Kiddush* prayer lessened during the day, from the elaborate formula in the evening, to a simpler prayer at noon, which included a repetition of the Biblical command to keep the Sabbath, to nothing more than the simple blessing on the wine in the afternoon.

For Schneider, it was all second nature. He had grown up with it, as had his daughter, and neither of them could even imagine eating anything without pronouncing a blessing over it first. Even something as commonplace as taking a drink of water called for a blessing. The purpose of creation, Rabbi Danilowitz had frequently declared in the synagogue Schneider had attended as a child, was so that men and women would one day be able to sanctify every aspect of their lives. If they could accomplish that, the old rabbi had said, then the Messiah would arrive, and the idealized, and much longed-for, World to Come would then become a reality.

It was Schneider's wish, as it was the wish of the rest of the Jewish residents in his building, that the day would come when their little community would grow to the point where they could afford to hire a full time rabbi of their own.

A community needed a rabbi if it was to prosper and grow. His presence conferred a degree of legitimacy on the congregation in the eyes of the less traditional Jews, whose rabbis, for the most part, were trained somewhat differently than Orthodox rabbis. An Orthodox rabbi was expected to be an expert on Jewish Law, to be familiar with all aspects of the Codes, ritual, and the dietary laws. He was the conscience of the community, the one who would point out when the people had begun to stray from the divine mandates brought down from Sinai by Moses.

A Reform rabbi was expected to be a marriage counselor, and generally not to bother his congregants too much.

Port Morrow Beach

As the sun began to sink into the Gulf of Mexico, Isaac Nathanson could feel the peace of the Sabbath departing as mobility returning to his body. This was his punishment, he was sure. Each Sabbath he would lay in his coffin, fully at peace with creation. But when the Sabbath ended the blood-thirst would return. Not too strongly, at first. Not so strongly that he couldn't control his lusts.

He could go several weeks without actually killing. Just taking a little here and there. Enough to sustain him, but not enough to inflict serious injury on a healthy victim. (Whose memory of the attack would be so tenuous that they could see Nathanson standing directly in front of them and not have the slightest idea who he was.)

But then the full hunting need would come again, and this time he would kill. It had been so since his "death" in 1684, and he had grown skilled at concealing his crimes.

At first, he had cut the throats of his victims with a sharp knife after killing them. It was unaesthetic, but it concealed the telltale marks of his canine teeth, which would have quickly given away what was happening in the eastern Europe of the 17th, 18th and early19th Centuries. In those times, people still *believed* in vampires.

Today it was easier. No one believed in vampires, except as characters in horror movies. And many of the recent crop of vampire movies had transformed the vampire into a generally sympathetic creature. In one film the beautiful vampire had been the unhappy victim of a virus. In another, Count Dracula was turned into a comic character, risking everything for the love of a flighty model.

And on television, two different actors had played the same character in virtually identical TV movies, with the second version, which moved the locale from Los Angeles to Toronto, serving as the pilot for a syndicated series, again featuring a tortured vampire who wanted nothing more than to somehow turn himself into a normal human being.

Even more interesting were a series of vampire novels, which had greatly enhanced the already present erotic potential of Nathanson's kind—at least in the imagination of anyone who was not a victim. The idea had always been there, even as far back as *Dracula*. There was something terribly seductive about a being who sustained his own life by taking the lives of others, and in the process conferred immortality on his victims.

Today, even in those communities where the word "vampire" had been connected with his victims by the news media, the official position was that the "vampiric" aspects of the cases merely represented a psychiatric disorder on the part of the killer, and that the effect was artificially produced.

Certainly, no one watched the graves of his victims, fearful lest they should be restored to life as vampires. Nor did anyone drive a precautionary stake through their hearts before they were buried. It was one of the benefits of the modern tendency to replace free will with a form of societal determinism in which no one was actually responsible for their own actions. Someone who drank the blood of the living could not, in the psychiatric opinion, be cursed by God—he was merely "acting out" his aggressive tendencies, which in turn were brought about by a sexually-repressed society, or childhood abuse.

Total disbelief, he thought, as full mobility returned, was a wonderful shield.

Chapter Seven
Monday, August 2, 1993

Benjamin County Sheriff's Department

The file was on Schneider's desk when he arrived at his office in the courthouse annex on Monday morning. This one, he thought, was going to be easier—but only to the extent that they knew who the victim was. The manager of the Winn-Dixie on Port Morrow Beach had called the Sheriff's Department on Sunday morning to see if they would do something about a car, which had been left on Thursday, and was still sitting in his parking lot. A check on the tag had given them a name, and a Beach address for the owner. The deputy sent to the address found only an irate landlady, whose chief complaint was that the tenant had seemingly gone away without making arrangements to board her dog.

About the same time, Elaine Gould's mother had called in, when her daughter failed to show up for her regular Sunday afternoon visit. Normally, a 25-year-old woman who missed a visit with her mother wasn't cause for much action on the part of a police agency. But when the same woman is listed as the owner of a car that seems to have been abandoned in a supermarket parking lot, and who takes off without making arrangements for her pet, the suspicion level naturally increases.

A deputy had driven to Mrs. Gould's home in North Port Morrow, and the identification portion of the case essentially ended at that moment. Pictures of Elaine were everywhere, and the deputy had been one of those who had responded to the original call when her body was found.

The deputy had gone back to his cruiser and called in for a detective to meet him at Mrs. Gould's house. The first detective had done the preliminary investigative work, then turned the case file over to Schneider, since the condition of the body made it seem almost certain that they were dealing with the same killer as in the Baring case.

And that, Schneider thought, after reading through the file, was probably where their luck would end. There had already been interviews with everyone at the Winn-Dixie, and none of them were able to remember even *seeing* Elaine Gould on Thursday, much less who she had left the store with.

For that matter, the Winn-Dixie wasn't the only store in the shopping center. It was merely the biggest, and the car had been parked in front of it. But there were ten other stores and shops in that particular center, so no one could say for sure that the victim had met the killer in the supermarket. It was equally possible the killer had simply met her in the parking lot, or in one of the other shops. About the only reason for suspecting the supermarket as the meeting place was that several books on "picking up girls" had suggested supermarkets and laundromats as the best places, and a serial killer was just as likely to take advantage of that fact as anyone else.

So Schneider decided the store was as good a place as any to start looking. He drove out to the Beach to do his own interviews.

Port Morrow Beach

He decided to start at the Winn-Dixie. The effect was a bit startling. The office manager greeted him like an old friend, but called him Mr. Nathanson.

"Schneider," he said, showing her his badge and I.D. card. "Detective Sergeant David Schneider, Benjamin County Sheriff's Department."

"You look just like him," the office manager said.

"Like who?"

"Zack Nathanson. Nice guy—regular customer."

"Well," Schneider said, "they say everyone has a double somewhere."

"So they say."

"But that's not why I'm here."

"I didn't think so, really. But you sure do look like the man. Height, build, hair color. You don't see a lot of guys with red hair, for some reason." She shook her head. Her own hair was blond, which considering her age was probably covering up a lot of grey. "Women, yes, but not men."

" Women," Schneider commented, "dye their hair. With men, you only get red when we're born that way."

"I suppose."

He took out his pen and notebook. "Did you know Elaine Gould?" he asked.

The office manager nodded. "Sort of. Another regular customer. I can't say I actually knew her, but I've seen her in the store enough to recognize her. She has a check-cashing card here."

"Did you see her in here on Thursday?"

"No. One of your people was here yesterday, you know, asking everyone if they'd seen anything."

"We like to be sure," Schneider explained. "Sometimes people forget things when you first ask them, then later on they remember. But they don't always bother to call us to *say* they've remembered."

"Oh."

"But you didn't see her?"

"No. And I was here from opening."

"Okay."

The office manager laughed. "He's younger than you, though," she said.

"Who is?"

"Zack Nathanson. And..." she looked at him carefully. "And I think his hair may be just a shade darker than yours."

I'll have to meet this guy, Schneider thought. The idea that he could have a youngerlooking double living in the same area struck him as, at the very least, curious.

•   •   •

While Schneider was interviewing other Winn-Dixie employees, and preparing to move on to the other shops in the center, Isaac Nathanson was sitting on his front porch, watching the traffic go by on Estuary Boulevard. He was currently in what he thought of as his "sipping" mode.

He'd find a girl, take a few ounces of blood, and then leave her, perhaps a bit weakened, but still very much alive. They never remembered, either. Something in his condition gave him that power over his victims. Even, to a lesser degree, over others. It was how, last week, he had sent out a mental command to everyone in the supermarket to forget he'd been there that day, or that they'd seen the girl.

Nathanson never thought of himself as evil. If anything, when he thought about it at all, he tended to think of himself as merely the first among many victims. His only real "crime" had been falling in love with that Polish innkeeper's daughter.

His father had been coldly furious. If he insisted on marrying the girl, then his father would sit *shivah* for him, mourning him as if he had died. It had been an ancient Jewish custom even then; the complete severing of allties to any child who married out of the faith.

From his reading, Nathanson had discovered that this was something which almost never happened today. Parents were now so terrified of alienating their children that they let them do whatever they wished. If the children knew that marrying the wrong person would mean they would never see their parents again, maybe fewer would do so, but the parents were now too "enlightened" to enforce that sort of rule.

Yet if Nathanson's father had been furious, Irena's father had been far worse. He had bluntly declared that there would be *no* marriage— not even if Nathanson had been willing to renounce his own faith and allow himself to be baptized into the Roman Catholic Church. (Which he had, indeed, been willing to do, even if not with any true sincerity.) Though the name would not be used until the 19th Century, Irena's father had been a true anti-Semite. He didn't think of Jews as people with a different religion; he thought of Jews as an infectious agent, and baptized Jews as the infection itself, dragging down the pure Polish stock into which they married.

Like the Nazis who came to power in Germany 248 years later, he really didn't care what a man's religion might be. He only cared who his ancestors had been. If they had been Jews, then he considered the man less than human, even if he had been baptized, converted, and taken holy orders!

But Nathanson had now had 309 years to reflect on his actions on that day. More than enough time to calm down and accept the reality of the world, which was rarely the idealized place young people all hoped for. At the time, his rage and grief had been so overwhelming that he'd thought nothing of cursing his father, his people, and his God, and then killing himself.

He'd had plenty of time to regret his actions, starting from the moment, two weeks after he had "died," when he'd regained consciousness in his coffin and gone hunting for the first time.

Chapter Eight
Monday, April 17, 1684

Kapelskof, Poland

During the two weeks since he'd dived head first into the street from the top of the synagogue, and been buried next to the two other suicides in a remote corner of the Kapelskof ghetto cemetery, a curious process had been taking place in the body of Itzak ben Reb Nosson Sh'muel.

Generally, a corpse follows a fairly straightforward course once it has been buried. Provided there was no embalming, the first thing that happens is that the digestive acids in the stomach begin to leak into the viscera, after the production of the mucous that protects the stomach lining has ceased. The defenses breached, the body begins digesting itself from within.

As this is happening, anærobic bacteria, always present, but prevented from multiplying in a normal atmosphere, suddenly find themselves in an oxygenless environment and increase exponentially. These bacteria literally consume the flesh as they grow, turning it into a liquifying mass.

Finally, insects and worms, entering the coffin through the holes which are always bored in the bottom of Orthodox Jewish coffins to insure that the body is buried in contact with the earth, consume the rest of the body. In the 20th Century, forensic pathologists would use the presence of certain insect larvae in a body as a guide to elapsed time since death.

These various mechanisms, in time, eliminate all of the soft tissue. After a period of several months, only the bones remain.

But Itzak's body was subjected to a different process. The fall had shattered his skull and broken his neck at the third and fourth cervical vertebrae. The latter injury was identical to that caused by the drop in a judicial hanging, and resulted in the severing of the spinal cord between the two vertebrae. Either of these injuries would have been sufficient to cause his death; the combination merely insured the result. But the series of entirely normal events which resulted in his death had an abnormal conclusion; his *neshamah*, his soul, had been prevented from leaving his corpse.

Over the course of two weeks, the broken bones in his skull and neck were restored to their original alignment and knitted firmly together. The nerve fibers also reconnected, and as the second Sabbath ended, consciousness was restored. His body was not yet mobile, but his mind was again functioning.

Now, two days later, an intuitive process began through which Itzak was able to control his body at the molecular level. Through sheer force of will, he reduced the density of his body and rose through the earth, regaining solid form when he was standing in the depressed part of the cemetery where the suicides were buried.

It was just after dark, and Itzak was grateful that his return had not occurred in the daylight, when someone might have seen him rise from his grave. And it was then that he realized something else. After having risen through the ground in his insubstantial form, he was suddenly aware that the reverse was now impossible. Deep in his mind, implanted there by the same divine source that had decreed his fate, was the knowledge that he could seek rest in his grave only on the Sabbath. For the six working days of the week he would remain awake, in the world of the living. In it, he thought, but not of it.

There was also a terrible weakness. The two week period, during which his shattered body had been restored, had taken its toll on his strength. He knew that he couldn't die; he also knew that he was experiencing a powerful desire to feed that very night.

• • •

Young Stanislaw, the pig butcher, threw the heavy wooden bar into its recess and set about cleaning up his shop. Part of a carcass was hanging in the rear, behind the table where he served his customers. He took this down off the hook, and throwing it over his shoulder, carried it into a back room.

The thick muscles in his arms bulged as he cut the carcass into smaller parts and pitched them into a wooden barrel filled with strong brine. In that period, salting was the best available method of preserving meat. In the winter he could store it in the unheated back room, where the frigid temperatures would keep the meat fresh. In the summer, it was the brine barrel for anything that didn't sell on the day he slaughtered the hog.

When he was finished, he went upstairs to his own rooms. The kitchen fire was low, so he added wood and stirred the embers to bring out more heat. He took a heavy iron pot from a hook on the wall, and filled it with water from the pump. It was rain water, collected from the roof, and stored in a cistern beneath the building. There was also a well, but the water from that could be drawn only on the ground floor. Why, he wasn't sure. The priest, who was an educated man, had told him that there was some curious force which would not allow water to rise more than 32 feet up a pipe, no matter how hard you worked the pump. His well was 29 feet deep, and the firstfloor pump was right at the upper end of that odd limit.

The cistern, however, was just below the level of the cellar floor, and a pump on the second floor could draw from it.

Stanislaw placed the pot on the fire, and threw several pieces of fresh pork into the water. After it had boiled for a sufficient time, he would have it for his supper.

Below, in the shop, he heard the sound of breaking glass. A moment later, a door creaked open. Stanislaw grabbed a butcher knife from the table and hurried downstairs. Whoever was breaking in had chosen the wrong shop, he thought. In many cities, the butchers constituted the emergency guard, since they were skilled with knives.

Now, he could see a shadowy figure just inside the back door.

"Who's there?" he demanded.

The figure turned toward him, but made no response. From the cut of his clothing, Stanislaw suspected his visitor was a Jew, which was puzzling. He was a pig butcher, and, for as long as he could remember, no Jew had ever so much as set foot inside his shop. They hated pork, he thought. Considered it unclean—as if perfectly good food could somehow contaminate a person. And Jews were simply not known as thieves; it was unheard of for one to break into a house or shop.

"Who are you?" he asked again.

Still no answer, but the figure moved toward him, into the light. Now he was sure. It was the tailor's son, the redheaded one who had—

No, Stanislaw thought, it couldn't be him. He was dead. But it certainly looked like him. He'd seen him many times, for if a Jew wouldn't patronize his business, he was willing to buy his clothing from a Jewish tailor. There was currently no gentile tailor in Kapelskof, in any case.

He had last seen the tailor, running away, on Easter Sunday, when he had joined the crowd inside the ghetto. That had been great sport, he thought. The priest had made it clear that the Jews were guilty of killing God, and the Gospel clearly proclaimed that the guilt was to be passed down from one generation to the next.

But something was very wrong here. It wasn't the place of a Jew to break in and attack a Christian. Jews were the victims; that was their place in the world—their fate and their sentence, for having rejected their Messiah. The priest had said so any number of times.

So why was this Jew here? And why wasn't he running away, fleeing in terror of his life at the sight of the powerful young butcher and his knife?

He held the knife in front of him now, the blade level, as the figure moved slowly toward him. Then the man lunged, and Stanislaw drove the knife deeply into his chest.

His assailant drew back, grunting, the knife still embedded in his chest. With an odd snarl he grabbed hold of the knife and wrenched it out, flinging it across the room. He didn't bleed. How was that possible?

Yet, hadn't this man killed himself? The dead couldn't walk around, could they? Not unless he was—*Upior?* The old people spoke of such things, but he'd never really believed in them.

Yet, if this man was *upior,* he would fear the holy, wouldn't he? Stanislaw grabbed a crucifix from a shelf near the door to the front of the shop, thrusting it out in front of him, waving the image of the Blessed Savior in this creature's face.

His assailant snarled, showing his teeth, the canines gleaming in the candle light, like an animal's fangs. He slapped the crucifix aside, laughing softly.

Stanislaw was backing toward the front room of the shop. There were more knives in there. Weapons. If one didn't work, then another would have to, wouldn't it? Hadn't he heard that you could kill one of these creatures by cutting off its head?

At that moment his attacker sprang at him, grabbing him by the upper arms. Compared to himself, Stanislaw realized, the man was quite weak. But at that moment he looked into his eyes, and at that moment the truth was driven into his mind. The eyes were dead. He was being attacked by a dead man, and something deep in his mind told him that it wasn't possible to kill someone who already dead.

Itzak drained the blood from the butcher's body as quickly as he could. As he did, he could feel the man's strength entering his body, adding itself to his own.

It was curious, he thought. As he had drunk deeply from the man's throat, his victim's thoughts had come unbidden to him. Odd to think that his death had been a kind of rough justice. The butcher had been one of those who had beaten Rabbi Shimon to death.

When he had finished, he laid the corpse on the serving table and used one of the man's own knives to slash his throat. Instinct told him that he had to conceal the nature of this man's death. Taking an odd pleasure in his restored strength, he lifted the butcher over his head and slammed his body down onto one of the meat hooks attached to the wall behind the butcher's block.

Then he walked out through the back door, and concealed himself in a small shed near the city gate. In the morning, when the gate was opened, he would take his leave of this city as rapidly as possible. There had been recognition in the butcher's eyes. And if the pig butcher, who had barely known of his existence in life, could recognize him, then it seemed reasonable that others, more familiar with him, could do the same.

The same instincts that warned him to conceal the bite marks in the butcher's neck also told him that there were ways in which he could be killed. The most vulnerable time, naturally, would be on the Sabbath, when he was confined to his coffin. Should anyone dig it up on that day, it would be possible to destroy him. And on the first night of his full resurrection, he was not yet ready for true death. That desire would not come for many years.

Nor would he truly leave Kapelskof for some time. A monster he might have become, but he remained a Jew, and his own death had not been the only evil on that Sunday. It had come to him, as he was killing the butcher. If he must kill, then he would choose his first victims from amongst other killers. From the butcher's mind, he had learned the names of all the others who had been involved in the rabbi's murder. Now he would kill them, drinking their blood, and gaining their strength in the process.

For if he had become a monster, he still retained much of the conscience of a man. Senseless brutality and murder now seemed to him as much a crime as they had always been. Looked at subjectively, his own killing made perfect sense. It was necessary in order to maintain his existence. That others would not see it in the same light made little difference to him; his own viewpoint was the only one that could possibly matter to him, for it was his own life he was most concerned with. And hadn't the Sages taught that one should consider that the world had been created for his own personal benefit? As, when you thought about it, it might as well have been, since the world could not really be said to exist for someone who wasn't in it.

So he would kill. That was how he was destined to sustain his own life. But if the necessity of killing could be made to serve a more noble purpose than mere survival, so much the better.

Chapter Nine
Monday, August 2, 1993

Benjamin County Courthouse

Sheriff Bill Mitchell had gone to the County Commission meeting with the specific purpose of asking for additional funds for his department. He expected the County Commission to turn him down. They always did. He was used to it, and it didn't matter very much, because he could always appeal to the legislature to overrule the commissioners. As County Sheriff, Mitchell was a constitutional officer, which meant his position was mandated by the Florida Constitution, and he was directly elected by the voters.

The commissioners, of course, were also directly elected, but in the way of government's everywhere, when a legislative body was given control of the budget of a department whose head wasn't actually responsible to them, they liked to hold back on funding. Their main concern was with the voters who elected *them*, and not with how the Sheriff was going to do in the next election. The commissioners, too, recognized that the Sheriff could appeal to the Legislature in Tallahassee for the additional funds, and the Legislature would then mandate them. And this would be fine—if the voters complained that their taxes had to be raised, the commissioners could point out that the Legislature was *making* them do it.

There was also a gentlemen's agreement of sorts in Tallahassee that, when a sheriff made such an appeal, the state representative and senator who had actually been elected from his area were allowed to vote "nay," and the others would approve the measure. That way the local legislators, too, could say it was somebody else's fault.

Mitchell had gone in expecting to have his budget shot down, and that was exactly what had happened. He hadn't been expecting what came next.

Ed Barron, the chairman, had started it.

"Sheriff," Barron had said, "You've had two young women killed on the Beach recently. What's being done about it?"

"Detective Sergeant Schneider is in charge of the case," Mitchell replied. "We're investigating."

"Do you have any suspects?" Andrea Corwin asked.

"Not yet. But it's still early."

"Haven't I heard that if a case isn't solved in the first 24 hours it may never be solved?" This was from Hiram Krause, who represented the Beach on the Commission.

"No, sir," Mitchell said. "That's not true. Cases that are solved that quickly usually involve an obvious suspect, like a husband, or a boyfriend. Or a known criminal. They're solved quickly because, most of the time, the perpetrator is obvious.

"But if there's *no* obvious suspect," he went on, "we have to work our way back from the evidence we have. It takes longer, but my department actually has one of the highest case clearance rates in the state."

"You need to find this killer damned quick, Sheriff," Krause said. "The business owners on the Beach don't like it. It scares the customers away, knowing there's a serial killer on the loose there."

"We haven't definitely established that, Sir," Mitchell replied.

Krause frowned. "You have two dead girls, who from their pictures look very much alike. They were both found on the beach, dressed the same way, and killed the same way. And a damned odd way at that. You going to try to tell us two different people did this?"

There really wasn't much question that they had a serial killer on their hands, Mitchell thought. But it was too early for the commissioners to be bothering him about it. The second death had occurred on Friday, and now, on Monday, these politicians were expecting him to have solved the case. Well, he was a politician of sorts himself, wasn't he? But he had been a professional law enforcement officer for 18 years before running for sheriff, with the last six as a detective.

Investigations took time, if they were to be done properly. What he had said was quite true. If you had an obvious suspect, you could frequently close the case very quickly. But when you ran into a true serial killer, who usually had no connection whatever with the victims except that he'd killed them, there was very little to go on.

The F.B.I. had a fairly good record of capturing serial killers, but they also took the credit in more than a few cases where their actual contribution had been marginal. The story was that the F.B.I. had been responsible for catching Bundy, but the truth was more prosaic. He hadn't been captured through their psychological profile, though it had helped He'd been captured because he screwed up an attempt to kill a girl, and she had been able to describe, and, later, identify him. It always became easier once you knew what the bad guy looked like.

The worst part now, he thought, was that Commission meetings were broadcast over all of the county's cable television systems. For all he knew, the killer could actually be *watching* as he tried to appease the commissioners without giving away any sensitive information.

Benjamin County Sheriff's Department

It had taken the commissioners almost an hour to finish with Mitchell, and when he left the meeting room he was in a cold rage. He entered his office through the private entrance off the courthouse atrium, which avoided the small band of reporters who had gathered in the Sheriff's Department lobby, and punched a button on his phone. "Is Schneider back yet?" he asked.

"No, Sir," his secretary replied.

"Well, as soon as he gets back, get him in here."

"Yes, Sir."

Port Morrow Beach

Schneider completed the interviews at the shopping center, feeling no closer to a solution than he had when he started. He went into a small snack bar at the far end of the center and asked for a cup of coffee.

"In a paper cup," he said. "Black." He would never have considered actually eating in the place, since it wasn't kosher, but coffee was made in an urn used for no other purpose, and the paper cup would be new. He also kept his hat on, so that no one would notice the *yarmulke* on his head, and perhaps conclude that it was permitted to actually *eat* in this place.

"No paper," the counterman said. "Styrofoam okay?"

"Fine." The material the cup was made of didn't really matter. Only that the cup be previously unused. In their fine details, the Jewish dietary laws could be extremely complex. But they served to elevate the spiritual level of those who observed them, and that was more than enough reason to keep them.

Schneider drank the coffee slowly. "Not very hot," he said.

"Drip coffee makers and lawyers," the counterman said.

"What?"

"The temperature. People used to make coffee in percolators. When you made it that way, you had to boil the water. It was the boiling that made the water go up the little pipe in the middle. Now everyone uses drip coffee makers. The water comes out at maybe 150 degrees and just sprays down onto the grounds in a filter. So now everyone's forgotten that coffee is supposed to be hot when you serve it, and if you give it to them normal they burn their tongues and sue you and you've lost your business."

Schneider smiled. He'd heard of a few cases of that sort. He'd always thought the juries were crazy, since coffee really *was* supposed to be hot. It hadn't occurred to him that a general change in the method of preparation could have had anything to do with it, though. Probably because his own coffee was still made in an ancient enamelware coffee pot on top of the stove.

"You live around here?" the counterman asked.

"No. Over in Cape Marl. Why?"

"You look like a guy I've seen around here a few times."

""In here?"

"No," the counterman said. "Never actually in here. But out in the parking lot."

"Somebody in the Winn-Dixie said the same thing," Schneider said. He realized that this was a different counterman than the one he'd interviewed two hours earlier.

"Has anyone talked to you about what happened on Thursday?" he asked.

"Something happened?"

"It's possible a young woman was abducted from this shopping center. At least, her car was found here, and the woman in question is dead."

The counterman shook his head. "Hadn't heard about it," he said. "But I went to see my daughter in Atlanta Thursday evening and just got back about three hours ago. I'm not really up on what happened while I was gone."

Schneider took out his I.D. "Did you work on Thursday?"

"Until 5:00 o'clock. Then I went home, got changed, and drove to the airport."

He took out the picture of Elaine Gould they'd obtained from her mother. "Did you, by any chance, see this woman while you were working?"

"This the dead girl?"

"Yes."

"I'm not sure. Maybe."

"In here?"

"No. Getting into a car."

"Do you remember what kind of car?"

"New Mustang convertible. Red." He nodded. "Yeah, it was with that same guy."

"What guy?"

"The one I mentioned before. You know, the guy that looks like you."

"She drove off with this guy?"

"I think so. I'm not positive, but he kind of stuck out, what with the red hair and being so tall. If I remember it right, he put a couple bags of groceries in his car and she was in the front seat."

Schneider asked a few more questions, getting the counterman's name and address, in case they needed him later. Which, if the lead he had provided proved out, they obviously would. He had been curious about this mysterious double before, but now he'd been given a new reason to look him up.

But there was a potential problem, too. The counterman remembered seeing this Nathanson fellow putting groceries in his car with the girl, and yet the people in the Winn-Dixie were certain he hadn't been in the store that day. How could you reconcile that?

This was always a potential problem with eye witnesses. Even when they remembered the people precisely, they sometimes had a tendency to confuse dates. Maybe Nathanson had picked up the Gould woman on a *different* day, and the counterman had confused the times. It seemed more likely for a single witness to be wrong about someone being there, than for fifteen of them to be wrong about him *not* being there.

In his car, he turned on the radio and called up headquarters. "This is Schneider," he said. "I need a tag and I.D. check."

"Go ahead, Sergeant."

"No number available. Run a check on Nathanson, first name Zack—Zebra , alfa, charlie, kilo, I think—middle initial unknown."

"Wait one."

He waited. In the communications room at the Sheriff's Department, the dispatcher would have punched up the name in the state's central crime computer. The answer came back a minute later.

"No record, Sergeant."

"Okay, run the name through auto tags and drivers licenses."

"Ten-four."

Schneider was thinking of a psychological treatment of serial killers he'd read. They seemed to start young, and usually started close to their homes before ranging out into a broader territory. The key to finding a serial killer, the author had suggested, was finding out where the first crime had been committed. It no more occurred to Schneider than it would have to the psychiatrist who'd written the book that, in this case, if they wanted to find the first victim they'd have to look in a small city in Poland, more than three centuries in the past.

"No Zack Nathanson," the dispatcher said. "There's a tag and license issued to an Isaac Nathanson, though. The tag is for a red, 1993 Mustang convertible."

"Have you got his license pulled up on the screen?"

"Affirmative."

"Does he look like me?"

"He does at that, Sergeant. Younger though, birthdate 4/18/69. That would make him 24."

"I need the address."

"He's at 22247 Estuary Boulevard, on the Beach."

"Thank you. I'm going over there now."

"Sergeant?"

"Yes?"

"The Sheriff wants you back here as soon as practical."

"Ten-four. I need to see this guy first, though. Might be a lead."

"Ten-four."

Nathanson was still sitting on his porch when the unmarked police car pulled into his driveway. The car was recognizable from the gas filler door, which had been replaced with a flat, polished piece of sheet steel with a good lock on it. The detectives took their cars home with them— though Nathanson didn't know this—and the department was taking no chances that someone would try to steal gas from them, or, potentially much worse, decide to pour a pound of sugar into the tank. Nathanson started slightly when Schneider got out of the car. He hadn't actually looked at himself in a mirror in more than three centuries, since he couldn't see himself even if he did, but he could be photographed, and the picture on his driver's license was sufficient to remind him of what he looked like. Which was exactly like the man coming up his front walk.

A policeman, he thought, his sensitive nose confirming the evidence of the car. You couldn't smell a man's profession, to be sure, but you *could* smell his sidearm. At least, Nathanson could. There was a distinctive scent to the cleaning solvents and oil used on firearms, as well as the sharp tang of the burnt powder that even the most careful cleaning usually missed.

He got up from his chair and walked to the edge of the porch. Schneider had his badge holder out, and was looking at him with an extreme degree of curiosity. Probably to be expected, Nathanson thought. You don't often meet yourself.

"Are you Isaac Nathanson?" Schneider asked. As if there was any doubt after seeing him.

"Yes."

"I'm Detective Sergeant David Schneider, Benjamin County Sheriff's Department. You have a few minutes?"

"Sure. You want to come inside, Sergeant?"

They went into the living room and Nathanson offered his visitor a seat on the sofa. Schneider didn't know it, but he was sitting on the exact spot where Elaine Gould had died.

The room itself was lined with bookshelves. The books, Schneider noticed, were in a number of languages, including, surprisingly, Yiddish. A multi volume set of Sholem Aleichem's stories and novels.

"You Jewish?" Schneider asked. It didn't have anything to do with the investigation, but he just felt like he had to know. If someone was walking around wearing his face, and had Yiddish books in his library, he just naturally wanted to know why.

"Yes," warily. "Is there something wrong with that?"

"Not that I've ever noticed," Schneider said, taking off his hat and revealing the crocheted *yarmulke* beneath it.

"But you figured that if I looked like you, and you were Jewish yourself, maybe I was related in some way?"

"Since two people pointed out the resemblance, I have to admit I was curious. And, of course, you don't see Sholem Aleichem in Yiddish in the average gentile's library."

"I don't suppose you do at that," Nathanson said. "And maybe we are related. Considering the physical resemblance, we certainly ought to be. Where do your people come from?"

"Poland. My grandfather came here in 1882 from a place called Kapelskof."

Nathanson smiled. "That's where my family hails from, too. So we're probably cousins of some sort." Cousins hell, Nathanson thought. This guy is my grand-nephew, with a whole lot of "greats" added on. Probably nine or ten generations removed.

Nathanson's younger brother, Pinchas, had taken the name of Schneider in 1736, when the prince decided that his Jews should have family names to make it easier for his tax collectors to keep track of them. Pinchas had also taken up their father's trade and named himself accordingly. "Schneider" was Yiddish for "tailor." And another David

Schneider, who had also borne a strong resemblance to Nathanson, had, indeed, left for America in 1882. This, then, was the result.

As for himself, when it became prudent to adopt a surname, he had decided to distance himself from his family and adopted a patronymic instead. Itzak ben Nosson Sh'muel became Itzak Nossonsohn, which was later mutated and Anglicized into Isaac Nathanson. Both were literal translations of his original Hebrew name. Isaac, the son of Nathan. His father's second given name, Sh'muel—Samuel—had simply been dropped.

"So," Nathanson said, "what can I do for you?"

Schneider took out the pictures of the two dead women. "I was wondering if you recognized either of these women?"

"I think I may have seen this one around here," he said, holding out the picture of Elaine Gould. "Don't recognize the other one, though." He felt it was safe to recognize the one who lived and shopped nearby. Probably even prudent. This detective wouldn't have shown up on his doorstep if he hadn't made some sort of connection—which was more likely with a local resident than with a tourist.

"They were both murdered. The one you recognized, probably on Friday."

Nathanson nodded. "I think I read something like that in the paper. How can I help?"

"Someone said they thought they saw her getting into your car Thursday afternoon in the Winn-Dixie parking lot."

Nathanson shook his head. "Not that I remember. Good looking lady, too. I think I'd have noticed her."

"Where were you on Friday?"

"Here, mostly. I decided to retire while I could still enjoy it."

"Retire?"

"As in not work."

"How do you support yourself?"

"My family made a lot of very good investments over the years. And my grandfather had built up a decent fortune by the time of the stockmarket crash in 1929. He invested very heavily after the crash and bought up every piece of stock he could get his hands on. A few issues never recovered, but the bulk of them climbed back to normal in a few months. I'm not sure exactly how much he made on that, but it was enough that no one in the family has had to actually work for a living since then." In fact, Nathanson had made those investments himself, and knew the amount of return to the penny, but he could hardly tell this detective that, could he?

"You didn't bring this girl home on Thursday?"

"No." Nor would they find any sign of her if they searched the house, he thought. Her clothing had already been disposed of, by the simple expedient of placing it in a garbage bag with a lot of other anonymous trash, and tossing it in a shopping center Dumpster up in Punta Ancha. And the box of women's bathing suits, even if they were found, were just a wealthy young man's courtesy for any unexpected guests who wanted to take advantage of his house's location on the Gulf of Mexico. There was a box of assorted men's suits in the same closet, just to firm up that concept.

As for any other physical evidence, there would be none. The same acute sense of smell that had allowed him to recognize the odor of Schneider's gun at 30 feet was also capable of locating even the finest hair from any person whose scent he knew. There wasn't so much as a piece of dandruff in the house by now. And since fingerprints were caused by the bodily oil on the skin's surface, and therefore also had a scent, each fingerprint had been sniffed out and eliminated.

"You were here all day Thursday?" Schneider asked.

"Most of the day. Not all."

"Were you at the Winn-Dixie on Estuary Boulevard?"

"No," Nathanson said. "But I was in the smoke shop next door to it that afternoon."

"This place doesn't smell like a smoker lives in it."

"I don't smoke. I read. The owner of that place stocks just about the best selection of magazines and paperback books in this area."

He also, Schneider thought, stocked one of the largest selections of pornographic magazines and video tapes. Something the sheriff had never managed to prove, even while it was common knowledge.

"Did you buy anything?" he asked.

"A *Popular Mechanics*. It's in the rack by the sofa, if you want to see it."

Schneider shook his head. "No need." The smoke shop's owner hadn't mentioned seeing Nathanson on Thursday. Of course, neither had he mentioned any of his other customers. And Schneider and the first detective had been asking about Elaine Gould, not Nathanson.

"Did you happen to meet anyone at that shopping center?"

"On Thursday?"

"Yes."

Now Nathanson smiled. "As a matter of fact, yes."

"Who?"

"A girl. Kari—or Sheri—something like that. We came back here and had a light supper."

"You're not sure of her name?"

"No. I met her that afternoon, and she was going home the next day. Chicago, I think."

"You just had dinner?"

"Supper, actually. And that actually was all, yes. I had some other things in mind, but it never happened. Probably why her name didn't stick."

"What did she look like?"

"Fairly tall. Good figure. Dark hair, about shoulder length. Very pretty."

Which, Schneider thought, was also a good description of Elaine Gould. Particularly at a distance, and seen through a shop window.

Even so, if it really had been Elaine the snack bar owner had seen with Nathanson, it would have been easy enough for him to invent an anonymous tourist who looked like her. Elaine was dead, and could no longer identify him. And this Kari or Sheri was back in, maybe, Chicago, where she would be impossible to find without a complete name.

Coincidences were common enough. As a police officer, Schneider was more aware of that fact than most people. But he also knew that coincidences could be contrived. And there was something about Nathanson that just didn't seem right. It was as if he was a little – too innocent seeming. The similar appearance of the women too obviously coincidental.

He was also aware that he wasn't going to get anything useful out of him now.

"Impressive library," Schneider said. It had nothing to do with the investigation, but Nathanson was the closest thing they had to a suspect at the moment. Getting friendly might help to put him at ease, and something could still slip out.

"This is just a part of it," Nathanson replied. "A very small part, in fact."

"Seems to be in several languages."

"I *speak* several. English, of course," which really wasn't 'of course,' but he was passing as an American and naturally claimed English as his native language. Since he'd been speaking it since 1807, it might as well have been. "Latin, Greek, Spanish, French, German, Hebrew, and Yiddish." He spoke 12 other languages as well, but this list seemed impressive enough, and accounted for all of the books he had at this house. In three centuries it was possible to learn as many languages as you wished.

"All I can manage is English, Hebrew, and Aramaic," Schneider said. "My Yiddish is sort of rusty."

"Any language takes constant practice if you want to remain proficient in it."

"True."

Schneider's beeper went off. The liquid crystal display was showing the Sheriff's private number.

"Well," he said, "I think I'd better be going now."

"Sorry I couldn't help," Nathanson said. "But stay in touch. I'm curious about the family connection. It might be interesting to see how closely we're actually related."

•   •   •

Schneider dialed the number, using the cellular phone in the car. Unlike the radio, the phone was difficult for anyone to monitor. For while it was astonishingly easy to hijack a cellular phone number and use it to make calls, there were no scanners made with cellular frequencies, which, in any case, might change several times during any given call. The fact that his beeper had displayed the phone number, and not a simple order to call in, generally indicated that what the Sheriff wished to discuss wasn't something he wanted the local news media—along with a thousand assorted busybodies with police scanners—to listen in on.

"Have you got anything on these beach killings yet?" Mitchell asked, not bothering with the preliminaries.

"Maybe, Sir. Too early to tell for sure."

"The county commission used my ass for a target this morning, Schneider. They yell at me, I get to yell at you. That's how it works."

"Always did, Sir."

"You got anything else to check on out there?"

"I think I'm done for now."

"But no suspects?"

"Possibly. Only possibly, though. One witness reported seeing someone with the last victim on Thursday, but I've done a preliminary interview with the suspect and there's nothing concrete. He admits recognizing her picture, but he lives out here, so a casual familiarity wouldn't be that unusual. And the employees at the Winn-Dixie are all positive that neither of them were in the store on Thursday. Also, he admits being in the parking lot with a girl who *looks* like the victim."

"You need to find her, then," the sheriff said.

"We can't. He says she was a tourist who's already gone back north, and he isn't sure what city, or even what her name was."

"Sounds pretty convenient," Mitchell said. "You didn't manage to get inside his house, did you?"

"Yes. But aside from the decor, nothing looked out of the ordinary."

"What was wrong with the decorating?"

"Nothing, Sir. It just seemed very Victorian looking for such a young man. From a 24-year-old living on Port Morrow Beach, I suppose I was expecting a lot more *casual* looking place."

"You think a search would do us any good?"

"You can never really be sure about that, can you, Sir? Anyway, I doubt if we have enough to convince a judge to issue a warrant. Our only witness saw them from maybe 50 yards away, so he obviously couldn't make a positive I.D. on the girl. And the description of this guy's 'tourist' sounds enough like her to provide a reasonable possibility of mistaken identity. I think a judge would probably prefer to err on the side of caution at this point."

"What do *you* think?"

The sheriff, Schneider thought, might not be a very good Jew, but he was definitely a good cop. And good cops knew that instinct was often as important as obvious facts. Cop instinct was, in any case, mostly subconscious deduction – the mind putting together all the little clues that hadn't registered on the surface.

"I think," Schneider said, "that he's probably the best lead we have. But I can't prove anything yet."

"So what do you want to do?"

"I think we should follow him around for a few days. Just see what he's really up to. He may just be a rich kid who's into casual relationships with tourists. But it's also possible he'll do something that will interest a judge, and we'll be able to get our warrant and search his house."

"Do you think he's likely to notice a tail?"

"Maybe," Schneider said. "He strikes me as pretty smart. He's only in his early 20s, but there's something about him that makes you wonder if he doesn't know things you haven't got around to learning yet. On the other hand, smart can also work to our advantage. If he thinks he's too smart to be caught, he might just do something stupid."

"Okay. Get on in here and file your report. I think we can spare one or two men to keep an eye on him for a few days."

Chapter Ten
Tuesday, August 3, 1993

Port Morrow Beach

Isaac Nathanson put the polishing cloth back in the drawer and examined the candlestick in the afternoon sunlight, which was pouring through the window over the kitchen sink. The polish was immaculate, as always. This was normal for him; keeping his home spotless not only created a more pleasant environment—which was important to someone who was "awake" 24 hours a day, six days a week—but also eliminated the evidence of visitors. Particularly of visitors Nathanson preferred to suggest had never been in his house.

The candlestick was American Colonial, hand crafted of sterling silver, and of an exquisite design. Not Revere—though Nathanson actually owned a silver tea service made by that well-known craftsman and revolutionary—the candlestick was, he felt, actually somewhat nicer. Revere had been a competent silversmith, certainly, but his renown came mostly from his activities on the eve of the American Revolution.

Nathanson had met Revere, during his first visit to then colonial America. That was when he had acquired the tea service. He hadn't been particularly impressed with the man, a silversmith—most of whose surviving work was actually in pewter—and dentist. Nathanson was sure he'd been a better silversmith than a dentist. But, in those times, even the best dentist was someone you avoided whenever possible.

The candlestick he had purchased five years ago, at an antique sale in New York.

He replaced the candlestick on its shelf, and washed his hands in the sink. There were several people on the beach, and when he had dried his hands, he walked out onto the back porch to watch the activity.

He had been sitting on the porch steps for about half an hour when he saw the girl coming down the beach. It was an odd feeling—like being suddenly transported back in time, though her costume was curiously out of sync with that feeling.

The girl was a blond, and not particularly tall. She wore her hair loose, falling about halfway down her back and was dressed in a skimpy bikini, which Nathanson considered an aesthetic disaster in the present era. Her figure was really too full for the bathing suit. Not fat, but much rounder than the current fashion, with wide hips, and heavy breasts that swayed as she walked.

She looked, he thought, just like Irena. Or, at least, just as Irena would have looked in a bikini—which she would obviously never have worn.

He hadn't thought of Irena in years, except with a pang of regret at throwing away his own life for her dubious affections. Once he'd loved her—but that had been more than three centuries ago, and there had been hundreds of relationships, and thousands of other women, in the intervening years.

Seeing the girl on the beach brought a lot of it back. The resemblance was striking. Even the same figure—too heavy by modern standards, though actually rather slender for the late 17th Century—and the same cascade of blond hair. Put her in an appropriate period dress and it would have been hard to tell them apart.

With a little effort, he could remember the last time he'd seen her. A very busy night, he recalled.

Chapter Eleven
Wednesday, May 10, 1684

Kapelskof, Poland

Father Itsvan Orloffski stood in the narrow opening at the top of the bell tower of Saint Ioseph's Church, looking down on the town. It offended his sensibilities that the most prominent thing to be seen from his vantage point was the ancient stone wall that surrounded the Kapelskof ghetto, with the Jewish houses beyond it. Why did the prince allow the Jews to remain there? They might, he admitted, contribute economically to the town, but they were a potential danger to the souls of the good Christian people who lived around them.

Orloffski was only too typical of a Polish priest of that time. He could read, which gave him an advantage over most of the local peasants, but for all his "education" he remained a remarkably ignorant man. His Church taught him that Jesus had been the promised Messiah. The Jews had rejected him, and therefore the Jews were cursed. By rights, they shouldn't even exist. How could God permit a people to live, when they had murdered Christ, and accepted the punishment for that deed upon themselves and all of their descendants?

Once, the Jews had served a purpose, as the only monotheistic people in a pagan world. But their day was past—their special place in God's scheme now occupied by the Church, and Jerusalem had been supplanted by Rome, which was the center of the New Israel. As for the Jews themselves, they should have long since been absorbed by the body of believers. Or destroyed, as a potential plague.

Yet they still existed. Orloffski knew nothing of psychology—the word hadn't even been invented yet—but it was precisely the psychology of the situation that was causing his problems. If the Jews, who were obsolete, still existed, then he was presented with the possibility that it might be *his* beliefs that were wrong. He could not accept such a possibility, so he did his best to prove that the Jews were truly cursed.

He had enjoyed a little success. On Easter, the peasants had paid enough attention to his homily to go into the ghetto and kill several Jews. They had even killed the old rabbi, who had been a thorn in Orloffski's side for nearly 30 years. And, so far, he had not been replaced. That would take time, and if the priest could arrange it, a great deal of time. A new rabbi would need a residency permit, for the number of Jews in the ghetto was carefully regulated. When there were too many, the excess were sent away, to make their fortunes as best they could in other cities or towns.

The prince would undoubtedly allow them to bring in a new rabbi, but Orloffski felt it was his duty to delay that. It seemed, to him, reasonable to require the Jews to wait a couple of years for a rabbi. Without a leader, they would be more vulnerable to conversion. And Orloffski was already planning his sermons, for the days when the Jews would be marched into the church, and made to listen to the Truth about their perfidy, and the crimes of their ancestors that could be expiated only by accepting Christ.

Orloffski told himself that he didn't really hate the Jews. His faith taught him to love all peoples, even the sinners, and to do his best to bring them to see the Truth. He thought he had succeeded with Itzak, the tailor's son, who had been secretly studying with the elderly priest, preparing for conversion.

But that fool, Wladislaw, had put an end to that. Imagine, forbidding the marriage, even if Itzak was willing to renounce his cursed origins and join the people of Christ! And so Itzak had killed himself, still unbaptized, which meant that he would be punished in hell for eternity. Twice damned—first, for being a Jew and rejecting his Savior, and, second, for killing himself.

The priest sighed. So many good intentions, and so often they were for nothing.

He turned and started down the winding stairs. It would soon be time for evening mass.

•   •   •

Irena walked at her father's side as they returned from the church in the dark. The streets were only fitfully lit by the dim glow from the windows of the houses. You had to be careful where you walked; not an easy task, when you could hardly see where you were putting your feet.

And there were other dangers. The prince's soldiers patrolled the streets after dark, but they couldn't be everywhere, and robbers were sometimes abroad. There had been several unexplained murders in the town in recent months. The soldiers' patrols had been increased, but people were still dying under the strangest of circumstances. Five men, all with their throats slashed, and yet there had been no blood.

There was talk of an *upior* in the town. Irena thought of the idea as foolish. Peasant legends and superstitions. Despite the best efforts of her father to prevent it, Irena had managed to educate herself. She could read, and her father was forced to admit that this might have some slight utility, since he was, himself, illiterate, and having a daughter who could read meant that he didn't have to depend on someone outside the family to keep his accounts.

But Wladislaw's ideas of female education stopped precisely at that point. His daughter could keep his accounts for him, but he saw no reason for her to pursue further knowledge. She was just a woman, after all, and her place in life was to marry the right man and give him a large brood of grandchildren.

They had differed on who the right man should be, too, Irena thought. For her father, the only real factor was that he should be of pure Polish stock. His financial status was less important. Irena was the only child, so her husband would naturally take over the family's inn when her father died.

For Irena, love was also a factor. And it was her curse that she had fallen in love with the wrong man. Itzak had been everything that her other suitors had not. He was tall and handsome, and, far more importantly, he was also truly gentle. The men her father brought home to meet her were usually crude, brutish peasants. Itzak had been literate in three languages, and had a knowledge of the classics which, though she didn't know it, was actually somewhat unusual for a Jew of that period, a traditional Jewish education being essentially limited to Talmudic studies.

They reached the inn, and Irena followed her father into the public room on the main floor. Old Ivan, the caretaker, was standing behind the long bar, pouring drinks for the customers. Mostly, these were exactly the sort of men Irena found most distasteful. Illiterate, cruel, and lazy, they spent most of their days in the inn, guzzling beer and wine, or gorging themselves on the big platters of heavily salted food her father always set out.

The food was free, provided you bought a drink first. The heavy dose of salt was what her father called an "incentive." It made the men thirstier, so they would drink more beer. And the food was the cheapest he could buy. Old bread, with the moldy crusts cut off; slices of meat that had been put in the brine barrel so long ago that even the butcher couldn't remember. Irena was surprised the customers didn't get sick from eating it.

Most of these men had wives at home, too. She wondered how many of them actually missed their husbands when they were here getting drunk, and how many were simply glad to be rid of them for a while. She suspected that, if she were married to any of them, she'd wish him to spend *all* of his time away from home.

If it was necessary for her father to find her a husband, she wondered, why couldn't he find her a sailor, who would at least be gone for months at a time? If she couldn't have the man she really wanted—and, now that he was dead, she obviously couldn't—then she would prefer to have one who didn't bother her too much.

Her father went behind the bar, and Irena walked through the door that led to the private quarters in the rear of the building.

•   •   •

The priest walked through the church, snuffing out the candles that lit the sanctuary. He wondered, sometimes, if the people actually listened to what he said. Or did they just come into the church because it was expected of them, and leave, none the better, when the mass was ended?

True, the people really didn't have to do much. They were there mostly as witnesses. The priest performed the ritual, and the only thing the congregation was required to do was to make the appropriate responses, and, if they had confessed and done their penance, come forward at the proper time and take the communion wafer onto their tongues.

But he had always wanted to make a difference. To make the peasants who comprised his congregation into better people. Into people for whom the sacrifice of their Blessed Savior was as real as it was for the priest.

"No one really listens," he said, as the entered the sacristy.

"Some do, Father," a voice said, from a dark corner of the room. "Some of them listen."

"Who?"

"It's just me, Father. Itzak."

The priest went pale as the tall, redhaired man stepped from the shadows. He was dressed differently now. More like a Polish merchant than a Jew, and his beard was gone, but it was unquestionably Itzak.

"It can't be," the priest said. "You're dead."

"If I was dead, I couldn't be standing here, could I? So I must not be dead."

The priest nodded. Had the Jews perpetrated an elaborate hoax on him, to rob him of this man's soul? To the priest, it seemed perfectly in character. The Jews would do anything to keep one of their own from seeing the Truth.

"I was told you were dead," he said. "That you'd killed yourself."

"Oh, I did. It just wasn't as permanent as everyone expected it to be."

Now what did that mean? the priest wondered. How could someone die, but not die permanently? Except for the Blessed Savior, death was always permanent. You couldn't come back.

"You're not wearing your Jewish clothing, Itzak," the priest commented. "Have you truly found God?"

Itzak laughed. "More than you can imagine, Father. I have been closer to God than *any* priest in the last few weeks. Heard his voice, even."

Now it was becoming clear. The man had suffered some terrible injury, and now he was mad. Hearing voices.

"And what did he say to you, Itzak?"

"He said that it was forbidden to take my own life. And that I must be punished for this, and for the blasphemy I spoke at the time. That I would live until the Messiah comes, resting only on the Sabbath." He smiled. "Not *your* Messiah, Father. He was a myth—just an ordinary man, who died and never rose. *Our* Messiah."

The priest blanched. What Itzak was saying was impossible. How could the Jews have been right?

"I'm afraid I have killed a few people since I last saw you, Father," Itzak said. "Stanislaw, the butcher, was the first. Did you know he was one of those who murdered Rabbi Shimon? And four more—all of them murderers on Easter past. Stanislaw told me who they were as he died. He didn't want to, I suppose, but his thoughts came to me as I drank his blood."

"*Retro, Satano, retro,*" the priest intoned.

"Why invoke *him*, Father? I'm not the Satan. I'm Itzak. Just another poor Jew that you'd thought to make a victim of your foolishness. And the Satan is no more than an angel, doing his job. Not a fallen angel, nor a powerful force for evil; just the angel who points out the things we do wrong, and prosecutes us in the heavenly court. He has no power over men—that's a myth *your* people invented, when *your* messiah failed to do what was expected."

Orloffski sat heavily in a wooden chair. "What do you want of me, Itzak?" he asked.

"Only your life, Father. Your preaching has been responsible for many deaths—for many murders. It is time you paid some penalty for your crimes."

"No! I sought only to do good!"

"Good does not come from evil, Father."

"And if you kill me, will you not be equally guilty?"

"I suppose I will. But that is *my* punishment, you see? I will live until *Moshiach* comes, and I will sustain my life with the blood of the living." He smiled broadly, showing the sharp canine teeth. "Not yours, though. I will not drink the blood of a man who has been responsible for so many deaths, for so many lies, and provocations. You I will merely kill."

Then, in a single, swift move, Itzak circled the priest, producing a long knife from his sleeve and slashing the man's throat right back to the spine. The priest's eyes opened wide, but he made no sound, dropping instantly to the floor as his blood spread out in a wide pool, gushing from the severed veins and arteries.

Itzak dropped the knife on the sacristy floor—it was one he had taken from Stanislaw's shop, and had the pig butcher's name branded on the handle. Let the prince's soldiers try to figure that one out, he thought. A murder weapon branded with its owner's name, but the owner himself dead for five weeks. He wondered if they would dig up Stanislaw's grave, to see if he had rotted yet. Even though he had been careful to eliminate the distinctive marks of his teeth on his victims, the lack of blood would surely suggest a vampire. And the belief was that the victim of a vampire would, himself, then become a vampire.

Itzak was now sure this was not so. There was a way, he had heard, in which the victim could be brought over. But it required more than merely having his blood drained by a vampire. It also required that the victim drink the *vampire's* blood.

Irena awoke with a start. Something was tapping gently at her window. She slipped out of the bed, pulling up the neck of her woolen nightgown, and walked to the window.

"Who's out there?" she demanded. In the darkness, she could see nothing but a vague man shape.

"Itzak."

Irena shuddered, but moved closer to the window. "Itzak is dead," she said softly.

"I'm not dead. It was our parents, Irena. Both of our fathers. Mine has kept me locked in the attic of his house since Easter, and yours has lied to you."

She wanted to believe this. It sounded like something her father would do. He hated Jews, but he would deal with one if he saw an advantage to be gained. And she knew that the Jews were just as firmly set against allowing their children to marry Poles as her father had been against her marrying a Jew. Would the two fathers have concocted such a story, just to prevent the marriage?

"Wait," she said. She walked to the hearth, where a low fire was kept burning at all times. In that period, before the invention of matches, fires were never permitted to go out, for it involved a great deal of trouble with flint, steel, and tinder to get them going again. She lit a slender twig from the fire, and used this to light a tallow candle, which she took over to the window.

The fitful light revealed the face through the wavy glass. It really *was* Itzak, she thought.

"Open the window," he said. "Let me in. We'll go away together and leave these people behind."

Irena nodded. Putting down the candle, she unhooked the latch and threw open the windows. Itzak climbed in. She was surprised by his clothing, and by the absence of his beard, wondering what it meant. Then, she realized, it could mean only one thing. He had actually gone to the priest and been baptized, casting off his Jewish identity. Her father wouldn't accept it, but it was sufficient for her.

"You've been to the priest," she said.

Itzak smiled, understanding her intended meaning. "I have at that," he said. "He was rather surprised to see me, as it turned out."

"We all thought you were dead."

He nodded. "I was. But I'm back now. Resurrected, and returned to you, my love."

"I feel restored to life myself, Itzak."

"Get dressed. If your father comes in, we'll have trouble."

She nodded and walked to the wardrobe. Like most houses of that period, the family quarters in the inn had been built without closets. It would not be until the 20th Century that architects finally decided that it was prudent to waste floor space on miniature rooms useful only for hanging up clothing. In the 17th Century, most people owned only two or three of any item of clothing in any case, so storage was less of a problem.

Irena pulled the nightdress off over her head and threw it onto the bed. Behind her, Itzak smiled. She had, he thought, a nearly perfect body. Full and rounded. It was a pity she would have no children, for she had the appearance of a woman who would bear easily.

She turned and smiled at him, still naked. Her breasts were full and heavy in the fitful candlelight. Her blond hair gleamed like pale gold as it cascaded about her shoulders. Not too long ago, he thought, he would have found it difficult not to simply throw off his own clothes and take her on the big feather-bed that took up most of her room. Now, he merely smiled.

"Hurry," he said.

Irena shrugged and pulled a dress on over her head. She had almost finished dressing when the door to the room burst open, to reveal her father, holding a lantern in one hand, and a heavy cudgel in the other. As the light fell on Itzak, the innkeeper nearly dropped them both.

"You! You're supposed to be dead!"

Itzak smiled broadly, so that Wladislaw could see his teeth, the sharp canines gleaming in the lanternlight. "Maybe I am," he replied.

"*You* killed him!" Wladislaw hissed. "You killed Father Istvan—and the others, too. Didn't you?"

"You said you'd been to see the priest," Irena said.

Itzak nodded. "I did see him. Only a little while ago. He was quite dead when I left. He's had dozens of people murdered in the time he's lived in this city—I was merely paying him back for his damned riots."

"First you kill Christ," Wladislaw yelled, "and now you kill his priest! You think you'll get away?"

"I'm quite sure of it, you pathetic little peasant."

The innkeeper rushed forward, swinging the club at Itzak's head. But Itzak simply reached up and grabbed the club before it could strike him. Then he straightened his arm, thrusting it upward, and tearing the cudgel from the innkeeper's hand.

"I'm sorry, Irena," Itzak said. "But it can't be helped."

With that, his head darted forward and down, his teeth ripping into Wladislaw's throat. The innkeeper went limp as the blood was pulled from his veins by an incredible suction.

When he released Wladislaw's body to fall in a heap on the floor, Itzak turned and smiled at Irena, who was looking at him in absolute horror.

"*Upior*?" she asked. "You?"

Itzak shrugged. "I'm afraid so. But *you* needn't fear me, my love. Come away with me, and you will never again know want, or fear, or hunger."

"How could you kill him?"

"He was standing in the way of our happiness, Irena. Can't you see that? And what was he, really? A little man of no real worth to anyone. A hater—a man who would very happily have killed *me* just now. Probably you, too, if you'd defied him."

"And what will you do to me, Itzak?"

"I am immortal. I'll live forever. So will you."

"As a monster? A creature of Satan?"

Itzak laughed. "Satan is a nothing," he said. "He does what he's told and nothing more. I know more about God now than I ever did. His is the *only* power. And there is a way for you to join me in this everlasting life. To have the power of life and death over lesser creatures. Over lesser men!"

He moved swiftly to her, grasping her arm in his left hand. His grip was too powerful to resist. With his right hand he tore open his shirt and, extracting a small knife from his belt, made a shallow slash in his chest.

He pushed her head down on his chest, forcing her mouth over the flowing wound. "Drink!" he demanded. The force of his will flowed out from him, and he could feel her sucking in his blood, her tongue lapping it up.

After a minute the wound began to close itself and the blood flow ceased. She lifted her head, her pretty mouth stained with the dark blood.

"Now," he said, "you will become immortal, and together we will continue our love forever."

His head darted down, his mouth fastening to her throat while the sharp canine teeth sank painlessly into her neck. He drank until she fell limp in his arms.

Gently, he placed her on the bed, and waited for her to rise and join him.

Chapter Twelve
Tuesday, August 3, 1993

Port Morrow Beach

But Irena had never risen from death, Nathanson thought. He had come to a realization after that. His condition was a punishment, and nothing more. Having the victim drink his blood accomplished nothing. Neither did repeated attacks, taking only a small amount of blood each time. None of the legends meant anything. Vampires were created by *God*, not by other vampires, and their creation was dependent only on the way in which they died.

In all the years since his death, he had met only one other vampire. That had been a "young" woman, very beautiful, and also with red hair. In fact, she had been some 400 years older than Nathanson, and had killed herself by leaping under the wheels of a heavily loaded cart in Satu Mare in 1258, after finding herself pregnant with her employer's child.

She, in turn, had known three other vampires, and each of them had also been a suicide. Each had cursed God at the time of their death, and been buried without ritual.

He smiled, thinking of her. He had known her for nearly 75 years now, and they kept in touch by letter and telephone on a fairly regular basis. Once or twice a year they would meet, for it is a little known fact that vampires are perfectly capable of normal sexual relations—but only with other vampires. There was a sexual connotation to their consumption of blood, to be sure, yet it was only a pale reflection of the heights of ecstasy they could reach through physically coupling with their own kind.

But with normal mortals, sex was impossible. Nathanson had tried, any number of times, but remained incapable of arousal with a living woman. Yet the slightest touch from Dinah had him ready in an instant.

But Dinah was, as far as he knew, the only female vampire in the world today. Of the three others *she* had known, one had been a female, but that one had been destroyed by the Baal Shem Tov in 1783. The other two were, themselves, lovers. Their homosexuality had been the reason for their dual suicide in the late 19th Century. They were also brothers, which Nathanson suspected made them doubly damned, for it added incest to their list of crimes against God.

As for Dinah—she was perfect. Too perfect, really. They met only once or twice a year, and then went their separate ways, keeping in touch only by telephone. They had long ago decided that it was better if they remained in different cities. Not only because, had they been together, the victim count would have doubled in the area, but because their physical proximity was too great a temptation. When they were together, they seemed to spend nearly every moment in bed. He suspected that, if they remained permanently together, they might both forget to eat and ultimately find themselves too weak to return to their coffins.

At the moment, he had other things to think about. The blond was now about 100 yards down the beach. Unless she had a car parked down there—which was unlikely—she would have to come back this way before long. And if Irena had never been restored to life, he still harbored a strange affection for her. One that might be briefly rekindled, given the chance.

Two hours later, Nathanson found himself peering in the window of an old house which, at some point, had been split up into a number of tiny apartments. The shade was up less than an inch above the window frame, and he was well concealed amidst a stand of heavy shrubbery.

Inside the ground-floor apartment, the blond had stripped off her bikini and taken a shower, and was now lying on the bed, holding a romance novel in her left hand, and absent-mindedly fingering herself with the right. After a time, she put down the book. Her left hand, which was now free, went to her right breast, her forefinger describing a circu-

lar motion around the hardened nipple. The middle finger of her right
hand was moving up and down at the juncture of her thighs, her hips
rising and falling as she worked herself into a frenzy. Her left hand
kneaded her breast, lifting it as she bent her head, her tongue darting
out to lick the nipple.

Now both hands were at her crotch, the right opening and caressing
from the front, while her left went behind her, the forefinger sliding in
and out, her whole body trembling as sharp, staccato gasps burst from
her lips.

And as she stopped shaking, and her breathing returned to normal,
she continued to caress and finger herself, starting the whole sequence
again, until she had brought herself to orgasm six times over the three
hours Nathanson remained hidden in the bushes. Six times, each more
intense than the previous, until, as she trembled and moaned with the
force of the final orgasm, she actually wet the bed.

When she had subsided the final time, Nathanson left his hiding
place and quietly entered the apartment, which had been left unlocked
the whole time. The blond was still basking in the afterglow, her body
spent, the whole room pungent with the mixed odor of woman and the
sharper tang of her urine on the sheets.

She looked up at him and smiled. He did as well, for the first time
noticing the painting on the cover of her romance novel. A beautiful
blonde, in the obligatory lowcut Regency gown, locked in the embrace
of a tall, redhaired man wearing what looked like a British naval uniform at least 50 years out of sync with the style of her gown. Nathanson
wasn't wearing a uniform—he was dressed in dark trousers and a white
shirt—but he realized that the girl was still high on the endorphins gen-
erated during her long masturbation session, and had somehow transported both of them into her book.

Her hand went to his crotch, caressing him through the fabric. He
frowned slightly. This happened from time to time, and he was always
hopeful, but he remained unaffected, and, with a sigh, bent over her
and fastened his lips on her throat.

•   •   •

There was a tremendous advantage to sand, Nathanson thought, an
hour later. You could bury someone quite deep, and after you'd filled in

the hole, there was nothing to show that anyone had dug there. Unlike normal soil, the sand simply flowed into the hole and blended with that surrounding it. Even if the damper sand from the hole showed up darker when the hole was first filled in, it quickly dried out, becoming indistinguishable from the rest of the beach. It was possible they would find the girl's body after a bad storm, but not otherwise.

He had decided to bury this one while he stood outside her window. The police would be looking for patterns, and it was better to remain consistent. The girl's resemblance to Irena had marked her out for him, but she was physically unlike any of the other victims. Better to hide her body, lest the search for the killer intensify even more.

Besides, he had noticed something odd earlier in the day, and he felt it might be safer to avoid anything obvious for a little while.

Chapter Thirteen
Wednesday, August 4, 1993

Port Morrow Beach

Deputy Edward Hanson sat at the far end of the bar in the Tropical Breeze Hotel, nursing a glass of Coca-Cola. Served in a cocktail glass, no one could tell by looking that there was no alcohol in his drink. He was supposed to be a guy cruising the Beach bars, looking for girls. That sort of guy would be drinking.

He had been sitting on the same stool for over an hour, ostensibly watching the baseball game being shown on the TV suspended over the bar. The degree of his true interest in the game was probably best demonstrated by the fact that he didn't know the score, and wasn't even sure who was playing. Or whether this game actually mattered, as far as the team rankings were concerned.

Hanson had never been much of a baseball fan. Certainly he had never cared about the game with the passion of his father, a diehard Cubs fan—which was the only sort, really—who had been infuriated when the leagues were split into divisions for no purpose other than to provide playoffs and increase the television revenue for the clubs. As far as the elder Hanson was concerned, the only thing the playoffs accomplished was to present the fans with the possibility of a World Series between two teams who might not have finished higher than fourth or fifth overall. Only *one* team in each league playoff would actually be the best team in the league, after all—the others would just be the best in their division. And with three divisions soon to start, the best team, even if it won the first set of playoffs, was faced with the prospect of playing a second set against a team that had spent the first set getting a good rest.

Some years, his father said, it wouldn't matter. If the top teams in each division were close enough in the overall standings, the ultimate victor would still have a better win-loss record and could arguably call itself the league champion. But if the top team in the league was so far ahead of the others that four games would make no difference, the worst could always happen.

Not, Hanson thought, that this game—he now realized it was New York and Baltimore—was going to make much of a difference in the standings. It was too early in the season.

At the far end of the lounge, the usual over amplified band was covering all the hit songs of the late 1970s. Hanson had been a teenager at that time, and couldn't understand what the older people could find in the music—mostly disco and low-quality rock—to be nostalgic about. To him it merely sounded trite and stupid. His own preferences ran more to Waylon Jennings, which was something you didn't find in the Tropical Breeze.

What you did find, at least this evening, was Isaac Nathanson. Hanson had been following him around for the last three evenings, and so far had seen nothing suspicious. The good part was that the surveillance job was a little extra money, and it got him out of uniform. He had to use his own car, but the Department would pay him 25 cents a mile for using it on official business, and he figured it didn't cost him more than a dime a mile to drive.

So far Nathanson had given no indication that he knew he was being followed. Hanson was the Department's expert on tailing people, and he knew he was good at it. Besides, this was Port Morrow Beach, where even in summer the bars and hotel lounges were normally busy. Mostly filled with young people looking for some casual sex, along with quite a few older men looking for younger women. Since men on the make tended to move from one bar to another as soon as they decided they weren't going to get any action where they were, a subject was less likely to notice he was being followed. Under the circumstances prevailing, it was common enough to keep running into the same people.

Nathanson was seated at one of the small tables. He could see the plain-clothes cop reflected in one of the narrow strips of mirror that were spaced at intervals on the wall behind the band. They weren't wide enough that anyone was likely to notice the absence of his reflection in one of them, but they did allow him to keep an eye on the cop.

The man had originally shown up on Monday evening. At first he had thought it might be a coincidence. Between the county Sheriff, and the city police departments in Port Morrow, Cape Marl, and Santiago Island, there were about 350 law enforcement officers in Benjamin County. It wouldn't be too unusual to run into one of them in a night club; cops liked to drink, after all, and had even been known to pick up women in bars. Statistically, cops were a total disaster when it came to alcohol abuse and divorce. They drank too much, chased women, and generally liked to unwind whenever they got the chance. Usually loudly and inappropriately.

About the only people with worse records for staying married were radio announcers and local TV personalities.

But the same cop kept showing up in the same bars with Nathanson. In one place wearing a sport coat, in the next in shirtsleeves. Twice he had been wearing glasses, each time with different frames. The best that could be said for his choice of disguises was that they weren't too obvious, like the fake beards that seemed to be favored by the clichéd movie and television types.

It didn't matter to Nathanson, of course. He'd known the man was armed by the smell of his gun, which wouldn't have been apparent to anyone else in the place. In Florida, that no longer guaranteed he was actually a cop, since a carry permit was now quite easy to obtain. That was also why the criminal element had started to concentrate on people driving rental cars, or those with out-of-state plates. Tourists were less likely to be armed, and thus were also less likely to shoot back when someone tried to rob them.

But there was a cop "look" to the man. And the frequent changes of appearance actually confirmed it. Someone looking to get laid wouldn't be doing that; someone who was trying not to be noticed would. Coupled with the fact that he had first appeared on the evening of the same day that Schneider had shown up on his doorstep, it left Nathanson with little doubt that the cop was there to keep an eye on him.

At the moment, Nathanson was watching the dance floor. There were a couple of likely candidates out there. The men they were dancing with had been sitting at the bar, and not with the girls, so it should be possible to approach one or the other of them when the music stopped.

The cop wouldn't be a problem. Having thoroughly satisfied his appetite the previous afternoon, Nathanson wasn't yet hungry enough to kill. When that time came, he knew it wouldn't be too hard to find the privacy he needed. And with any luck the cops would decide that following him around was a waste of time before he felt the need.

Cape Marl

Schneider sat in the living room of his apartment, wondering just how long this meeting would go on. The other board members were crowded into the room. Since Florida's corporation laws required ten board members for non-profit religious corporations, the board consisted of 10/13th of the male membership.

This evening, there was an eleventh person present. Rabbi Dov-Ber Hershkovitz had applied to the congregation for the High Holiday position they had advertised in one of the national Jewish newspapers. While the little congregation was unable to afford a full-time spiritual leader, they *could* put together enough money to bring in a rabbi for the Holidays.

Usually they didn't hold in-person interviews, since it would have been the congregation's responsibility to pay the candidate's air fare and lodging. But Hershkovitz was retiring from a congregation in Cleveland, and thinking of moving to the Port Morrow area, which meant that he was there on his own and they were able to take advantage of the fact.

"You can sing?" Sam Heilman asked. If they were going to hire a rabbi for the Holidays, they wouldn't be able to afford a cantor as well. Some years the little congregation had a rabbi, other years a cantor—mostly, they tried to hire a rabbi who could sing.

"Some people seem to think so," Hershkovitz said. The rabbi was perfectly aware of the reason behind the question. He also knew that Jewish law decreed that if a congregation could afford to hire either a rabbi *or* a cantor, but not both, the cantor was preferred. Unlike their

Reform and Conservative counterparts, Orthodox rabbis were hired for their scholarship and knowledge of Jewish law, and not because of the way they conducted services. In many congregations, the rabbi never actually led the services, as that was the cantor's job.

"How long were you in your Cleveland pulpit?" Schneider asked.

"Forty-one years. They were my sponsors when I came to this country, and since we got along so well I just never left."

"So where were you from, originally?" asked Mort Cohen.

"I was born in Warsaw, and learned in the Yeshiva in Lublin, which is where I received my *s'micha.* I had a congregation in Krakow for a year, before the war started. When it did, I decided it would be a good idea to leave. I said this to my congregation—that they should leave—but most of them didn't listen, so the majority died in the camps."

"Where did you go? During the war, I mean?"

"I was lucky. I spent most of the war in Tokyo. Enemy territory, in a sense, but the Japanese version of anti-Semitism was more theoretical than practical. The Japanese really dislike all foreigners, but they're usually too polite to mistreat them in actual practice."

"My brother might disagree with you on that," Heilman said. "He was captured at Corregidor and spent the war in a Jap POW camp."

"Ah, well—*I* wasn't a prisoner. There's a curious thing about the Japanese character; a prisoner of war is presumed to be less than human, because the Japanese code of *bushido*—their code of the warrior—holds that a human being would obviously commit suicide rather than surrender. They didn't think as we did, and, I suppose, they still don't."

"But you came to Cleveland when the war was over?" Schneider asked, trying to get the discussion back on track.

"In 1951. I worked with the Jewish Welfare Board in Tokyo right after the war, while I was waiting to get a visa. There was a large Jewish refugee population there during the war, but when it was over the majority of us were more than ready to return to a western country. I think there may be about 400 Jews living there now—most of them diplomatic personnel."

"How do you view a rabbi's function in the general community?" Cohen asked.

"For a High Holy Day position, I'd say fairly limited. After all, you're only in town for three or four days at the most. But I presume you're asking because I've said I will probably move here permanently, so let me discuss the question from the point of view of a retired rabbi."

"Who would be the only Orthodox rabbi in the county," Schneider interjected.

"So, maybe an active retirement, then?" Hershkovitz said, smiling. "I'm 79, which I don't think is particularly old. My parents, may their memories be for a blessing, were killed by the Nazis, may their names be erased, but my grandfather lived to 96, and everyone else in the family tends to be long lived. So retiring, to me, mostly means that I will no longer have the responsibility of fulltime involvement with a congregation.

"But in the community I retire into, I would still be active. Obviously, I would attend your little congregation in any case. I've seen the others. Yours is the only congregation that has a *mechitzah,* so, from my viewpoint, yours is the only *shul* I can attend. I would not be 'your' rabbi, in the usual sense, since you wouldn't be paying me—but I would be available if my services were ever needed for some reason."

Port Morrow Beach

Hanson was getting bored. It was an inherent condition with police work. That was one thing none of the TV shows ever managed to get right, because if they made police work as exciting as it *really* was no one would ever watch. On TV you got *only* the exciting parts, while the infinitude of boredom that separated the action presumably took place during commercials.

Nathanson had danced with one young woman, then gone back to his own table. Just now he was dancing again, with a different girl, a petite blond who didn't at all fit the pattern of the killer's victims.

The first girl Nathanson had danced with had made Hanson a little hopeful. She'd been a tall, athletic, brunette who had matched the pattern perfectly. But when the dance had ended, so had the contact. Hanson hadn't seen either of them write anything down, or pass the other a note or card, so if they weren't exchanging phone numbers the dance was, probably, just a dance.

The girl he was dancing with at the moment, however, was pressing tightly against him. If he was going to take someone home, it would be her, Hanson thought.

Nathanson finished the dance and walked back to the table where the girl had been sitting. They sat down together, and he summoned a waitress—who was dressed, rather incongruously for a lounge that was decorated in early Polynesian—in a maroon velvet costume that looked like a skirtless version of what Hollywood thought Victorian hookers had worn. The fitted bodice was cut quite low, with white lace trim around the square neck, framing her upthrust breasts, and the bare suggestion of a shirt's drapery revealed a bottom suggesting ruffled, black-lace pants worn over black net stockings.

He gave her the drink order, then turned back to his companion. "So what do you do?" he asked the girl, whose name was Margie. A nickname, naturally, to go along with her petite frame and upbeat personality. She just didn't act, or look, like a Margaret.

"I work for a doctor."

"You're a nurse?"

"I wish. No, I'm a transcriptionist. You know—he dictates stuff into a tape recorder and I type it up later."

"Sounds interesting."

"Sometimes. If you like spending all day listening to reports of clogged arteries, sclerotic livers, and blunt-force trauma."

Nathanson frowned. "What kind of doctor do you work for?"

"He's the County Medical Examiner."

Now Nathanson smiled. Margie, without knowing it, had just guaranteed her continued existence. She had also guaranteed that, whatever her opinion on the subject might *really* be, she was about to fall in love.

The drinks arrived. "Do you like to read?" Nathanson asked.

"Actually, yes."

"What sort of books?"

"A lot of novels. But serious stuff, too. And for some reason I keep picking up these books full of useless information. You know the type—does clockwise and counter-clockwise mean anything if you own a digital watch, and why does a watch work that way in the first place? That sort of thing."

"I think I have a few of those at home myself."

"You want to dance again, Zack? I kind of like this slow stuff."

"Sure."

Cape Marl

Rabbi Hershkovitz seemed to be just what they were looking for. He'd chanted a couple of the major prayers from the Yom Kippur service for them, impressing everyone. Even Sam Heilman, who, being a cantor's son, was a difficult man to impress.

More importantly, it appeared that the board members had also impressed Rabbi Hershkovitz. Mort Cohen, who was also the building manager, in addition to being a past-president of the congregation, knew that a groundfloor apartment had just become vacant. It was one of the larger units, a three-bedroom, with two bathrooms, and would be ideal for the Rabbi and his wife. The fact that it would get one more gentile family out of the building, replaced by Orthodox Jews, was also a bonus.

Port Morrow Beach

Nathanson and the girl had talked and danced for almost three hours, then left the lounge together, holding hands. Hanson followed them as they walked to Nathanson's car, keeping well back so as not to be noticed. Once he was sure that they were getting into the car, Hanson climbed into his own, picking up the radio microphone as soon as he'd started the engine. He had no intention of giving himself away by making a personal approach, but if Nathanson really *was* their killer, he figured he could remove any threat to the girl by arranging for a simple traffic stop. Nathanson had downed at least five large drinks in the last two hours, and there was simply no way for him not to be over the legal limit.

Nathanson pulled out onto Estuary Boulevard, heading south. It was a little after 1:00 o'clock in the morning, and traffic was light. The early drinkers had long since gone home, and the hardcore drunks would be grimly sticking it out until the bars closed at 2:00 am.

The red Mustang was easy to follow. Nathanson was obviously heading for home. He was also, Hanson noticed, keeping remarkably good control of the vehicle, considering the volume of alcohol he'd consumed. Hanson had watched the bartender mixing the drinks—they had all contained the appropriate volume of booze. But Nathanson was driving so well that Hanson was beginning to wonder if the sector car was even going to have an excuse for stopping him.

Probably, he thought, it would come down to the time of the morning. The majority of people on the road now would be coming home from a party or a bar. That fact alone gave the deputies some reason for stopping them. It would be nice, though, if Nathanson would run a traffic signal—which would be a little hard, since there were only two on the beach, and both were well behind them—or make an illegal lane change. If the sector car, which he knew was waiting in a 7-Eleven parking lot about a mile ahead, had been around to see Nathanson come out of the Tropical Breeze parking lot—where there was a bar—that, in itself, would have given probably cause for a stop.

Hanson looked down at his speedometer. He was keeping an even distance, and it was holding steady at 45—exactly the speed limit. Hanson's personal car didn't have a certified speedometer, such as they had in the patrol cars, and which would be required to clock another car in order to issue a speeding ticket, but it was accurate enough to tell him that Nathanson was staying within the limit.

Nathanson passed the 7-Eleven, and a moment later a car pulled out of the parking lot and took off after him. Hanson smiled as the blue lights came on. By the time Hanson caught up, the red Mustang was pulled off the road about half a mile from Nathanson's house.

Hanson continued on past them without slowing down, or looking over. He'd go down through Belle Springs and return home that way.

The patrol sergeant was wondering just what was the matter with people who had nothing better to do than to annoy senior deputies. He'd pulled out every trick he could think of, from walking a straight line, to nose-touching, to blowing through a breath analyzer. His professional conclusion was that, whatever Hanson had seen this guy drinking, it didn't have any alcohol in it. He knew Hanson had considered it important to pull Nathanson in. But the sergeant didn't know why. He wasn't even sure what Hanson was working on at the moment.

He performed a quick search of the car, which was allowed in a routine traffic stop. There was a loaded revolver in the glove compartment, but that was perfectly legal in Florida, and had been for years. The trunk was empty, except for the spare tire and jack, and a bottle of windshield washer fluid that was held upright with a bungee cord through the handle.

But no drugs. Nothing that would justify an arrest, or even a temporary detainment. And the girl was very obviously there because she wanted to be.

Lacking any evidence of impairment, or of any criminal action, the sergeant had no choice but to return Nathanson's driver's license and let him go.

Nathanson got back into his car and continued home. It had been neatly done, he thought. The cop who'd been following him had obviously called in a different cop to try to arrest him. And it would have worked, had he possessed the metabolism of a normal person.

But alcohol, like everything else he might eat or drink—other than human blood—was simply not absorbed by his system. It passed right through him and was eliminated without having any effect.

He pulled the car into the garage and walked into the house, with Margie holding his hand. She came into his arms as he locked the front door, rising up on her toes to kiss him. His hands cupped her buttocks, lifting her off her feet as she wrapped her legs around his waist.

He carried her into the bedroom that way, lowering her gently onto the bed. "I want you to make love to me," she said. "All night long."

Nathanson smiled. "Your wish is my command."

Slowly he undid the buttons on her shirt, pulling it off. She stood up as he unhooked the waistband of her shorts and lowered the zipper, pulling the shorts down her legs for her to step out of them.

Now she was standing in front of him, dressed only in white cotton panties and a gauzy nylon bra. He reached up and unhooked the bra between the cups, exposing her small, firm breasts. With a smile, he ran his tongue around the right nipple, which hardened instantly. As he sucked and licked her breasts, her hands pressing the back of his head, he pulled down her panties, all the while gently caressing her firm bottom.

His mouth moved down from her breasts, his tongue trailing over her flat stomach and into the patch of blond hair between her legs. Margie sighed and sat down on the edge of the bed, opening her legs and spreading herself apart for him as his tongue flickered over the inner softness of her.

•　　　•　　　•

Twenty minutes later, she was asleep in his bed, missing five ounces of blood and hopelessly in love with him. The blood would regenerate itself by the time she woke up, and she would have no memory of its loss. And, while their only actual lovemaking had been his oral ministrations to her, she would also remember taking him into her and the perfection of a shattering mutual climax that had never really occurred.

Nathanson sat on the bed beside her, still fully clothed, the taste of her blood and her intimate, musky juices mingling in his mouth. It was a pity he was unable to truly make love to a mortal woman, he thought. She had really tried, opening his trousers and taking him into her mouth as he licked her, but nothing had happened—though her memory would inform her that it had.

And her employer was the one who examined his victims. So much the better for him if he had the woman who typed up those reports in his power. It would give him an extra edge. Perhaps help him to recognize any progress in the investigation. Margie wouldn't be quite as good as, say, the sheriff's secretary, but she would certainly be useful.

Perhaps most importantly, the fact that Margie would walk out of his house in the morning and go to work, just like any other day, would help to remove some of the suspicion from him.

He knew Schneider suspected him. The fact that there was now a plain-clothes cop following him around merely confirmed that fact. And, after all, he really *was* guilty, wasn't he? If his grand-nephew was suspicious, it merely proved that he was a good detective. On the other hand, Nathanson thought, it was extremely unlikely that Schneider would ever be able to *prove* anything. He had a little more than three centuries of experience at convincing people that he was innocent of all the deaths that could, rightly, have been laid to his blame. And he possessed powers of suggestion that could be used to implant false beliefs, or to remove evidence from the minds of investigators.

Not that he was planning to use those powers on Schneider. But a plan was already forming. It only required the proper circumstances— and the proper subject—to be placed into effect.

Chapter Fourteen
Sunday, August 8, 1993

Benjamin County Sheriff's Department

Schneider felt as if he was back where he'd started from. The surveillance on Nathanson had come up with nothing. He'd picked up a girl in a hotel lounge on the Beach, which had potentially been promising. But the girl hadn't fit the physical type of the first two murders and, in any case, he'd taken her back to her car early the next morning, looking not only none the worse for wear, but positively euphoric.

In fact, Deputy Hanson had reported, Nathanson had also driven in to Port Morrow the next evening and collected the same girl at her apartment. They had then gone back to the Beach, and once more spent the night in Nathanson's house. Hanson had seen them go in, and he'd seen them come out in the morning. He was quite sure that no one had left the house all night.

On the same morning, a new victim had been found on the beach at the end of Earl Wilson Park. The Medical Examiner's report indicated that she had been killed during the time when Nathanson was definitely in his house. The report also indicated that this was undoubtedly the work of the same killer.

So now it was back to an endless round of interviews with hundreds of people, most of whom knew absolutely nothing. Just about as much, he thought, as *we* know. Once again, the latest victim was anonymous. There had been no identification found with her. As before, she was just a bloodless, bikini-clad body on a lonely stretch of beach. Once again very fit, and with the same shoulder-length black hair.

Which was why Schneider was in his office on a Sunday afternoon, even though it wasn't his scheduled weekend. The detectives worked one Sunday in every four, and his had been two weeks ago. He wasn't actually due to work a Sunday again until the 22nd.

But there were reports to read. And there were others to write. With the third death, the sheriff was seriously thinking about asking for Federal assistance on the case. The F.B.I. had specialists in this sort of thing; psychologists, working out of the F.B.I. Academy at Quantico, Virginia, who had made their careers out of looking into the minds of psychotic killers, and figuring out just what made them tick.

Now it was up to Schneider to put together whatever they had on the three cases, and to have a presentation ready if Mitchell made the decision to call in the Feds. Schneider suspected that the decision was already made, or why go to the trouble?

Of course, it would also help him with his own investigation. The three cases were clearly connected, and there had to be some common thread linking them together beyond the unusual methodology and the general physical similarity of the victims. The assistance of an F.B.I. shrink couldn't hurt. Neither would the added resources of the Federal investigators. Benjamin County had one of the better labs in Florida, but the whole thing would fit into the fiber section of the F.B.I. Lab.

So maybe the Feds would be able to find a previously-unknown connection between the victims. They were all athletic. Did they work out at the same health club? No, Schneider thought, it couldn't be that, The Baring girl had been from New York, and actually *worked* in a health club, but unless the killer was also from New York, he couldn't have known her from that.

The Gould girl, of course, had been a local, born and raised in North Port Morrow. She had belonged to a health club on Pittsburgh Avenue, the local designation for U.S. 41, and there were investigators checking out the other members. But they had already determined that the Baring girl had never been a guest at that facility. According to the manager of her timeshare, she had done her exercising by the pool, to the delight of the male guests, and the irritation of those of their wives who hadn't been in good enough shape to join the impromptu classes.

And since the latest victim was still unknown, Schneider had no way of knowing if she belonged to *any* health club. Or did she just exercise at home? The Medical Examiner also indicated that she was probably in her mid to late 30s, which would make her several years older than the others. Probably you couldn't tell from even a fairly short distance, though, since she was also in excellent physical condition. There was a suspicion that she worked in some type of outdoor job, since her face and arms were more darkly tanned than the rest of her body. Maybe the killer had seen her in that way? Doing some kind of work? The phone company sometimes brought in outside contractors to install new lines. Was any of that going on now? he wondered. And if it was, had one of the installers suddenly stopped showing up for work?

Of course, he thought, there was always the possibility that they were dealing with a psychopath, in which case the only connection between the victims may have been that they happened to look like his mother, or like his old third-grade teacher, or like whoever he was vicariously killing.

How did you really get inside the mind of a serial killer? He had read that, in most of these cases, the victim was rarely the actual object of the killer's anger. The victim merely *represented* his hate—or anger—or even his fear. Each time a serial murderer killed a new victim, he was, in his mind, actually killing someone else. Perhaps someone who was protected from his overt action, such as a parent. The murderer couldn't kill his mother, for instance, so he vicariously killed her by killing other women who looked like her.

Was that what was happening here? Did the three dead women look like the killer's mother? Or like an old girlfriend? Schneider remembered a psychological study of the Jack the Ripper murders that suggested the killer was a man who had caught a venereal disease from a prostitute, and took to killing other prostitutes as a type of revenge. The Ripper would have been called a serial murderer today, he thought. In any case, the condition of the bodies had made it obvious he was terribly angry about *something*.

Schneider also remembered that the Ripper murders remained unsolved after the passage of a century. He knew that Scotland Yard had had a suspect, but that there had never been an arrest or a prosecution.

At the same time, there were obvious differences. In the present murders, the chief distinguishing feature was the total lack of blood. In the Ripper murders, blood had been everywhere. And the Ripper hadn't so much killed his victims as slaughtered them. He'd even taken away pieces of the bodies, and one of his letters to the police indicated that he had fried and eaten a kidney.

But the one, distinguishing feature of the Ripper murders had been the obvious *anger* directed at the victims.

Could the same sort of thing be operating now? Had their unknown killer been hurt in some way by an aerobics instructor, and decided to kill athleticlooking young women as revenge? Schneider had to consider all possibilities, even the seemingly silly ones.

The only thing he was fairly sure of was that the killer was a man. As far as he was aware, there had only been one female serial murderer—in Florida, curiously enough. A rather unattractive prostitute whose victims had been truck drivers. The only thing he really remembered about the case was that Jean Smart, who'd played her in a TV movie, had been much too attractive to be realistic.

Of course, the entertainment industry liked to glamorize both killers and their victims. In every movie ever made about Jack the Ripper, his victims had been played by young, and very attractive, actresses, and the Ripper himself was usually a leading man type. In reality, all of the victims had been rather plain, and a couple were downright homely. What the real Ripper had looked like was anybody's guess.

Those murders had started with a relatively minor degree of violence to the bodies, and progressed to the extreme mutilation of the final victim. Schneider, who had read several books on those Whitechapel killings, had sometimes wondered if everyone had been following a false trail. They had, after all, been trying to find someone who wanted to kill prostitutes. Possibly, he thought, they should have been looking for someone who wanted to kill a *particular* prostitute, and slaughtered the others to obscure the motive. Had the murders stopped with Polly Kelly because she was, in fact, the only *intended* victim?

And could the same thing be operating here? Elaine Gould was, as far as he knew, the only local girl who had been killed up to this point. Should he be looking more closely at her, and think of the others as camouflage? It was something to think about.

Port Morrow Beach

Nathanson was sitting in a rocking chair on the front porch of his house. Next to him, in a second rocker, Margie Calloway was sipping from a tall glass of lemonade.

The cops, Nathanson had noticed, were now gone. Thursday had done it, he thought. As far as the Sheriff's Department was aware, he'd spent the entire night in the house with Margie.

As far as they were aware.

In fact, he had used his influence over her mind to cause her to fall asleep. Once she was out, he had simply walked out of the front door, actually greeting the lurking deputy. The cop hadn't noticed a thing, for in that greeting Nathanson had entered his mind and literally removed himself from the deputy's memory picture. It was, on a mental level, the equivalent of the tricks artists and filmmakers now did with computers, when they manipulated the individual pixels in the image to remove what was there and then paste in an extension of the background.

That was technology catching up with him, he thought. In the old days it had sometimes reminded him of the powers of the heroes of the pulp magazines he would sometimes read—except that, unlike The Shadow, Nathanson didn't need a mystical cloak in order to become invisible to others. He merely had to mentally inform them that he wasn't there, and they became incapable of seeing or remembering him. It was rather like the effects of nitrous oxide on a dental patient. While he was under the influence of the gas, the patient could feel the pain, but was effectively paralyzed and couldn't react. And when he came out of it, he couldn't remember the pain.

It was much the same with Nathanson. If he exerted his will over someone, they certainly could see him—their eyes stayed open and continued to function normally—but the impression was prevented from imprinting on their memory. Even *he* didn't know just how it worked. He only knew that it did.

He hadn't used his car. The problem with a red Mustang convertible was precisely that it *was* a red Mustang convertible, which made it fairly conspicuous. As the unknown witness when he'd picked up Elaine Gould had reminded him, even *he* couldn't influence *everyone* not to notice.

Admitting to having picked up a different girl, with a similar physical description, was nothing more than a ploy. He knew it and Schneider knew it. But, given the locale, it was at least plausible. The Beach was always crawling with tourists, even off season. And anonymous one-night stands remained a popular sport for both tourists and locals.

But it would have been better if no one had noticed them. And his power to influence the minds of others was limited to a fairly short range. Nor did he usually exercise those powers on someone that he didn't know was watching him.

Since the deputy who'd been watching him now presumed he was still at home, it had seemed a bit foolish to go out in a car that might be recognized. That sort of thing could cause the Sheriff's Department to reevaluate their agent's report. If their deputy said he was home, but his car was seen on the road, it wouldn't be hard for them to believe that he had managed to slip out while the deputy wasn't paying attention. And that would keep their suspicions alive.

So he had gone with the cliché movie image of a vampire by dressing entirely in black. To make the costume complete, he'd put on black leather gloves, and pulled a black hood over his head, the eyes covered by a single layer of black gauze that allowed him to see out, but would prevent his eyes from reflecting any ambient light.

It was a fact recognized by the military, but generally not well-known by civilians, that in the dark a human face made an excellent reflector. This was one reason that combat soldiers wore camouflage paint. (The other reason was that, by putting dark colors where the natural highlights were, and light colors where there would normally be shadows, the result was something that didn't look very much like a face from more than a few feet away.) Even black soldiers wore the paint, since the oil on the surface of their skin was just as capable of reflecting light.

But the eyes couldn't be painted, and the human eye, while lacking the reflective retinal cells found in the eyes of felines, still stood out rather clearly in a direct light. A thin layer of black, loosely-woven cloth, stretched tightly in front of the eye, became transparent to the wearer, but was opaque to an onlooker. The hood itself was tight, but covered with ragged strips of black cloth that effectively broke up the outline and removed it from the usual pattern of human shapes.

Dressed as he was, Nathanson had been very nearly invisible. He had walked down Estuary Boulevard, keeping close to the brush, and stopping whenever a car approached. To the drivers who happened to glance in his direction he was simply a shadow, and since he wasn't moving he became invisible. That was another lesson he'd learned from studying military training manuals. When you're caught in the open by a sudden light, don't dive for cover—freeze right where you are. The human eye sees motion more easily than stillness in a poor light. If it's moving, you notice it. If it's still, it frequently becomes difficult to tell whether you're looking at a person, a tree stump, or just an odd shadow.

He'd noticed the girl the previous day, when he'd driven down Estuary Boulevard and into Belle Springs to buy some supplies for the house. She'd been on the upper porch of a rental duplex, dressed in a black bikini and riding an exercise bike to the accompaniment of a blaring radio.

When he returned in his melodramatic disguise that evening, he circled the house once, to make sure it was safe. Then he walked up the outside stairs and knocked on the door.

Before the girl had time to react to the black-clad spectre on her landing, he had entered her mind, compelling her to step back and allow him to come into the house. Old legends to the contrary, he no more required an invitation to enter a house than he was vulnerable to sunlight.

His acute senses told him that she was alone, so he removed the hood. Despite all of his internal protestations that he had worn it as an extra technique for remaining invisible, he knew that it was least as much his own sense of the melodramatic that had caused him to take the extra step.

He led the girl—who, seen close up, now appeared to be considerably older than he had thought, perhaps in her late 30s, though in remarkable physical condition—into the bedroom. She was wearing nothing but a long T-shirt.

"Take that off," he commanded.

She did as he had ordered, pulling the T-shirt, which had reached to her knees, off over her head. He was right about her condition. Her body was slender, with large, full breasts, a flat stomach, and a slim waist.

As she pulled the T-shirt off, the muscles in her torso moved under her smooth skin, making him feel the usual anticipation.

"Sit down," he said.

She sat on the edge of the bed, looking up at him with a mild curiosity registering on her face. There were tiny lines around her eyes that hinted at some outdoor occupation. The eyes themselves were a deep blue, almost violet.

He sat beside her on the bed, his right hand moving over her body, cupping her left breast, and feeling the nipple harden at his caress. It was not an induced reaction. The part of her mind that registered pleasure was entirely unaffected by his influence over her conscious actions. It simply reacted to the touch as it was programmed to do, without the restraint that would normally have been imposed by the conscious mind.

He bent his head, his lips brushing the sensitive skin of her throat. His teeth pierced cleanly through the skin and into the carotid artery. The result had to be painful, he thought, yet the reaction, at least in the women, was always one of intense, sensual pleasure.

He could feel the life flowing out of her, adding to his strength. Yet he noticed, even as her body spasmed in the final orgasm that accompanied death, that the usual pleasure was missing for him. He felt no true need to kill, and the greatest pleasure was always obtained after a period of abstention.

But another need was there. The need to draw the police away from him; to force them to concentrate on finding a different suspect. If he was at home, with a deputy outside his house to confirm it, and a "girl friend" who could testify—believably—that she had been with him the entire night, it would become obvious to anyone confronted with these 'facts' that someone else had to be the killer.

Now, sitting on his porch with Margie, Nathanson smiled. It was amazing how simple it was to fool people today. The late 20th Century was, in many ways, a surprisingly innocent time. The highly sophisticated modern civilization had discounted anything that science was unable to explain. Vampires didn't exist; they were mythical creatures, dreamed up, perhaps, to explain epidemics. But *real* vampires? Science said that once someone was dead, that was it. Life could never be restored to a dead body.

So even when the evidence all pointed to a true vampire, the coroners, and the police investigators, and the psychiatrists and psychologists all insisted that such an explanation was impossible, and that, at most, they were dealing with a psychopath who *thought* he was a vampire.

In the same way, since Nathanson still looked like he was 24-years-old, everyone would believe he was really that age. And since he could walk around in daylight, handle crosses, and even take a bath in holy water if he felt like it, they would never believe he was a vampire, even when all of their other senses were screaming that he was.

The idea that there was such a thing as a Jewish vampire was also outside the normal realm. Vampires were a part of *Christian* mythology, and they were supposed to act in a particular way. He didn't, so, of course, he couldn't be a vampire.

Chapter Fifteen
Wednesday, August 11, 1993

Benjamin County Sheriff's Department

Schneider sat on one side of the long table in the Sheriff's Department's main conference room. Deputy Hanson, once more dressed in his dark-green uniform, was seated beside him. Sheriff Mitchell was pouring himself a cup of coffee. His copies of the files were set out at the head of the table. Weeks of work, Schneider thought, now reduced to four thick stacks of laser-printed forms and reports.

Across from Schneider, Special Agent Burton Henley had a duplicate set of files spread out before him, along with another stack of thick folders, each bound with a heavy rubber band, that he had brought with him from Quantico. Henley held a PhD. in clinical psychology. He was also an F.B.I. Special Agent, and his particular area of interest was in tracking down serial killers. He had so far been responsible for the capture of eight, which everyone agreed was a suitably impressive record.

"So we are obviously dealing with a serial killer," Henley said, after Mitchell had resumed his seat.

"We sort of figured that out for ourselves," Mitchell said. His tone somehow failed to convey the awe that the F.B.I. was supposed to engender in local cops. (Most of whom were sometimes grateful for the assistance in complicated cases, but more often thought of the Feds as an infernal nuisance who just got in the way on simple cases. Mitchell had called the F.B.I. in, but the resentment was reflexive.)

"I don't think you're alone on this one, Sheriff," Henley said. "This guy looks entirely too familiar."

Schneider looked up from his notes. "This isn't a local boy, then?"

"I don't think so. Both the method and the physical description of the victims match a whole string of similar killings across the country."

Schneider nodded. So much for the idea of finding the first murder, and then seeing if any of the suspects lived or worked nearby.

"We thought we had someone," Mitchell offered. "Except the third victim was killed when we knew our suspect was at home."

"Are you certain he was really home?"

"I was outside his house," Hanson said. "He never left the whole night. At least not from the front. And we had another man on the back of the house, so he didn't go out that way, either."

"Just to be sure," Schneider added, "we also interviewed his girlfriend. She's a county employee, and I've known her family for quite a few years. She had no reason to lie. And she confirmed that he was with her all night."

"So it sounds like you've eliminated that suspect," Henley said. "Nothing unusual. There almost always seems to be at least one very likely type who turns out to have absolutely nothing to do with the case."

The Sheriff picked up the latest file. "This last victim we haven't even identified."

Henley smiled. "*We* have." He reached into his briefcase and took out a copy of a fingerprint card. "Your latest victim had her prints on file."

"She had a record?" Mitchell asked.

"No. She was a Naval officer. A doctor, to be exact. Captain Donna Slodine, U.S. Navy Medical Corps. She was on leave from the *Eisenhower*. I understand she commanded the medical detachment for Sixth Fleet. One of our people has already notified Navy Personnel in D.C., and I expect you'll be hearing from them sometime today as far as disposition of her remains."

The sheriff nodded. He had momentarily forgotten that the F.B.I. fingerprint files held literally millions of fingerprint cards, the majority of them taken from entirely innocent people. Every police officer in the country had his prints on file. So did everyone who had ever applied for a gun license, had his house broken into—the victim's prints were taken so they could be eliminated as evidence, and copies of the cards were routinely sent to Washington—or worked for the government. The final category included all military personnel.

J. Edgar Hoover had even started a voluntary campaign to finger-print everyone in the country, but the idea had never caught on, some-what to the regret of police officers and medical examiners with anony-mous corpses on their hands. At least lately, when computers could match even single prints with relative ease. In the old days, the classification system employed required a full set of prints, and it might have taken a skilled examiner several weeks to sort through all the cards and find a match, which meant that, most of the time, no one ever actually tried.

"You said the method and victim types fit other murders?" Schneider asked. "How many?"

Henley looked at his notes. "That we're aware of, 137."

"Be nice if we could catch this guy, then," Mitchell said. "How long's he been at it?"

You could almost see the sheriff's mind working, Schneider thought. Numbers like that very likely meant that they were dealing with the record holder—the worst serial murderer in history. If *their* department could capture him, Mitchell would become famous overnight. Even if it meant that Benjamin County took on a more notorious aura for a while.

"We're not actually sure," Henley said. "For that matter, we're not even sure that we know about all of the victims. He seems to have moved around quite a bit, so it's possible that if he only killed a single victim in a particular jurisdiction, we might never have heard about it. An iso-lated killing isn't as likely to make it into our data base. But the first one we know about was. . ." He looked in a thick file folder. ". . .December 5, 1978."

"Then that *definitely* rules out Nathanson," Schneider said. "Unless he started when he was nine-years-old."

Mitchell nodded. "Agreed."

"Or he really *is* a vampire, and he's 300-years-old," Hanson com-mented, earning disgusted looks from the others.

"No such things," Henley said. "Vampire-*style* killers, yes. But no real vampires."

"Our medical examiner agrees on that point," Schneider said. "He thinks some sort of machine was used to extract the blood."

"So look for someone with an appropriate machine," Henley said. "Though I'll be damned if we've ever been able to figure out what it could be, and we've been trying for several years."

"Have you seen this sort of thing before?" Mitchell asked.

"I believe," Henley said, "that this fellow is unique. Most of the other so-called 'vampires' I've heard about were pretty inefficient when it came to actually sucking out the blood. From a psychological viewpoint, the blood drinking seems to fulfill some sort of fetishistic desire. One that we caught four years ago claimed that it gave him possession of the victim's soul."

"*Ki ha'dam, hu ha'nefesh,*" Schneider commented.

"What?"

"From the Torah, in the twelfth chapter of *Devarim—Deuteronomy* in English Bibles. 'For the blood is the life.' At least that's how it's usually translated. But you can also translate '*nefesh*' as 'soul,' which I suppose could imply that the soul is actually in the blood."

Henley smiled. "Interesting. But do you think our killer is likely to be conversant with the nuances of Hebrew? I've got a PhD., after all, and I've never heard that before."

"You wouldn't have to know Hebrew," Schneider said. "You can find 'the blood is the life' in a King James Bible. Or in a copy of *Dracula*, for that matter. For a literal translation of *nefesh* as 'soul,' I suppose you could find a source in English without too much trouble."

"Good point. But, in any case, that was the opinion of only *one* of the 'vampires' we've caught. All of them seemed to feel that drinking their victim's blood would provide them with some sort of benefit, though.

"And we've had the same sort of concept in dealing with the 'cannibal' types. They eat parts of their victims because they think it gives them some sort of special power. Something like the Moslem idea that if you kill an infidel in a holy war, he becomes your slave in the afterlife."

"What do you think might motivate our guy?" Mitchell asked.

"I really don't know. I've been trying to figure this fellow out for years, and nothing seems to make any sense. We know he can't be a 'real' vampire, because we know perfectly well that there's no such thing."

"Which leaves us where?" Mitchell asked.

"Still trying to find an answer."

Hanson leaned forward with his chin propped up on his fist. It never once occurred to anyone in the room—not even to him—that he had blurted out the real answer in a moment of whimsy. He was really at the meeting only to report on the surveillance. He wasn't a detective—just an ordinary road deputy who had a talent for following people around without being noticed. A talent based mostly on his being one of those people no one ever actually seemed to remember.

"Haven't you worked up some kind of profile?" Schneider asked.

"Sure," Henley replied. "I just don't happen to think it's a very good one."

"Why not?"

"For as many killings as we've connected to this one man—at least, we assume it's a man—there are no clear patterns other than a preference for tall women with dark hair and athletic builds. He costumes the victims before leaving them, but he isn't consistent on the costumes." Henley shook his head. "Not quite right—he's consistent in each *city*, but the way he dresses them changes whenever he shifts his location. So does the way he poses the bodies. In fact, the only absolutely uniform indicator is the almost total lack of blood in the victims' bodies, and the tooth marks on their necks."

Mitchell was looking at a chart Henley had prepared. "He gets around a lot, doesn't he?"

"Quite a bit. And, like most serial killers, he doesn't cooperate by doing anything unusual. At least, nothing beyond killing people. I have a feeling that when we find him he'll seem terribly ordinary."

"And the neighbors," Schneider added, "will all tell us how he was such a quiet fellow—one you hardly noticed at all."

"Exactly. If serial killers were all raving lunatics who ran around foaming at the mouth it wouldn't be that hard to catch them. But they're not. They look just like everyone else, and generally *act* like them, too. Ted Bundy was a charming, personable young man, and quite handsome, too. John Wayne Gacy was a gentle fellow who liked to play the part of a clown at kids' parties. David Berkowitz was so ordinary that even the people he worked with at the Post Office never suspected him of anything. Not even of having a life. The only multiple murder cases where the murderer is obvious tend to be the ones where some psycho shoots up a restaurant or office, and kills all of his victims at once."

"Those just give the muggers' lobby an excuse to try to talk congress into disarming the victims, anyway," Hanson offered.

Henley smiled. He agreed with that idea, but the Bureau's official position was that whatever the President wanted—and the President figured no one had a basic right to keep someone else from killing him unless he could do it without a gun—was what was right. Just the sort of nonsense you'd expect from a draft dodger, of course. Henley had honestly believed that the only thing actually wrong with the Viet Nam War was the refusal of congress to declare war on the North and let the military go in and clean the place out. Something he now recognized could have been done with impunity, for unlike in Korea, China would not have come into the conflict, since the Chinese hated the Vietnamese on *both* sides of the D.M.Z.

"Maybe," he conceded. "But that really has nothing to do with the case at hand."

Chapter Sixteen
Thursday, August 12, 1993

Tropical Breeze Motel, Port Morrow Beach

It had been a gloomy day, and Gail Irwin was wondering if there was such a thing as a 'miserable-weather' discount at her hotel. It had been warm enough, but so humid that she couldn't stand being on her balcony for more than a few minutes at a time. Not that there was much of a view; her room was on the front of the hotel, and from the balcony she could get a clear view of Estuary Boulevard, which at this point was crowded with souvenir shops and swimsuit boutiques, a convenience store, and behind them, the backs of several houses on a short, parallel street.

If she looked very hard, she could also see a little of the back bay, which was considered a particularly undesirable place by the locals. Lined with mangroves, it was impossible to build anything on either shore. You weren't allowed to cut down mangroves—fish were more important than people.

Now it had started to rain.

In the first week she was there, it had rained only once, and she'd been able to spend a lot of time on the white sand beach on the other side of the hotel. The second week was turning out very different, with daily thunderstorms, and rain so heavy that walking three feet in it was like stepping into a shower turned on full blast. The travel agent's brochures had never mentioned this sort of rain, which a clerk at the 7-Eleven across the street from her hotel had told was nothing more than normal summer weather in Port Morrow Beach.

So why did you think *room rates were so reasonable at this time of year?* Like many people who work for a living, and get the standard two weeks in the summer, Gail had forgotten that tourist season, in Florida, started around Christmas and ended the day after Easter. There was a reason for it, too. In Florida, the summers were hot, filled with swarms of mosquitos, and punctuated by 80% of the annual rainfall. In the winter it was cooler, but still quite warm by Northern standards, and that was when the people with the money arrived.

She walked over to the bed and turned on the television. The remote control was attached to the bedside table on some kind of swivel. This was fine for watching TV in bed, she thought, but a damned nuisance if you wanted to sit in one of the chairs. From those, the remote was out of reach.

She slowly flipped through the channels until she found an exercise show. Frowning—the beach where the show was taped was nice and sunny—she stripped down to her bra and panties, pulled on her aerobics shoes, and started to work out. If she couldn't swim or work on her tan, at least she could keep in shape and, maybe, work off some of the frustration in the process.

It never really occurred to her that the vertical blinds which normally covered the sliding glass doors leading to the balcony were open, and that she might be putting on a good show for a young man staying in a rented house behind the 7-Eleven, who had been scanning the hotel with binoculars. Her bra and panties, after all, were *less* revealing than her bathing suit.

Gail took considerable pride in her appearance. She was smart enough to recognize that she owed her greatest debt to heredity, which had given her a tall, slender body and natural good looks. Moderate exercise had firmed up her body, and she had a stylist back in Chicago who kept her shoulder-length black hair looking perfect.

The vacation on Port Morrow Beach had been her roommate's idea. They both worked in the corporate offices at Sears, and this year had coordinated their two weeks off so that they could go to Florida and enjoy themselves. As far as Gail could tell, Judy was having a *great* time.

She'd met an accountant from Scarsdale on the first day and Gail hadn't seen her since, unless you wanted to count catching a glimpse of her across the dining room, or out on the beach, draped over her new boyfriend.

Gail dropped to the floor and began a series of exercises which were supposed to firm up the inner thigh muscles. It really wasn't that bad, not having Judy around; it was the new boyfriend she felt sorry for. Judy wasn't exactly known for her steadfast devotion to any man she couldn't see on a daily basis. He'd go back to Scarsdale, Judy would go back to Chicago, and their torrid romance would come to an abrupt end.

The show finished with some cool-down exercises and Gail switched off the TV. Her bra and panties were sodden with sweat, so she threw them into a corner, took off her shoes, and walked into the bathroom to turn on the shower.

Across the street, the young man, who had been excited before, was now even more rapt. He had seen the girl bouncing around in her lacy white underwear, and then she had taken it off and spent a few moments standing in her room, facing him, stark naked. He wondered how soon she would come out, and how long it would take her to get dressed.

Cape Marl

Rabbi Dov-Ber Hershkovitz stood in a corner of the third bedroom and watched as the movers brought in the last of the tall bookcases. The movers had put the furniture on the truck last, which allowed them to take it off first and set it up before they started bringing in the boxes. That way, there was a place to put things away.

The biggest problem had been the rebbetzin's piano, a seven-foot Knabe grand. Florida condominium living rooms weren't usually built to accommodate substantial furniture. But the movers were experienced, and found a way to fit it in and still allow room for the sofa, love seat, and chairs.

The rebbetzin herself was in the kitchen, boiling water. She would pour this over the two stainless-steel sinks, which Mrs. Cohen had assured her had already been *kashered* by the ladies of the congregation. Sarah Borodaty Hershkovitz, the daughter of one Orthodox rabbi and the wife of another, had her own standards. Even though the sinks looked spotless, she would *kasher* them again, just to be sure.

She was delighted with the kitchen. The builder had planned on attracting Jewish residents from the start, and had designed the kitchens with the special needs of Jewish cooking in mind. The kitchen was built with counters along both long walls. At the far end was a large refrigerator, with an upright freezer beside it. The building was 15 years old, and she'd been told that the Port Morrow area had only had a kosher butcher for the last four months. Before that, everyone who wanted to keep kosher had to drive across the state to Miami to buy meat. If you kept a kosher home, you had a freezer.

The long-time members of the Benjamin County Jewish community —mostly Reform and Conservative Jews—were confidently predicting that this kosher butcher would go the way of the fellow who had tried carrying kosher meats in the late 1960s. That experiment had lasted six months, after which the man had taken down the "kosher" sign and started selling ordinary meats.

For some reason, Mrs. Cohen had told her, most of the local Jews simply couldn't get it through their heads that having a kosher butcher fail in a community of 500 Jews had very little to do with its chances in a community of 5,000. The community had grown a lot in the intervening years—the mindset, however, had not.

Each of the two long countertops had a sink, a food preparation area, and a stove, with a self-cleaning oven. A microwave hung over each stove, with a vent hood attached beneath it. Above and below each counter were capacious cabinets.

Observant Jews never eat meat and dairy products together, and keep separate sets of dishes, silverware, cookware, and utensils for each category of food. Following the general custom, Sarah Hershkovitz had red handles on the meat pans, and blue on the dairy. The same color motif was carried over into the china; the dairy had blue rims, and the meat had red rims. The silverware, which couldn't be color-coded, was of two very distinct patterns.

In Cleveland, she'd had two refrigerators, but it was possible to keep things separate in a single unit if you were careful. The necessity for a freezer at the time the condo was built had made separate refrigerators impractical.

Rabbi Hershkovitz was still in the third bedroom, which was now rapidly filling up with heavy boxes of books. As they arrived he began to unpack them and place them on the shelves. The extra bedroom had been one of the things that had sold him on moving to this community. There would be room for a personal study. Like all rabbis, he owned a huge number of books.

The rabbi was actually enjoying himself. Moving was something of a new experience for him. He'd lived in the same house in Cleveland for 41 years, moving in on the day he arrived in that city to take over his new congregation. But the house, where he had raised his five children, belonged to the shul, and now that he had retired it would become the home of his successor at Ansche Israel.

His eldest son was the rabbi of a congregation in Miami, and had urged him to move there. Rabbi Hershkovitz had thought that Florida was a good idea, but had vetoed Miami. True, there was a large Jewish community there. Over half a million, if you included the strip of cities running north from Miami to Delray Beach. But his son would expect his parents to live close to him, if not in his house, and to attend his synagogue. His son was a Conservative rabbi, and his father simply could not bring himself to worship regularly in a synagogue where men and women sat together. On a visit, possibly, but not every week. The Rav had forbidden it, hadn't he?

He took out the slender volume of *Sefer Yetzirah*, the *Book of Formations*, which was the oldest source of Kabalistic knowledge, written by the patriarch Abraham almost 4,000 years ago. The rabbi was thoroughly familiar with Jewish mysticism—something that a person might never guess from his sermons, which were more in the tradition of modern Orthodoxy. With this book, it was said, a person who was sufficiently knowledgeable could actually create a *golem*, a humanoid creature made of clay and brought to "life" through the use of the proper kabalistic formulae.

Rabbi Hershkovitz had his doubts on that point, but many years before the Rabbis had been sufficiently convinced that such a thing was possible to issue a ruling that a *golem* could not be counted toward a *minyan*—the quorum of ten men required for public worship. A *golem* was alive—sort of—but it didn't have a soul. That ruling had been cited recently to forbid saying *kaddish* in a computer-generated "virtual *minyan*," on the grounds that cybernetic images also lacked souls.

And there was the well-known story of the Maharal of Prague, Rabbi Yehudah Loewe, and the huge, mute servant who had suddenly appeared at the time of a blood libel, and vanished when the threat to the community had been averted and the slanderers exposed. God had given life to Adam, whom he had molded out of clay, and implanted a living soul in his body. The Maharal had also molded a man of clay, and given him life, but *not* a soul, and written the word "*emes*," "truth," in the soft clay of his forehead.

When the first letter, *aleph,* was rubbed out, "*emes*" became "*meis*," or "death," and the golem ceased to live. It was a reminder of true reality, for Hebrew letters were also numbers, and *aleph* had a numerical value of one, which was representative of the primary characteristic of God, who was an absolute unity. And any "truth" that lacked the presence of God was no truth, but merely another course leading to death.

The rabbi smiled, putting the book in its place on the shelf and reaching into the box for another.

Benjamin County Sheriff's Department

Schneider picked up another case file from the thick stack Henley had brought with him. Each case was essentially the same as every other. A young woman, between the ages of 18 and 27, was found in an isolated location, with all of the blood somehow drained from her body. The shortest was 5' 7', and the tallest had been an even 6'. They all had black or dark brown hair, and each had been in excellent physical condition, with a good figure and normal weight. From the pictures that accompanied the files, each had been somewhat better than average looking. A couple had looked like models. Captain Slodine was outside the age range by 11 years, but she had looked young enough to fit in with the others.

In all but two cases, there had been no evidence of any recent sexual activity. In the two cases where semen had been found, the condition of the genitals seemed to indicate that it had got there with the victim's cooperation, and had nothing to do with their murders. And, in both cases, their boyfriends had confirmed that opinion.

There were, it seemed, some variations in the costuming patterns. The three who had been found on Port Morrow Beach were all dressed in bikini bathing suits. The suits themselves had been manufactured by two of the largest makers, and could have been purchased anywhere in the United States. One advantage of U.S. reluctance to join the world on the metric standard was that you could always recognize American clothing by the size labels. Particularly on shoes and undergarments, which everywhere else were labeled in centimeters. He'd been more than a little surprised the first time he'd seen a European bra, which had been labeled size 89. Some odd visions had flashed through his mind before he realized that 89 centimeters was really just a hair over 35 inches.

Five women had been killed in Milwaukee, and there they had been found dressed in long winter coats and nothing else. The coats had been just as anonymous as the bikinis. Again, they were all from major manufacturers and available anywhere in the northern half of the country.

In Atlanta, the nine victims had been found topless, dressed in hot pants. The Atlanta killings had been among the earliest, in the mid-1970s, when hot pants—and a tendency toward public nudity—were still more or less in style.

Schneider pushed the files aside. The only variable seemed to be the clothing. None of the known victims had been found wearing her own clothes. Which raised the obvious question, what had happened to the clothes they'd been wearing when they met the killer? Did he still have them? Would they find a closet full of women's clothes when they finally caught this guy?

He opened the file he'd started on Nathanson. They had just received a copy of his most recent credit report, and Schneider thought he might as well file it, even if they'd now eliminated Nathanson as a serious suspect based on his age when the killings began, and his seemingly unshakable alibi for the time of the latest killing.

The man had moved several times in the last five years, he noticed. The credit history began in Seattle, in 1987, when he'd applied for a Visa Card. The application had been approved, and he'd purchased several thousand dollars worth of household items over the next three months. The bills had been paid as soon as they fell due.

The file showed a total of nine credit cards, all of them frequently used, and none showing an outstanding balance. This seemed to go with what Nathanson had said about his family's financial standing; he seemed to use the credit cards for convenience, and not, as most people did, to allow a bill to be stretched out over time.

Schneider thought for a moment, then dug into the other pile of files. Three women had been killed in Seattle in 1987, during the months immediately after Nathanson received his first credit card.

Where did he go next? Las Vegas, from May 1988 through October 1989. There had been no killings reported there. Was Seattle just a coincidence? Schneider had been a cop long enough to know that you always had to consider that possibility. But, he thought, you also had to consider that Las Vegas was host to a huge tourist industry, with several million people visiting every year. And it was surround by a desert. Someone could have killed *50* women there, hidden the bodies in the desert, and no one would ever know. In that sort of city, you didn't check for murders in this kind of case—you checked for missing persons cases where the descriptions matched.

And there were plenty of stories out of that town suggesting that the desert was already the final resting place of half the crooked gamblers in the western United States. At some point the city would expand outward sufficiently for foundation excavations to clear a lot of missing persons cases.

Schneider continued down the credit report. The next move had been to Akron, where Nathanson seemed to have stayed for six months. Once again there were no killings.

But five women had been killed in Cleveland's southwestern suburbs during the same period, and Akron was no more than an hour or so away. Was he living in one city, and doing his hunting on the other end of Route 8?

Then Nathanson moved to Manhattan. And there Schneider was faced with a problem very similar to Las Vegas. New York didn't get the same tourist trade, but there were over eleven million people living within the city limits, and an annual murder rate in the thousands. (Which, curiously, on a deaths per 100,000 population ratio—which was how murder rates were calculated—made New York City statistically *safer* than Port Morrow, which last year had registered *eight* murders.)

During the time Nathanson had lived in New York, only a single death that seemed to fit the pattern had been reported, and that was actually in Hoboken. Again, it didn't prove anything. How could they be sure the killer was dressing up all of his victims and posing them? Couldn't he have simply killed some and hidden the bodies?

And from New York he'd come to Port Morrow Beach. Schneider had already checked with the phone company, and Nathanson had arrived five weeks before the first death.

Coincidence? That was always possible. But Schneider didn't like coincidences, even while he had to recognize that they existed. And it occurred to him that the first local victim had been *from* New York. Was that a connection? And, if it was, how did you get around the fact that Nathanson would have been only nine-years-old when the first murder was committed?

Port Morrow Beach

Gail Irwin stood under the hot shower, letting the pulsing spray from the adjustable showerhead massage her back muscles. The day was lousy, she thought, but she'd at least managed to get a good workout and now she could relax for the rest of the afternoon.

Across the street from Gail's hotel, her young admirer was sitting on the edge of his bed, using his binoculars to keep an eye on her room. The window was high enough that, from outside, no one could see that he was naked below the waist. He'd checked the angles carefully on his first day in the room.

There was a slick-paper porno magazine open on the bed beside him, which he glanced down at between peeps at the hotel. In the part he was slowly leafing through, a young blond was doing to a middle-aged man exactly what he wished he could get the girl across the street to do to him. His right hand—he was holding the binoculars left-handed—was busy in his lap, and he was wishing it was the girl's mouth on him instead.

He saw her coming out of the bathroom, drying herself off, and his hand speeded up. With the binoculars she looked to be no more than 30 or 40 feet away, and he was almost drooling over her near-perfect body.

Then she started to dress, which spoiled the whole afternoon for him. At least, he thought, she'd put on her panties and a pair of old jeans first, leaving her beautiful breasts exposed to his sight for an extra minute or so. It wasn't that he preferred breasts, really. It was just that, with the binoculars and the construction of the female body, you could only see a woman's genitals when she opened her legs for you, but her breasts were right there in front of her, always in plain sight as long as they were uncovered.

As she buttoned her shirt, the young man put down the binoculars and concentrated on the photographs in the magazine. He wasn't quite finished.

• • •

Isaac Nathanson stood on his back porch, looking out over the Gulf of Mexico. The beach was deserted, except for an elderly woman who was dressed in a yellow raincoat, and slowly making her way north at the edge of the surf, looking for shells. The best shelling, everyone said, was actually on Santiago Island, but there were usually a few people carrying the tell-tale plastic buckets after every storm.

On a sunny day, there would usually be several people with their towels and blankets spread out on his beach. That was one of the problems with modern Florida, he thought. When he had lived in Miami in the late 1940s, the beach in front of a person's house was considered private. You could run a fence down to the high tide line and chase away anyone who got between you and the ocean.

But not now. Since the mid-1970s, Florida courts had interpreted the property laws in favor of the trespassers. If you lived on the beach, then your front yard essentially became public property. Everything from the water to the mean high-tide line was now classified as public property, and anything above it fell into a gray area. The general rule seemed to be that, as long as you got there by walking on the public beach, you could sit on the private parts as well.

Inside the house, the phone starting ringing. Nathanson looked at his watch. Just after 5:00 pm, so that would probably be Margie, wondering if she would see him that evening.

•   •   •

Gail Irwin walked back across Estuary Boulevard, the plastic bag from the 7-Eleven in her right hand. The weather had cleared shortly after 6:30. Too late to get out on the beach, but at least it seemed they would have a nice evening.

She walked through the lobby, taking the elevator to the seventh floor. The little pin next to the key slot was still retracted, which meant that Judy hadn't brought her new friend back to the room and locked Gail out again.

The room was empty. Gail put the bag on the table. Two chili dogs with cheese and onions, and a can of regular 7-Up. It was her one absolute rule—no diet sodas. The logic of those things was beyond her. The only nutrient of any kind in most sodas was the sugar, so if you eliminated that, then you might as well just drink water. And more than a few studies had suggested that diet sodas actually made people *gain* weight, since the sweetness without any actual nutrition just made you hungry.

The chili dogs were an indulgence, and would impose an extra twenty minutes of aerobics in the morning. But it was her vacation, and vacations were *for* indulgence. Vacations were also, she thought, for sex—an idea Judy seemed to have taken to heart, but which had so far eluded Gail.

Cape Marl

Rabbi Hershkovitz closed the prayer book and kissed the cover before replacing it on the shelf of the schtender—a small, standing desk. It was fully dark now, and outside the study window he could see the lights of a large cabin cruiser making its way up the canal.

The canals had been one of his first lessons about Cape Marl. The community had been developed from marshes and pastureland in the mid-1960s by the simple expedient of digging a vast network of canals and using the excavated dirt to fill in the wetlands. Mort Cohen had told him that it was a system which was no longer possible, what with the passage of wetland preservation laws that now seemed to require a Federal permit to fill in a wet spot in a gravel driveway.

The canals also meant that a short drive was frequently a much longer drive, for many of the streets simply ended at one side of a canal and started again on the other. You might have to drive a mile out of your way to travel a few hundred feet. Or buy a boat.

The rabbi picked a book off his shelf and settled into a comfortable chair. It was going to be interesting, he thought, living in a community where he had no real responsibilities. Most of his life he'd had the responsibility of a congregation, or of an entire community.

It had started with the little shul in Krakow, where he had gone immediately after being ordained. The threat of war had told him that it might be wise to leave, but before he could make the appropriate arrangements to travel to Palestine the Germans had invaded. On the following Sabbath he had delivered a long address to his congregation, telling them that, after hundreds of years, it was time for all Jews to get out of Poland.

No one had listened, but he had set out in an easterly direction. A Japanese consul had issued transit visas to several hundred Jews, despite orders to the contrary, which had enabled the young rabbi to spend the war in Japan. As for the diplomat, though he was now considered a true hero in Israel, his selfless act in defiance of his government's orders had destroyed his career.

Even in Japan, Hershkovitz had been responsible for a community. There were a number of rabbis, including several truly great figures in the Torah world, exiled in Japan. But to the small community living in one district of Tokyo, Rabbi Hershkovitz was their rabbi. He had gained this position after two years as assistant to Rabbi Haskel Borodaty, who had been an important leader of that segment of the Polish Jewish community in Tokyo before being killed in an air raid in 1942. He had also, in 1941, married Borodaty's daughter, Sarah.

After the war, he had stayed in Tokyo until 1951, when a small congregation in Cleveland Heights had been in need of a rabbi, and agreed to sponsor his immigration. He'd been there ever since.

And now he was retired. He would be the only Orthodox rabbi in Benjamin County, but he would not be *employed* by this community, and that would make a difference.

Port Morrow Beach

About 10:00 pm, Gail found that she was hungry again. The drapes were still open, and she had yet to notice the young man in the darkened window across the street. He was still looking up at her through binoculars from time to time.

She picked up her purse and walked out of the room. As she crossed the street, her admirer was standing in the shadows beside the 7-Eleven, watching her. He had put his trousers back on, but one of his porno magazines had still been open on the bed when he left his room.

Gail went into the store and bought another 7-Up and a bag of barbecue potato chips. She didn't notice the young man watching her through the plate glass window, nor did she realize he had followed her back across the street after she had paid for her snacks.

He caught up with her in the hotel parking lot, wrapping one arm around her waist and putting his hand over her mouth. She was strong, but she had never studied any martial. arts, and so had never learned how to apply her strength to self defense. In a moment he had her behind a camper-van, hidden from the street by dense plantings.

His hand across her mouth was pulling her back, keeping her off balance. His other hand was now under her shirt, which he had ripped open, sending the buttons flying, roughly pawing at her breasts. Then his hand moved down, fumbling with her belt and the button at the top of her jeans.

She continued to struggle, knowing what was coming. He took his hand away from her mouth for a moment, but before she thought to scream he had slugged her on the corner of the jaw. It didn't knock her out, but it dazed her, and he was able to unzip her jeans and pull them down around her knees.

He ripped off her panties, and she could hear the sound of his own zipper being lowered. He had her bent over now, and she could feel him pressing into her from behind. There was a sharp pain as he thrust into her, pumping away like a lunatic, tearing and abrading the tender, unprepared tissue within her. And after only a moment she could feel him stiffen, driving himself deep into her and flooding her with his unwanted essence. Still, she couldn't scream. Couldn't really react.

And then, suddenly, he let go of her and she fell onto the asphalt surface of the parking lot. As she looked up from the pavement, her attacker seemed to be hanging in mid-air, and it was a moment before she realized that someone was standing over her, holding the half-naked young man off the ground by the throat.

She heard a sharp "crack!," like a muffled shot, and her attacker's body spasmed and went limp. The other was still holding him up by the throat with a single hand, but now his head was tilted at an odd angle, his eyes bulging, his tongue protruding from his mouth. She felt something warm, and realized that her attacker's neck had been broken, and his bladder, divorced from conscious command, was emptying itself across her legs.

Gail pulled herself away as the other threw her attacker down as if he were discarding a sack of trash. He turned to look at her, smiling. A tall man, not too old, with red hair.

Nathanson offered the girl his hand, helping her to her feet. She was a mess, he thought. The buttons on her shirt were all gone, and it now gaped open, one breast exposed to his view while the other remained covered. The fastener on her bra, made of plastic, had broken where it joined the cups. Her jeans were still down around her knees, and there was blood on her upper thighs, mingled with her attacker's ejaculate, which was running out of her. He could see her panties hanging across a bush, where her attacker had thrown them after ripping them off.

"He can't hurt you any more," Nathanson said.

Gail nodded, bending to pull up her jeans. It took her longer before she realized her shirt was also open. Her hands still trembling, she twisted the shirttails on either side and tied them together beneath her breasts.

"Thank you," she said.

"People like that one have no place in a civilized society," Nathanson replied. It was curious, he thought. He had killed hundreds of people since his "death," most of them young women. But this was different. He usually killed because he had no choice in the matter. This dead man, though, was a far worse sort of predator. One who attacked for the pleasure of it, or because it gave him some perverted feeling of power. The pleasure Nathanson took from drinking the blood of his victims was *coincidental,* not causative.

Well, this *thing* couldn't hurt anyone now. His neck had snapped as easily as a thin twig, and now he lay on his back on the pavement beside the van, exposed and stinking from the contents of his bowels, which had also escaped as he died.

But now Nathanson was faced with a curious moral dilemma. The girl was precisely the physical type he preferred. Should he rescue her from a rapist, and then kill her himself? Does the rescuer become the murderer?

"Are you staying here?" he asked.

She nodded, looking around for her grocery bag. For some reason finding it suddenly seemed vital. It was an irrational thought, she realized. She had just been raped, and she was worried about losing a bag of potato chips and a 7-Up! Did that make any sense?

"You should get to a hospital," Nathanson said.

"No. I just want to get back to my room." It now seemed terribly important to take a shower. Her reactions were entirely normal, but she didn't realize it. There was nothing in her experience upon which to base a comparison.

"Do you?"

She looked up at him, for the first time letting her eyes meet his. Seeing something compelling in them. And yet, she also saw a choice to be made. As if her next words would have a permanent effect on her life.

"Maybe not," she said.

Chapter Seventeen
Friday, August 13, 1993

Benjamin County Medical Examiner's Office

"We have a new element," Edgars said. "This time it looks as if our boy has added rape to his repertoire.'"

Schneider put down the book he had been reading, a paperback edition of an English translation of *Michtav MeEliyahu,* a popular Jewish ethical text. "Did he leave us any evidence?"

"So it would appear. Someone has washed her genital region, but there is semen in her vagina, along with bruising, and other marks on the body, consistent with rape."

"Somehow, that doesn't really sound right," Schneider said. It was one of the curious things about the beach killer. There had never been the slightest evidence of any sexual molestation, unless you considered the fact that the bodies had obviously been stripped and dressed in bathing suits. And there was no way to tell if he stripped his victims before, or after, they were dead. If this was really the same serial killer the F.B.I. was looking for, dressing up his victims in a consistent costume was a kind of trademark with this guy. But none of the previous victims had been raped. It didn't make any sense.

"You think maybe we have a copycat?" the doctor asked.

"You tell me, Doc. You've examined all the bodies."

Edgars shook his head. "I don't think so. I still can't figure out how he's getting all the blood out of them, but I also can't imagine how anyone else would manage, either."

Schneider nodded. "What about the other one?" The bad guys had been busy on the beach last night, he thought. Two bodies. The second was a guy from Columbus named Smith, according to his driver's license. He'd been found sprawled on his back in a parking lot with his neck broken, and his genitals hanging out of his pants.

Edgars shifted the other chart onto the top. "Fracture of the third and fourth cervical vertebrae. Classical death by hanging, as a matter of fact."

"We don't need any hangings on the beach," Schneider said, remembering an incident in the late 1970s when a group of beach residents had almost managed to lynch a purse snatcher after he'd injured an elderly woman. They'd had the rope around his neck, with the other end thrown over a second-story balcony, when the deputies arrived. A major had been disciplined for citing the incident as an example of poor response time, indicating that he thought the deputies had got there too soon. Letting them hang the guy—he'd been a six-time loser, as it turned out—might have been satisfying to half the department, but you weren't supposed to say that sort of thing in public.

"It wasn't a hanging," Edgars said. "Just that sort of fracture. But it was done manually. Bruises on the victim's neck indicate he was manually strangled before his neck was broken. Strangled one-handed, by the way, so whoever killed him is obviously extremely strong and has fairly large hands."

"Anything else?"

"Looks like he was jumped while he was making out."

"You mean because his pants were open? You sure he wasn't just taking a leak?"

"Very sure. He had dried vaginal secretions on him, mixed with semen and a little blood."

Schneider had an odd thought. "Can you get a blood type?" he asked.

"We're working on it. Why?"

"What if our friend Smith in there was raping our other victim, and our serial killer got hold of him and broke his neck for his trouble?"

"And then killed the girl after he rescued her?"

"Why not? The only thing we really know about this guy is that he drains all the blood out of their bodies. That doesn't mean he wouldn't react if he came across a rapist. Even a murderer can have a conscience and a sense of public duty, as long as it doesn't infringe on his own activities."

Edgars smiled. "Now that's something to think about," he said.

Chapter Eighteen
Tuesday, August 31, 1993

Port Morrow

The crowd shuffled along the gravel path behind the docent, stopping as they passed through the gate and came to the sidewalk on O'Brien Boulevard.

"Now, we'll have to wait here for a moment," the docent announced. "Mr. Elison had his laboratory on this side of the street, but he built his house on the river side." He pressed the traffic light control button mounted on a post by the crosswalk. "As soon as the cars stop, go on across and wait for me on the other side. I don't walk as fast as I used to."

The docent was in his late 70s, and despite his protests of decrepitude, could still walk a mile in 17 minutes. His complaining about his aches and pains was mostly for show. And it gave him an excuse to point out that Theodore Elison had come to Port Morrow every winter, starting in 1891, because of his *own* rheumatism, which had been aggravated by the winters in New Jersey.

"The house, which you should just about be able to see now that we've got across the street," he continued, "was built in 1891. In fact, it was built at Mr. Elison's factory in Paramus, New Jersey, in sections, and shipped down to Port Morrow by train. When the pieces got here, local workmen were hired to put the whole thing together. So the Elisons actually arrived in Port Morrow at the same time as the parts of their house, yet only had to spend a week in the Hotel Rusk before the house was ready for them to move in.

"Of course, the house was a little old-fashioned, for all that. Mr. Elison insisted on gas lighting fixtures, since he'd made his fortune after inventing a new type of gaslight mantel that gave a much brighter light than the older fixtures. The same general type of mantel is still used on camp lanterns."

Karen Rubenstein found her mind wandering. The elderly docent was delivering a speech he had given in front of hundreds of other tours. He was good, she thought, but the subject matter wasn't as interesting as it might be. Karen was a high school teacher—she was an expert on what got people's attention and what didn't. Besides, as an inventor, Theodore Ellison had never been more than second rate, most of his developments having been made in the area of pure science. He'd made plenty off the gaslight mantel—before practical electric lights came along and displaced them with an even brighter, and safer, alternative. But the majority of his developments had simply provided a basic discovery that others had exploited. Elison was simply the most famous resident Port Morrow could boast.

What was holding much of her attention at the moment was the fact that her vacation was nearly over. School would be starting in exactly one week. In Florida, she had discovered, it had already started. Her system still followed the traditional schedule, with school opening on the day after labor day. She didn't have to leave until Thursday.

It was hot, she thought. It would probably still be more than hot enough at home, too. A local weatherman had pointed out the previous evening that in the last 50 years, Port Morrow had recorded fewer days with temperatures over 100° than Cleveland. Having grown up in the Cleveland suburbs, Karen had no trouble believing that. The summer rains, the weatherman had said, tended to keep the temperatures down by cooling things off.

It hadn't rained today, though, and didn't seem likely to do so.

Karen had dressed for the weather. At least, she *thought* she had. She was wearing a sleeveless, white cotton top and dark blue shorts. Her feet were encased in sensible walking shoes—the canvas type, that would breath better than the more pricey leather varieties. She was starting to regret the choice of a top, though. They'd spent quite a bit of the tour out in the sun, going through the estate's extensive gardens, and she was sweating. The top was clinging to her more than she liked, making her wish she'd worn a bra; the damp top was outlining her nipples a bit too clearly, and thin white cotton has a tendency to become semi-transparent when it gets wet.

"Over here, we have Mr. Elison's swimming pool. This was the first one ever built in Port Morrow. It was originally fed from an artesian well, so there was no need for a filter. We had to put one in a few years back, though—the state changed the water laws and free-flowing wells were outlawed. Seems they were causing ground water problems, and, well, in Florida most of the water comes from the ground."

Maybe a broad-brimmed hat, Karen thought. Something to keep the direct sun off her face. It was too bad they couldn't go for a swim in the pool. She smiled. She didn't have a suit with her, and if she was afraid her clinging top was going to scandalize anyone who saw her, what would they think if she threw off all her clothes and dove into the pool naked? Not exactly proper behavior for a schoolteacher.

Benjamin County Sheriff's Department Gun Range

Schneider fired five rounds as rapidly as he could. A complete waste of time, he thought. The road deputies carried 9mm Model 92 Berettas, which were highly accurate in the hands of a competent marksman. Their accuracy and reliability was why the department—not to mention the U.S. military—had picked them as the standard issue sidearm. As a detective, however, Schneider was normally armed with a .38 caliber Charter Arms "Undercover" revolver. It was an adequate defensive weapon at close range, but at any distance over five yards the two-inch barrel and rudimentary sights made actually hitting anything more a matter of luck than skill.

His own weapon had been modified slightly. A gunsmith had fitted a new hammer, which lacked the spur that could sometimes catch on clothing—a disaster if you needed the gun in a hurry. He had also removed the cylinder latch button, which tended to loosen after firing a few rounds and created a danger of jamming. Since the front of the cylinder pin was unsupported, the cylinder could still be opened by pulling forward on the pin. The front sight had also been removed, to allow for a smoother draw—not much of a loss, since it had never helped much anyway.

Schneider opened the cylinder and dumped out the spent cases. The little Charter held only five rounds, which made it easier to conceal. Since a jacket wasn't always that practical in Florida, Schneider carried the weapon in an ankle holster.

"All clear!" the rangemaster announced. "Check your targets."

Schneider walked down the concrete lane to where a standard silhouette target was stapled to the rails. There was none of the big-city, electrified target retriever nonsense to be found in Benjamin County— you stapled the targets to a wooden railing and backed up to where the proper distance was marked on the concrete path, then walked back down after you'd fired to check the results. Schneider wasn't expecting much. Twice a year, when he actually had to qualify, he brought out the Ruger Security-Six revolver he'd carried in his days as a road deputy. The rest of the year he practiced with the Charter, secure in the knowledge that the last time a Sheriff's Department detective had been called upon to fire his service revolver at anything other than a target had been in 1924.

This time he was quite pleased with the results. Three of the five shots were in the stomach area. The fourth was in the shoulder, and the fifth had missed entirely. In actual combat, you tried for a gut shot. Not only was the abdominal region the largest target, but a hit there was almost guaranteed to stop the assailant from continuing any sort of hostile action, since it would be extremely painful.

Port Morrow

Nathanson was sitting quietly in a study carrel in the Port Morrow Library. Telephone directories from six different cities were spread out in front of him, and he opened each one in turn, copying down the telephone numbers and addresses of real estate companies. So far he had filled five pages on a yellow legal pad.

He looked upon the work as a form of insurance. He would have to leave the area eventually, and it was useful to have a list of people who would be able to help him relocate.

Generally, he would maintain a degree of continuity. In each new community, he would present a connection to the previous, using the tax laws to make a property exchange when he sold one house and bought another, so as to avoid a big capital gains tax.

But he didn't need to. A great deal of his cash was invested in an ostensibly public corporation, of which he was the only major share-holder. When necessary, he would simply change identities and sell his stock to his new self. Or, in some cases, allow himself to inherit it by turning into his own son or grandson.

There was other money, too. A separate corporation held title to several hundred acres of woodland in the Colorado Rockies. At the center of the property, buried some 30 feet under the floor of a natural cave, was a stock of gold bullion worth several million dollars at current prices.

Safe deposit boxes in a number of cities each held over a million dollars in cut diamonds. Each was in a different name, and he had the appropriate identification for each. Diamonds had the advantage of being portable, and could be sold with relative ease. By simply letting his beard grow out, and putting on appropriate clothing, Nathanson could dispose of his stones in the New York diamond district, where his perfect Yiddish—which was, after all, his native language—allowed him to fit right in with the *chassidic* Jews who had come to dominate the diamond trade for precisely the same reason that Nathanson had invested in that area. Diamonds were small, extremely valuable, and could be taken along when the latest version of the Cossacks decided to start killing Jews again. Or, in Nathanson's case, when it appeared that someone was about to catch up with him.

Whenever possible, Nathanson liked to keep a large part of his money in non-cash forms, which could be moved from one place to another, and disposed of with much less trouble than currency. If he had relied only on money, he would have lost everything several times over as various European governments recalled their banknotes, or, in the case of the Russians, started a long-term experiment with a political system utilizing a currency that had absolutely no value beyond their own borders.

In all, Nathanson was worth over 400-million dollars. Only about a twentieth of that was "visible." The rest was a closely held secret, unknown to anyone else, but always available in an emergency.

Port Morrow Beach

Karen Rubenstein pulled the rental car under the house and shut off the engine. One of the quirks of the insurance laws in Florida was that the newer houses on the beach had to be built with their first floor above the highest projected storm surge level. As a result, they were built on tall pilings, which left room for parking under them. Some owners had enclosed the space to create big family rooms, which was permitted as long as the walls were flimsy and would break away if the Gulf of Mexico rolled over the island, but no one was allowed to create actual living spaces—meaning bedrooms—at ground level. Most just left the space empty, which provided a good place to park the car without the extra expense of building a garage.

She had rented the house on Estuary Boulevard from the dean of boys at her school. He never used the place himself, having inherited it from one of his aunts. From what he'd told Karen, his aunt had never lived in the house either, but had bought it as a rental property, strictly for investment purposes.

Karen had no doubt that he had been right. Everything about the house reeked of "rental." The furniture was very "Florida," with gay prints and fake bamboo frames. What her father, who had sold furniture, called "borax." Cheap, and not very well made, but capable of looking good for a few years. It was the sort of furniture that was sold to people just starting out in life—or to people who wanted to furnish a house they weren't planning to live in themselves.

The kitchen was the same. Name brand appliances, to be sure, but bottom of the line. In fact, as far as she could tell, the only things in the place that were actually top quality were the air conditioning unit and the ceiling fans in every room. Since the landlord paid the electric bill, a little extra spent on more efficiency in those areas would actually result in long-term savings.

But, if the furnishings were less than elegant, and the kitchen only adequate, at least the rent was cheap. Karen had paid only $400 for the month, which was actually below market even in the summer. And $2,100 less than what the house rented for during the season.

She went around to the back of the car and took the bag of groceries from the trunk. Just enough to get her through the rest of her stay. She carried the groceries up the outside stairs and let herself into the house, putting the bag on the counter in the kitchen.

She had left the air on while she was out, and the house was pleasantly cool. She opened the drapes that covered the sliding glass doors at the end of the living room, revealing the "redwood" deck, with the beach beyond it. The silvered window film gave the view an odd grey tint, making the sky look a little gloomy, though it was, in fact, clear and sunny. From outside, Karen knew, the film was reflective, which not only kept the sunlight from fading the furniture, but also prevented anyone outside from seeing in during the daytime. At night it had the opposite effect, reflecting the interior of the room, but providing a clear view from outside. At night, she kept the drapes closed.

Karen walked into the front bedroom and took off the white cotton top, which had been reduced to a shapeless, sodden mess by the heat and sweat. She kicked off her shoes and pulled off her shorts, then removed her panties as well, tossing them onto the pile of dirty clothes in the corner.

She didn't bother dressing. Truth be told, she was a "private" nudist —someone who tended to go around naked at home, but didn't strip off in public places, like nudist camps. Just before she headed home, she'd do up all of her laundry, using the washer and dryer in the kitchen, also while nude, and in that way be able to pack only clean clothing. Karen liked to think of herself as quite practical. As often as not, the image was correct.

The cool air from the ceiling vent felt good on her bare skin. Since the silver window film assured her privacy for several more hours, she walked naked into the living room and sat down in the big armchair in front of the television, with the drapes wide open.

Cape Marl

Chayah Schneider stepped down from the school bus a block from her building, waving good bye to her friend Shari Feldman. Shari, she suspected, thought that she was a little odd, but Chayah was used to that by now. It wasn't easy being the only Orthodox kid at Cape Marl High School. There were a lot of things that the other kids wanted to do, but that she couldn't. Going out to eat, for instance, was a normal part of high school life, but there were no kosher restaurants in the area, so Chayah only ate out when she went on vacation with her father to visit her grand-parents in Brooklyn. Nor did she go to the football games that seemed to constitute the real reason for the existence of the school, since the games were always on Friday night. She figured she was in school to get an education, but you'd never know it during football season.

She didn't date, either. Her father wouldn't have objected, she knew, as long as the boy was Jewish. But Chayah had long ago realized that she was every bit as Orthodox and committed as her father, and so she had decided to forego dating until she was ready for marriage. At that point, she would go to Brooklyn, get a seminary education, and stay with her grand-parents for a while. Brooklyn not only had kosher restaurants, but also had a large supply of Orthodox bachelors.

So she confined her social life to casual friendships with the other Jewish girls at Cape High, and accepted the fact that the other girls, who were mostly Reform or Conservative, thought of her as impossibly "old-fashioned."

Chayah looked at her watch. It was 2:38 pm, which would give her time to start on her homework before getting busy with supper. Had she ever bothered to think about it, she was well on her way to becoming the ideal Jewish wife, at least in the domestic area, having had several years of practice in keeping house and cooking for her father.

Port Morrow Beach

Karen switched off the television, after deciding that there was nothing on worth watching. She stood up and stretched. Now what? she thought. She smiled. Her students would never believe this, even if they could see her—which she was damned glad they couldn't. At the high school, Karen Rubenstein was looked upon as a terrible prude, with her long skirts, sensible shoes, and baggy, vested outfits that did a pretty good job of concealing her figure. The bifocal glasses she habitually wore in school, with their heavy frames, added to the image of the oldmaid schoolteacher.

Not that she was all that old. At 26, she was actually only about ten years older than most of her students, and she had been teaching for six years now. When she had started, the prim outfits had been adopted, more than anything else, as a way of distinguishing herself from her students. If she dressed the way she normally did—she actually liked short skirts and tailored blouses that would show off her legs and figure —she had looked too much like one of the students. As for the glasses, she had a little trouble focusing at short distances, and while she really just needed reading glasses—the upper half of the lens was plain glass— the bifocals also enhanced the image of maturity and authority. Away from school, the glasses went into her purse, and were brought out only when she had to read something.

And her students certainly wouldn't believe that their teacher was now wandering around a rented house on Port Morrow Beach, stark naked, and casually scratching her bare behind. It was the wrong image. One she would keep entirely private.

She walked back into the bedroom and took a bathing suit out of a dresser drawer. It was a stretchy onepiece, in a tropical print, and made of a "tan-through" material that allowed much of the ultraviolet light to pass through. The cloth was actually rated as SPF15, and worn with the same strength sun block, it had the effect of allowing her to get an all-over tan without having to lay out in the sunlight naked, or spend money on a tanning booth. If you pulled the material away from your body, you could actually see through it, but when it was worn normally it appeared as opaque as any normal cloth.

Properly dressed, Karen opened the sliding glass doors and stepped out onto the deck. She walked to the edge, looking down at the beach, which was only lightly crowded this afternoon.

To her left, she could see the next door neighbor coming out onto his back porch. She had always liked the look of the old house, with its deep, wrap-around porch on two sides, and another deep porch at the back. There had been no hurricane laws in effect when the neighbor's house was built, she thought; it sat close to the ground, surrounded by ancient trees, and looking as if it had always been there.

The neighbor looked up and waved, then sat down in a chair and started to read a book. Karen took the towel she had over her arm and draped it over the chaise lounge, then sat down and leaned back onto it.

• • •

Isaac Nathanson found it difficult to concentrate on his book. He had known the house next door had been rented because there was a car parked under it, but before today he hadn't actually seen the renter. Now he had, a tall, fit-looking brunette. Just the sort he liked.

But there was an obvious danger. Schneider certainly still considered him to be, at the very least, a possible suspect—even if an unlikely one. Did he dare go after someone living next door? He could hardly claim he didn't know her, even if he would be telling the truth. Who, really, knew their neighbors today? Schneider, probably, living in that Orthodox enclave in Cape Marl, where his neighbors were also the members of his congregation. But most people hardly saw their neighbors, and often didn't even know their names.

So perhaps, he thought, there might even be a degree of safety in simply going next door and taking this young woman. She was too close. Such an obvious victim that only a lunatic would pick her. They thought of him as a serial killer, and such people chose their victims at random, generally staying well away from their own homes. Even when they killed at home, like the Gacys and Dahmers, they would bring the victim from elsewhere.

But could he rely on psychology to shield him? He knew he was going to have to move on eventually, but he actually liked this house, and living on the Beach. It was the sort of place he might consider keeping as a vacation home after he left. A place where he could go for a few weeks every year, though he would never again be able to hunt in this place once he had moved away. If the killings stopped when he left town, it would strengthen their suspicions, but prove nothing. If they resumed as soon as he returned, however, he would inevitably become the most obvious suspect once again.

But for the moment, he was concerned only with the girl next door. Could he take her and remain free? It presented a nice challenge.

Cape Marl

Chayah had supper ready when Schneider returned home at 5:30. The Orthodox Jewish version of a cheeseburger, which was made with an *ersatz* burger composed of soybeans and other vegetable products, along with a casein binder. Despite looking and tasting like beef, the patty was actually a dairy product, and so could be eaten with a topping of cheese.

"You have a good day?" Chayah asked.

"Not bad. At least, no one found any dead women lately, which is kind of a relief. Maybe this guy has left the area."

"Is that good, *Tateh*?" Something in her tone suggested that it probably wasn't.

"I think so, Chayah. If he leaves, then he won't kill anyone else."

"Here, you mean?"

"Here? Oh."

"But somewhere else, he'll keep killing."

Schneider smiled at his daughter. In another year, when she graduated from high school, he would send her to live with his wife's parents in Brooklyn. She'd already applied to Stern College at Yeshiva University, and if she was accepted would work toward a degree in Jewish education.

And, with any luck, she would meet a nice young man from the rabbinic program at the same university. With her knack for seeing through to the core of the matter, she would make an excellent rebbetzin.

"So you don't really want him to go away, do you, *Tateh*? What you want to do is catch him."

Schneider nodded. "True. But with that we aren't having much luck."

Port Morrow Beach

Karen pushed herself up off the chaise and stood up. She had been on the deck for a little over an hour, which was probably enough, even with the tan she had acquired during the month she had been staying on the Beach. No use getting a nice tan, then overdoing it right at the end of your vacation and burning.

Her neighbor, she noticed, was still reading on his back porch. He glanced up at her and smiled. She raised her right hand and waved. "I love your house!" she called.

He put his book down and walked over to the railing. "So do I," he called up. "Would you like to see it?"

"I'd love to."

"So come on down and I'll show it to you."

The girl disappeared into her house, and a moment later he could see her bare legs, quickly followed by the rest of her, coming down the outside stairs on the far side of the house. She was still wearing only her bathing suit, which Nathanson found quite appealing.

She came around the beach side and up onto the back porch. He found himself oddly thrilled by her beauty. Her figure was nearly perfect, and the thin material of the suit, damp with perspiration from being in the sun, moulded itself to her like a second skin. The nipples of her full breasts were clearly outlined, and the unlined crotch defined her womanliness to anyone who cared to look.

"It really is a great old house," she said. "Hi, I'm Karen."

"Zack."

"Is that a first name or last?" she asked.

"First. Well, Isaac, actually. Why don't you come inside, and I'll show you around the place."

"Okay."

He actually gave her the full tour, starting in the kitchen, and ending in the master bedroom. There she came willingly into his arms, pressing her perfect body against him, her lips open as she kissed him.

His hands moved over her body, feeling her respond to his touch. His lips brushed her throat, but as his teeth penetrated he began to receive her thoughts, and after taking only a few drops of blood he kissed her and backed away.

She was Jewish.

His first act as a vampire had been to kill the pig butcher, Stanislaw, who had been among those who murdered Rabbi Shimon. He had eventually killed all of the men who had beaten the old *tzaddik* to death, along with the priest who had incited them to riot in the first place.

Over the last 309 years, he had killed hundreds of people. So many he had lost count, one death finally seeming to blend into all the others.

But he had never killed another Jew. He didn't think he had any real qualms about doing so—but, when the opportunity presented itself, as now, he was unable to do it. He could take a little blood. Never enough to hurt them. Never enough even to weaken them. But that was all.

So this girl would live to return home, to her school room, and to her normal life. She would not even be aware of the tiny amount of blood he had taken from her. The very fact that it had happened would compel her to forget.

The memory she would take away would be of the house, and of a gracious host. And she would remember his kisses, and his embrace, and an evening spent in each other's arms. An evening of sweet, wonderful lovemaking that actually was nothing more than an implanted memory.

•　　•　　•

Karen had just left when Nathanson's phone began to ring. He walked across the kitchen and picked up the receiver.

"Hello?"

"Itzak? This is Dinah."

He smiled. "Where are you calling from, my love?"

"Atlanta. I'm at the airport, and there's a flight leaving for Port Morrow that would get me in just after midnight. I was thinking of taking it, if you wouldn't mind picking me up at the airport?"

"I can think of nothing I'd like better."

"Flight 807." She made a kissing noise over the phone. "See you in about two and half hours, okay?"

"I'll be there."

Chapter Nineteen
Wednesday, September 1, 1993

Port Morrow International Airport

The flight arrived right on time. The airport was going through one of its periodic security binges, and Nathanson had to wait amidst the pack outside the concourse checkpoint. At least for the moment, no one without a ticket was being passed into the gate area.

Dinah was the last passenger to emerge from the roped-off gateway. She always did like to make an entrance, Nathanson thought, and this was to be no exception. She was wearing her flaming red hair long, flowing across her shoulders, and framing her perfect face, with its full lips and green eyes. She was dressed in a pleated skirt, made of some sort of plaid material, and a white blouse, with short sleeves ending at the middle of her upper arm. Except for the detail that her long, slender legs were covered with nylon and not knee socks – and that she had left the top three buttons of her blouse open, so that the upper curves of her perfect breasts were exposed—she looked like a grownup version of a pedophile's fantasy of a Catholic schoolgirl.

She looked to be about 20-years-old, which Nathanson thought wasn't too bad for someone he knew had observed her 758th birthday in February.

She came into his arms and kissed him, her tongue probing his mouth. Her breasts pressed against him, the nipples hard through the thin material of her blouse.

"I've missed you," she said.

"So have I. Who are you, by the way?" It was an entirely practical question. Dinah changed her name a lot more often than he did.

"My last name, darling, is currently Gehritty. Of course, it does bring with it that dreadful Anglicized pronunciation of my first name. But I can live with that for a time, as long as I get to see you once in a while."

The known vampires of the world, Nathanson remembered, were now evenly divided between Jews and gentiles. The incestuous, homosexual brothers were ostensibly Roman Catholic; Dinah was Jewish, the daughter of an impoverished Romanian rabbi, who had grieved at her death, but had never known to say the prayers that would have released her from her curse. One of her brother's descendants was now the leader of a small group of *chassidim* in Israel. A group, curiously enough, with absolutely no connection to Satu Mare, where Dinah had been born and died, though the largest of the *chassidic* dynasties was derived from that city. (Which they called, in Yiddish, "Satmar," the Romanian name having the unfortunate meaning—at least as the name for a group of very Orthodox Jews—of "Saint Mary.")

Another of her brother's descendants, totally unaware of his relationship with the rebbe—or even that he was of Jewish descent—was a television evangelist. It had been estimated that there were at least 500,000,000 people who were direct descendants of the Jews of the Middle Ages who were utterly unaware of that fact, their ancestors having long ago apostatized.

In Hebrew, her name was pronounced "DEE-nah," but, since she was now passing herself off as an Irish American, he would have to remember to call her "DIE-nuh" in public.

They walked through the terminal together, arms around each other's waists, looking for all the world like young people in love. True enough, except that neither of them was remotely young, and while they really were in love, that love was to a degree compelled upon them by the simple fact that neither was aware of anyone else who could bring true passion to their physical relationships. Or, for that matter, with whom they could even have a satisfying physical relationship.

Taking the escalator down to the ground floor, Nathanson noticed a teenaged boy at the bottom, staring wide-eyed, and self-consciously tying his shoe while looking up the escalator. He seemed to be having a great deal of trouble getting the laces fastened properly. Nathanson had a pretty good idea of what was distracting the boy.

"Are you wearing any underwear?" he asked.

"What do you think?"

"I think that boy is trying to get an eyeful."

Dinah grinned. "You're lucky there are people on the 'up' escalator," she said, "or I'd flash him and *really* embarrass you."

He shook his head. "Let's just get your luggage," he laughed.

The drive back to the Beach was made in Nathanson's usual safe and sane way, with all speed limits carefully observed. It wasn't easy. He had the top down, and once they hit the relatively deserted section of O'Brien Boulevard, Dinah opened two more buttons on her white blouse and spread it open to let the cool night air flow over her bare breasts.

"That," she said, "feels much better. It's too damned hot down here."

Nathanson grinned, trying to concentrate on his driving. "You're a vampire, my love," he said. "You don't perspire, and you don't suffer in the heat. You're just trying to turn me on."

And doing, he thought, a damned good job of it.

"You could just be right," Dinah replied, smiling wickedly. She spread her knees as far apart as the seat allowed and pulled up her plaid skirt, confirming Nathanson's suspicion that she wasn't wearing panties. Her nylons were held up by a black lace garter belt.

Her right hand covered her red pubic patch, the middle finger dipping in and massaging herself. "Now that," she said, "*really* feels good."

He found himself wishing he'd taken the long way home, through Belle Springs. It would have avoided the builtup part of the Beach, and there was a park where they could have pulled over for a time.

Dinah's left hand moved across the car and came down in his lap, her fingers working on him through the material of his trousers. "My old friend," she sighed. "Think it would be okay if I take him out and lick him until we get to your house?"

"I don't think so. And in another mile we're going to be getting to the part of the Beach where there are people wandering around, so you might want to at least cover your breasts."

"Prude."

"Only when necessary."

Dinah refastened her blouse, but kept her hand working in her crotch. Nathanson wondered if he should stop and put the top up. The girl was a hopeless exhibitionist, and made her "living" as a stripper, which allowed her to show off her body in a "socially acceptable" manner, and also let her meet hundreds of men every week, insuring an adequate food supply.

They got through the busy part of the Beach without attracting any undue attention, and ten minutes later he pulled the car into the garage. Next door, the lights were still on, and Nathanson wondered what Karen was doing so late. Starting her packing, perhaps?

"Great house," Dinah announced, as they entered the living room. "Now where's the bedroom, and how fast can you get out of those clothes?"

Chapter Twenty
Sunday, December 1, 1918

New York City

Nathanson jumped back onto the curb as a yellow taxicab tooted its horn. He watched it go by, still unsure of how he felt about automobiles. They were noisy and unreliable, but they were also faster than horses on paved roads, and at least you didn't have to watch where you were stepping once they passed.

He had arrived back in New York on the first available ship after the Armistice had gone into effect—Nathanson had never cared for wars, which he considered a terrible waste of human life that rarely settled anything permanently, but he had gone to Europe as a correspondent for the *Tribune*. It paid him a small salary, which he didn't really need; and it had also placed him close to the front, where his own victims had gone utterly unnoticed in the general carnage.

"Be careful," a soft voice warned.

He turned, smiling into the face of a beautiful young woman in a grey dress. Her clothes were a little old-fashioned, but somehow suited her. Her picture hat was poised atop a mass of flaming red hair, which was pulled back from her face and fastened up.

"I guess I wasn't paying attention," he said.

"Are you from out of town?"

"No. But I've been away since we got into the war. I'm a writer for the *Tribune*. Isaac Nathanson."

She smiled. "I think I've read some of your stories. You seemed to take a different point of view than the rest of them. As if you didn't really approve of *any* war."

"You mean our great patriotic adventure to make the world safe for democracy? The peace won't last. Wilson will try, but you can count on Congress to shoot down any of his ideas that might bring about a lasting peace. And the French are still mad about the Franco-Prussian War, so their ideas of a peace treaty will run to the punitive. The Germans will take it because they have no choice, but in a few years they'll be rearming, and they'll start something even worse within the next 30 years."

"You interest me, Mr. Nathanson. Are you by any chance married?"

"No."

"Then perhaps you'd care to buy a nice single lady a light lunch?"

He smiled. "I would if you're the single lady."

"I am. And there's a nice little delicatessen just down the block that serves a delicious hot pastrami." She touched his arm. "You're Jewish, I suspect?"

"Guilty."

"Of course you're guilty. It's our specialty."

Nathanson laughed. Some, he thought, are guiltier than others. This had not been his first war, after all. Much as he loathed the conflicts as a waste of potential, he had gravitated to them over the years. Never as a soldier—that would have been impossible, with the necessity of resting in his coffin on the Sabbath—but always in some capacity that allowed him to be close to the front lines. There was less satisfaction in the blood of young men, to be sure, but in the midst of a war there was also less suspicion. And there were often women around. The prostitutes who hovered near the battlefields, waiting to service the troops. Or the women in the towns nearby.

But wars had a way of ending. Then he could go back to his preferred prey. He glanced over at the girl walking beside him. Much more satisfying, he thought. He had never killed a Jew, but there was something about this girl that suggested he should make an exception. An aura, for want of a better term.

They were at the delicatessen in a few minutes, and found seats at a small, linoleum-covered table in a corner. The owner's wife came over to the table with a pad and pencil.

"So what's for you?" she asked, in Yiddish.

The girl answered in the same language, with what Nathanson recognized as a Romanian accent. "A pastrami sandwich," she said. "And cut off the fat."

"Corned beef," Nathanson said, also in Yiddish.

The woman went back to the counter to put in the order, and Nathanson looked curiously at the girl. "You speak Romanian Yiddish," he said, "and you speak English with no accent. How is this?"

She smiled. "Does your English sound Polish?" she asked. "I came here as a child, of course. My parents never spoke anything but Yiddish at home, but I learned English in school, and from my friends in the neighborhood. And you, by the way, don't have any noticeable accent, either."

"Elocution lessons," he said, grinning. "You should have heard me when I first got to this country." Which had been during the presidency of Thomas Jefferson, though he wasn't about to mention that little detail.

"Fifty cents," the waitress said, putting down the plates. "You pay now."

Nathanson put a silver dollar on the table. "You keep the rest, eh?"

"Are you always that generous?" the girl asked, after the woman had left.

"She reminded me a little of my mother," he said.

"Oh."

Both attacked their sandwiches, though neither actually ate very much. "You're not really hungry?" Nathanson asked.

"Maybe not too much," she admitted. "But I wanted to get to know you."

"Would you like to go somewhere else, then?"

She nodded. "I have a little flat on the next block. If you don't think that's too scandalous."

"I just got back from France. *Nothing* strikes me as particularly scandalous any more." And it will give us some privacy, he thought, though you may soon wish it didn't.

"Then let's forget the food and go to my place."

•   •   •

The girl's flat was typical of those built in the late 19th Century to house the tremendous influx of immigrants to New York. On the second floor, directly above a religious bookstore, the flat comprised three rooms at the front of the building, its two windows looking out onto the street.

The door opened into the kitchen, which was the central of the three rooms. At the back was a small bedroom, the window to which opened into the bottom of an airshaft. There was a sink and bathtub in the kitchen, with a porcelain-coated metal cover that would allow the tub to serve as a low table.

The toilet was in the hallway, shared with the flat on the other side of the hall.

The girl took off her hat, which had been transfixed by a six-inch hatpin, and placed it on the tub cover. With a few deft movements, she loosened her hair, letting it fall about her shoulders. "Much better," she said.

"You are extraordinarily beautiful," he commented, meaning it.

She walked over to him and put her arms around his waist, looking up at him with a coy smile. Her body rubbed sensuously against him, and he suddenly felt himself beginning to respond.

"What's the matter?" she asked, startled at his expression.

He shook his head. "Nothing, really. Just. . ."

"Just what?"

"You're having an interesting effect on me."

She brought her hand around to his crotch and took hold of him, squeezing gently. "I think it's a very *nice* effect," she said.

"So do I. Just unexpected."

The girl laughed. "*I* expected it. I was *hoping* for it, in fact."

He bent and kissed her, feeling her mouth open, her tongue slipping between his teeth. There was no denying it. He was responding in exactly the way any man would to a beautiful woman. And it made him extremely nervous.

Her hands were fumbling with the buttons on his fly. In a moment his trousers had fallen down around his ankles, and the girl was on her knees in front of him, her tongue tracing his length, her lips opening to take him in. It was really out of character coming to her flat. He knew she was Jewish, and he never attacked Jews.

Or was *this* the real reason? Had he somehow sensed that he would respond to this particular girl, and it was the nearly-forgotten pleasures of the flesh, and not a desire for blood, that he had been feeling? He had never *killed* another Jew, but he didn't think he had any qualms about making love to one.

After a time, he pulled her to her feet. "Why don't we go into the bedroom?" he said.

She licked her lips. "Good idea. I think I'm over-dressed, in any event. Don't you?"

He just nodded. It was curious. He was exerting no effort whatever into influencing her actions. And his body was reacting in a way that he had last experienced with Irena, in the barn behind her father's inn, a week before he had "died."

He sat on the edge of the bed, watching the girl undress. The room was sparsely furnished. A full-sized bed dominated the little room. There was an armoire in one corner, and a dressing table, with the frame for the mirror empty, and showing only the wooden backing. Fortunate, he thought, for had the mirror been intact she would almost certainly have noticed that he did not reflect in it.

Her shirtwaist dropped to the floor, so that she was standing before him in her ankle-length skirt and nothing else. Her breasts were perfect, the nipples dark brown, the points firm knobs.

"Take off your clothes," she said. "You look silly like that."

He did as he was told.

She unbuttoned her skirt and let it fall to the floor. Her silk under-pants quickly followed. Sitting on the edge of the bed, she rolled her silk hose down to her ankles and pulled them off. Then she stood again, arms at her side, smiling at him as he threw off the last of his clothing.

She went into his arms, her right hand taking hold of him and stroking gently. Her head pressed against his chest. "Do I make your heart beat faster?" she asked, looking up at him, her ear pressed against his chest.

A moment later she suddenly pulled away, a look of utter astonishment on her lovely face. Very softly, she asked, "Or do I make your heart beat at all?"

Damn!! he thought. He had been so preoccupied with the astonishing fact that he was responding in a normal sexual manner to this girl that he had completely forgotten to exert the conscious control of his body required to simulate a heartbeat and respiration. He shook his head, his look one of sad resignation, and then slowly smiled, his lips pulling well back, so that the extended canine teeth showed for the first time.

She laughed. "Wonderful!" she cried.

Now it was Nathanson's turn to look astonished. If anything, he had expected some show of fear. This girl seemed absolutely delighted.

"I knew you were Jewish," she laughed, "and I brought you up here anyway. And now I know why."

She came to him and threw her arms around him, her hips grinding against him. "And you're not a pansy, either!" she laughed. "Where have you been hiding all these years?"

The girl pushed him back onto the bed, leaping after him, her legs straddling his body, her hand guiding him into her. She began to move in a slow rhythm, up and down, her breasts rising and falling as she rode him, a broad smile on her face, showing the corners of her mouth.

It was then that he knew. The missing mirror on her dressing table wasn't broken. It had been deliberately removed. And with that realization came a strange peace. It was as if a missing element had at last been restored to his existence.

An hour later, they lay side by side on the bed, each totally delighted to have found the other. Her name, she had told him, was Dinah Roth. Or, at least, that was what she was now calling herself, since her parents had brought her into the world long before Jews had surnames.

She was 683-years-old, and had been a vampire for 663 of those years. The curious effect of this was that, physically, she would always be four years *younger* than Nathanson, who had been 24 at the time of his suicide, though chronologically she was 425 years his senior.

She had been lightly stroking him as she told him about herself. Soon he would be ready again, she thought. As a female vampire, she was entirely capable of having sexual relations with normal men. When she brought him up to her flat, knowing he was Jewish, that had been all she really expected. She was beautiful, and she knew it, and she could provoke an erection in a priest when she put her mind to it.

But there was no possibility of a lasting relationship with a mortal. She had tried in the past. After a very few years they would begin to notice that she never aged. And they would question her need to be away from them at frequent intervals.

Most of all, they would wonder why she vanished every Friday evening, and didn't reappear until the following night.

And the sex was less than fully satisfying. Something had always been missing. Now she thought that she might have found it.

It was different for Nathanson. For him, sex with mortals was impossible. Dinah merely had to be receptive, opening herself for any man she found appealing. But there is something in the character or makeup of a male vampire that makes them hopelessly impotent with mortal women. The feelings are there, but the body refuses to react.

Meeting Dinah had been a revelation. If he was impotent with mortal females, he could function very well indeed with a female vampire.

Dinah smiled, opening her legs as he lifted himself above her. This, she thought, is going to be wonderful.

Chapter Twenty-One
Wednesday, September 1, 1993

Port Morrow Beach

Isaac Nathanson ran the pine board through the planer in his garage and added it to the stack beside the workbench. Dinah had pulled him into the bedroom the moment they got home, and they had been there continuously for 14 hours. Now she was resting, sated for the moment.

The two of them had seen a lot in the last 75 years. Her very existence had been a revelation for him, all those years ago. He had almost resigned himself to the idea that he was unique. She had changed that, providing a constant that served to anchor him to the physical world.

She had told him she was planning to stay for a while. Perhaps even as long as a few weeks. If that was the case, she would need a place to rest on the Sabbath. He was nearly finished with the boards, and before long would be able to begin assembling them, using short pieces of quarter-inch dowelling as fasteners. A coffin, after all, was just a simple box, and he had years of experience in building them by now.

There were some things that you couldn't simply go out and buy. Not without exciting a certain degree of curiosity on the part of the seller. Coffins were sold by funeral homes, and the seller generally expected to deliver it to a cemetery after placing a body in it. Home delivery was not the normal practice.

Nathanson ran the final board through the planer, then selected the three that would be used for the bottom. He placed them on the bench, making sure that the planed edges fit together with no gaps. With a carpenter's pencil, he marked the tops of the board where they met. Then each board was placed in the vise, clamped tight, and drilled for the dowels. A special dowelling jig on the drill insured that the holes were exactly centered in the boards, while the pencil marks, carried over to the edge with a small square, insured they would line up properly.

He put a dab of waterproof glue in each hole, inserted the dowels, and used six pipe clamps to pull them together until the glue set.

An hour later, he had the bottom, top, sides, and ends glued up. He would let them set until the next day, then remove the clamps and assemble the coffin.

When he went back into the house, Dinah was sitting on the recliner in the living room, reading Montague Summers' *The Vampire: His Kith and Kin.* "He doesn't know all that much, does he?" she commented.

Nathanson smiled. "Doesn't seem to. Mostly just a collection of old legends and stories."

"I really like this house," Dinah said. "It has character. Most places in Florida are decidedly lacking in that these days. Like little developers' insipid notions of what houses are supposed to look like in subtropical regions."

"I know what you mean. Pretty, but not very functional, and probably uninhabitable without air conditioning."

"A lot of men think a little perspiration is sexy—as long as you don't overdo it. I use a plant mister, myself."

"Are you trying to tell me that you actually regret being entirely unaffected by heat and cold?"

"No. Just one of the things I do to enhance my sex appeal. When you're dancing on a stage under hot lights, the customers sort of expect you to sweat a bit. Besides, I've always sort of enjoyed playing with my food first."

Nathanson laughed, sitting down on the sofa. He was directly opposite Dinah, and could see the triangle of red hair between her slightly-parted legs. She was wearing one of his dress shirts, completely unbuttoned, and nothing else.

"You know," he said, "I *do* have someone who thinks she's my girlfriend, so there are going to be evenings when you'll have to disappear for a few hours. Maybe even the whole night. She's my source inside the Medical Examiner's Office, so I need to keep her happy and healthy."

"How do you keep her happy? You're a vampire. You know you can only function sexually with me—or with someone like me. And, as far as I know, there *isn't* anyone else like me."

"She doesn't know that. As far as she's concerned, I'm the greatest lover she's ever encountered. And don't tell me you've never planted a fantasy in someone's mind."

"I don't have to, remember? Just because a male vampire can't get it up except with a female vampire doesn't mean that a mortal can't get it up with me. I may not get as much satisfaction out of it, but that doesn't mean that the *man* doesn't."

Nathanson nodded. "I suppose that would bother me a little less if you weren't the only female vampire in the world. You can have anyone you want, and I can only have you."

"I don't know that I *am* the only one, Itzak. I don't *know* any others. Not since Golda was murdered by the Baal Shem Tov. But that isn't saying I'm unique. You'd been around for over 200 years before I knew *you* existed, after all. And people still kill themselves. It stands to reason that once in a while one of them will do so in just the right way, and we'll have a new colleague."

"Who will probably be a male." Statistically, most suicides were young men.

"I should be so lucky," Dinah said. "Besides, if he is, he's just as likely to wind up joining the brothers, isn't he?"

"At least that would leave you with me, wouldn't it?"

She grinned. "I suppose it would at that." Her right hand slipped under the shirt and began to massage her left breast. "How are you feeling, by the way? Rested?"

"Horny."

"Great." She slid forward in the chair. "Why don't you come on over here and lick me for a while, then I'll return the favor."

Chapter Twenty-Two
Tuesday, September 6, 1993

Benjamin County Sheriff's Department

"There's still nothing really suspicious," Hanson reported, "unless you think there's some significance to the fact that he seems to be cheating on his girlfriend."

Schneider shook his head. "Probably not. Unless the girl he's cheating with is a tall, athletic brunette."

"No. Average height. And not a brunette—she's another redhead. I saw her come out onto the front porch in a bikini just before sundown last night." He smiled at the memory. "She's one of the most beautiful women I've ever seen. Perfect figure—looks like a dancer."

"She's a redhead?"

"That's right."

"You sure she isn't his sister?"

"Not unless he's into incest. At least, my sister has never grabbed *me* by the crotch and tried to put her tongue all the way down my throat."

"Okay," Schneider conceded. "A new girlfriend. Are you sure he's still seeing Margie Calloway?"

"He was with her last night. The redhead has a rented car, and she took off just after sunset. Nathanson left a couple minutes later and came back with Calloway. She spent the night there. I'm not sure where the redhead went."

"Okay. Did you get the tag on the redhead's car, by the way?"

"Sure. I had Sandy check it through the computer. The car is rented to a Dinah Gehritty, and the company's records show her as being from D.C."

"Any record?"

"Not even a parking ticket."

Schneider shrugged. "Not much we can do, then, is there? Let it go for now. I still have a feeling this is the guy we want, but there just doesn't seem to be any way to shake his alibi and prove it."

"What about his girlfriend? Do you think she'd change her mind about where he's been if she found out he has a new playmate?"

"Maybe," Schneider admitted. "But *you* were there, too, in case you didn't remember?"

"Well, yeah—good point—"

"And you can hardly change *your* report, can you? He's got two witnesses who can place him at his house when Captain Slodine was being killed, and one of them is you." Schneider frowned at the report. "But for all that, I still think he's probably the guy we're looking for."

Hanson nodded. "Too bad we don't seem to be able to prove it."

Port Morrow Beach

Dinah Gehritty sat at a small table by the poolside bar at the Tropical Breeze, a cafe umbrella providing a degree of shade. She was dressed in a white bikini that left very little to the imagination, covered with a white lace pool jacket. Like most natural redheads, Dinah was quite fair. Unlike many, her skin was clear and unfreckled.

She had spent the night at the Tropical Breeze, while Nathanson was entertaining Margie at his house. There was no jealousy, for Dinah realized that Margie was really nothing more than a convenient alibi for the night of one killing, and a good source of information. She also knew that the girl meant nothing to Nathanson, and would be fortunate if he didn't kill her before he left Port Morrow for good.

Dinah could provide him with the one thing that no one else in the world could supply. Actual, physical lovemaking, in which he could be a fully active participant. The reasons why a male vampire should be impotent with mortal women were simply not known. Nathanson had never reported any insights on that matter, and Dinah certainly had nothing to contribute. And it wasn't the sort of thing you could discuss with the local urologist, either, for doctor-patient privilege or not, the average physician would certainly consider a vampire to be less a patient than an infectious organism. It was a normal part of a doctor's occupation to kill disease germs, as well as other things that were dangerous to human life.

While Nathanson had been mentally inducing false memories in Margie, Dinah had been creating a few genuine memories for a college football player from Boston. It seemed only fair, even if there was less satisfaction than she might have received from her longtime lover. Male vampires might not be able to function sexually with mortal women, but with a female vampire they could not only function normally, but very nearly endlessly.

Human males got tired too quickly, she thought. She smiled into her drink. Of course, the average human male couldn't pick up a Plymouth with one hand, either. A male vampire could.

And perhaps the lessened satisfaction she felt with mortal lovers was the counterpart of the male vampire's congenital impotence. The nature of her female organs meant that sex was always possible. She merely had to open her legs. But even the most skilled lover produced little more than a slight tingle. Nothing at all like the waves of passion she felt with Itzak.

She looked across the pool, her eyes hidden behind dark glasses, to where two young women were sunbathing, lying on their stomachs, with their bra straps unhooked for a better tan. Dinah had seen them come out of the building a few minutes earlier. Both tall, with dark, even tans. Their hair was black, cut shoulder length, and they moved with the practiced ease of professional dancers.

Both had blue eyes, and while their breasts weren't large, they were high and well formed. Their stomachs were flat, their legs perfect.

They were also identical twins.

Dinah kept her eye on the twins, careful to seem to be looking elsewhere. Her drink was one of the bartender's more exotic concoctions, served in a coconut shell, with two kinds of rum and a lot of fruit juice. It seemed to be intended to get someone very drunk very quickly. As far as Dinah was concerned, it might as well have been water. Within an hour it would pass right through her system and be flushed away.

　She actually missed food. She could eat and drink, and often did. But there was no particular pleasure in the act of eating. The taste was no longer there; eating was nothing more than a form of camouflage— a way of appearing more like a mortal human being than an undead body animated by a spirit that would have preferred to truly die and return to its Creator. The food wasn't even digested—it just moved through her system and passed out in the same form.

　The girls were reaching around behind them and fastening their bra straps now. Not quite in unison, they both sat up on their lounges and swung their smooth legs around, pulling them up in front of them. One of them, she noticed, was now looking at her. She tilted her head back, brushing the fingers of her left hand through her hair, arching her back in the process, so that her breasts strained at the tiny cups of her bikini top, the lace coverup slipping aside.

　The girl's sudden intake of breath would have been inaudible to a normal person at that distance, but Dinah heard it clearly. Interesting, she thought. There might just be some possibilities here.

　Dinah placed her drink on the table and stood up. With a sly smile, she lowered her dark glasses, looking over the frames at the first twin. She was rewarded with a reflexive preening motion as the girl unconsciously adjusted her hair back off her face.

　Very casually, she walked around the pool to where the twins were sitting. The first never took her eyes off her. The other, she noticed, was ignoring her completely, and exuding an aura of complete disdain for her sister. Dinah thought this might work out even better than she had anticipated.

● ● ●

　Nathanson picked up the phone in the kitchen, where he was busy putting away the breakfast dishes. Margie had stayed later than usual— something to do with having to work late on Friday, and getting a half-day off in compensation—so they had eaten a light breakfast about 9:00 o'clock.

　Feeling particularly naughty, he had recalled some of the things he had done with Dinah the previous day and used those memories to create his illusion in Margie's mind. He had also taken a couple ounces of blood. Just enough for a snack, yet not so much that she was likely to notice the loss. It created a stronger bond, and he had noticed that when Dinah was around he often forgot to eat.

It was Dinah on the phone. "Your friend gone?" she asked.

"Yes. I'm just finishing the cleaning up now."

"Make the bedroom presentable. I'm bringing home a present for you."

"Like to give me a hint?"

"It comes in a matched set."

"That helps a lot."

"I think you'll be pleased, darling. See you in fifteen minutes."

Nathanson replaced the phone and finished the dishes. Now what was she up to? he wondered.

He walked into the bedroom and stripped the bed, throwing the sheets into the hamper. There were fresh sheets in the linen closet, and it took only a few minutes to make up the bed. Just for a lark, he also put on a new spread. One of the maroon satin ones he'd purchased a few years earlier, when he had done up a New York apartment in what the decorator called "early decadent."

He was doing a little tidying in the living room when he heard Dinah's car pull into the drive.

•   •   •

There was something a little odd looking about the three of them. The two girls with Dinah were obviously identical twins. They had dressed differently, but their hairstyles and makeup were exactly alike. One was wearing jeans and a denim shirt, with black leather sneakers. That one was looking at Dinah with an undisguised hunger that said volumes about her sexual preferences.

Her sister was wearing a mid-thigh-length skirt over panty hose and low heels, and a white, fitted blouse, open at the throat. From the way she was looking at her sister and Dinah, he was fairly sure she was straight.

"This is Zack," Dinah told the girls.

"Hi."

"My friend here is Tina," Dinah announced, indicating the sister in denim. "And her sister is Gina. I got them both to come out her by telling Gina you'd be here."

Nathanson smiled. "Glad you convinced her."

"Your friend was suggesting a sort of orgy," Gina said. "I was hoping you could convince my sister of the error of her ways."

"I *like* group things, actually," Tina said. "I just don't usually let *men* participate."

"I bet them that you could tell which was which, even if they didn't give you any clues," Dinah announced.

Nathanson frowned. "What did you bet?"

"If you can't tell, you only get Gina. If you *can* tell, then Tina will sit on your face. That's the most she'd promise, though."

He laughed. "You have odd ideas, dear."

"Perverse, ain't I?"

"Absolutely. That's why I love you."

Dinah herded the two girls into the bedroom, but closed the door when Nathanson made to follow. "You have a wait a few minutes," she said. "And take off your clothes before you come in."

Nathanson shrugged and went back into the living room. Through the window, he could see someone moving into the rental next door. An older couple, this time. No one to attract his attention.

The twins, however, were perfect. He suspected that Dinah had a bit more than a little sex in mind when she brought them home. Provided, of course, that no one knew they had come there.

"Got your clothes off yet?" Dinah called, sticking her head out the bedroom door.

"Just a minute." He stripped and went into the bedroom. Dinah had turned off the lights, and adjusted the aluminum miniblinds to provide a soft, but adequate illumination.

All three of them were naked. Dinah was sitting on the edge of the bed, while the twins were standing beside it, their expressions carefully neutral. He didn't think any normal man could have told them apart. Except for a tiny mole on the lower curve of the left breast of the one nearest the dresser—which would be hidden when she was dressed, and therefore couldn't be called a clue—they were absolutely identical.

He walked back and forth in front of them a couple of times. "Do I get to touch them before I say which is which?" he asked.

"No," Dinah declared. "No touching until you make your choice. We don't want you trying to decide who's who based on how they respond to you."

He put on a petulant frown. After a moment, he put his arm around the twin with the mole. "This one," he said, "is Gina."

"Are you sure?" she asked. They even sounded alike.

"Unless you were introduced to me with the wrong names."

The one he was holding smiled and kissed his cheek. "This might be fun after all," she said.

"How the hell did he do that?" Tina asked. Now she was going to have to let a man eat her—and God knew what else her sister would try to make her do with him.

"You smell different," he said.

"Yeah, right."

It was the absolute truth, he thought. It was just that the difference in scent was so subtle that a normal man would never have been able to detect it. For someone who could smell the cleaning solvent on a policeman's gun at 30 feet, however, it was easy.

Gina smiled at him, hardly needing to look up. Naked and bare footed, the girls were only a quarter inch under six feet tall. In heels, she would almost have been able to look him right in the eye. "Even our mother can't tell us apart most of the time, if we're dressed alike. She usually has to rely on the dog. He always goes to Tina first."

"Like I said, you smell different."

"He's part bloodhound," Dinah commented. "If he wasn't already rich, he could go into the perfume business and make a fortune with that nose."

"Now," Gina said, "since I won the bet I get to set the scene, and that includes my sister doing something with a *man* for a change. So, Zack, you go lay down on the bed, face up. Little sister, I want to see you with your snatch where he can get his tongue into it."

"He'd better do it right," Tina said, petulantly, "or I'll pee on him."

Nathanson looked over at her. "Oh, now *there's* a real incentive."

But he did as he was told, and a moment later Tina was hovering over his face, her calves under his arms, her thighs on either side of his head.

The other two were bending over his crotch, their hands gently massaging him, lips and tongues joining to bring him up. He was responding, which he knew was Dinah's touch. But it was Gina who suddenly straddled him and slipped him inside her.

As she moved up and down on him, he could feel Dinah's hand massaging him just below her, sustaining him. Once he was up, he thought he might have been able to maintain an erection, but he wasn't sure, and the female vampire's touch was reassuring.

Tina was starting to move her hips now, responding in spite of herself as his tongue moved over her.

Dinah, left without an available outlet, was massaging his balls with her left hand, and masturbating with her right.

A soft moan came from above his head, and he looked up the front of Tina's body, past her small, firm breasts, with their hard pink nipples, to see her looking down at him with an expression combining ecstasy with astonishment at what was happening. Her body was quivering, and she was thrusting her vulva against his open mouth. He could taste the passion oozing from within her, and he let his hands move across her smooth behind, pulling her into him.

Her sister was moving faster now, her hips rising and falling in an ever-increasing rhythm. Suddenly she pressed herself down against him, groaning, and he could feel the muscles inside her spasming, as if trying to pull him in even deeper. Gripping and releasing while her body went limp, and she leaned back, supporting herself on his upraised knees.

As Gina had exploded, Tina had begun to relax. But she didn't move from her place, and after a very short time she was once again pressing herself against his mouth. "I could learn to like this," she commented.

Gina rolled off of him, and he could feel Dinah's mouth closing over him, taking her place without giving him a chance to pause.

Tina's thighs were pressing against the sides of his head, her body again quaking as another orgasm took hold of her. Her hips were moving in a short, rolling motion, her wet, fragrant center suctioned to his lips. After a final, long shudder of satisfaction she rolled off him, thoroughly spent.

Now Gina straddled his face, lowering herself against his mouth as she bent over his body. Her nipples brushed his upper abdomen, and he could feel her tongue working its way in just under Dinah's lips.

Dinah gave a sudden start, and he realized that Tina had moved in behind her and was now expressing her usual sexual nature as she licked her upraised privates.

A moment later he erupted, his seed—sterile and functionless in a vampire, but still present—pouring out into Dinah's hungry mouth, and running down him to where Gina avidly licked up the excess.

And Dinah was gasping, too, her own hips moving to the rhythm of Tina's flickering tongue, her nipples hard and tender as they rubbed against the satin spread.

She kept him in her mouth, bringing him up again after a few minutes. Gina pulled Dinah upright, so that she was squatting on the bed, her genitals spread open above Tina's face. The straight sister took Nathanson's hand and pulled him toward her, positioning him between her sister's drawn-up legs.

There was no resistance as he entered her, and Tina's hips began to move in response to his thrusting. Again he felt the clutching spasms as she came. She was more like her sister than even she had imagined, he thought.

He was leaning forward, his arms fully extended, while Dinah pressed her mouth against his, their tongues probing. The contact with her continued to exert its influence as he pumped his hips, driving himself in and out of Tina, until he again felt the congestion in his loins, and he was shooting into her.

After a time, they all collapsed onto the bed, each fully used in their own fashion. In a few minutes, the twins were asleep, and Nathanson led Dinah out into the kitchen. Neither of them bothered to dress.

"You brought me a really nice present," he said. "I haven't done that with a mortal woman in over 300 years."

"Seems almost a pity to eat them now, doesn't it, darling?"

He nodded solemnly. "It does at that. Especially considering we've already eaten both of them several times this afternoon."

Dinah groaned and shook her head. "I never really cared for puns, you know."

"Are we sharing?" he asked.

"I think that would be nice. Why don't you have Gina and I'll take Tina. I think we'll get the best cooperation that way. Tina will definitely let me come on to her—that's how I got them here in the first place.

Though considering that she let you fuck her, maybe she's turning? And right now Gina thinks you're the sexiest thing to come along in the last hundred years."

"It really does seem a pity, though."

"Do you want to let them go?"

He shook his head. "I don't think so. After all, they both fit what I'm sure the police think of as my 'victim profile.' We do need the nourishment, and I presume you were careful about being seen?"

"As careful as I *could* be, considering I found them in a pretty public place."

"How were you dressed?"

"My white bikini, with the lace coverup."

"Maybe we should let them go," he said. "If you were dressed in that outfit, every man within a mile is sure to have noticed you."

She smiled. "Not that they'd *remember.*"

"That's what I thought once. Only someone didn't get the message that he wasn't supposed to notice. That's why the sheriff keeps sending people to check me out."

"Are they around now?"

"No."

"Then why worry?"

"I suppose you're right, my love. Now, do you want to play with them some more? Or are you getting hungry?"

Chapter Twenty-Three
Wednesday, September 7, 1993

Belle Beach

By the time Schneider arrived, there was already a crowd. He put the deputies to work shooing the spectators away, then went up to the crime scene. Or, at least, to what would have to pass for the crime scene, since he was certain that this was the same killer, and thus this would only be a disposal site, not the actual murder scene.

Twins, he thought. Identical twins.

There was a variation this time, he noticed. They seemed to be sharing a pair of bikinis between them. The one on the right was wearing a black bottom and a silver metallic bra, while the one on the left had a black bra and a silver bottom. Typically, they were lying on their backs, big towels spread out under them, as if they were just getting some sun.

The assistant Medical Examiner finished his examination. "Looks like the same killer," he said. "Working overtime on this one. Looks like were probably killed at least 15 hours ago, judging by the temperature, and the general condition of the bodies."

Schneider nodded. "Thanks. The lab crew should be done before long and you can take them back for the posts." He turned to the lab technician, who was taking photographs, since there was nothing on the beach to dust for fingerprints. "Be sure you bag their hands," he said. "Maybe this time we'll get lucky and one of them scratched him."

Benjamin County Medical Examiner's Office

"Something new has been added," Edgars said, coming out of the autopsy room shortly after 11:00 pm.

"You found skin under their fingernails?" Schneider asked, somewhat hopefully.

"Nothing that good. But they both had sex shortly before they were killed. I can't find any signs of force. No tearing or abrasions. Both of them seem to have been fully lubricated at the time of entry, so I have to conclude that the sex was consensual."

"Please tell me there's semen that didn't come from their regular boyfriends."

"There was semen. But I'm not sure just who it came from. Damnedest stuff I've ever seen."

"What do you mean?"

"Zero motility. This was in number one's mouth, so it had to have been deposited very shortly before she was killed. Otherwise she would have either swallowed it, or brushed her teeth and eliminated it that way.

"But all things being normal, the sperm should still have been alive. And we found more in number two's vagina, and that was just as dead as the first sample. In the first case we might have argued that the saliva had killed it—you'd be surprised just what that stuff can destroy—but the vagina is definitely a sperm-friendly environment."

Schneider was nodding and writing in his notebook. "Would you say that means we'll be able to identify the killer by his semen?"

"If you can get a sample. But how are you going to do that? The courts aren't about to let you make a suspect provide a sample. If he's innocent he might do so voluntarily, just, to clear himself. But if he's guilty—or just bloody minded, for that matter—I seem to recall a few rulings that would say compelling him to jerk off into a sample jar presents a Fifth Amendment problem. Like the way the courts have always ruled that people who are barred from owning guns don't have to register them if they do, since it would be admitting they were committing a crime by having the gun."

"Good point, Doc."

"Otherwise, this looks exactly like all of the others. Right down to the tooth marks on the throats. I think he might have a new machine, though."

"What makes you think that?"

"There's a slight difference in the marks. The punctures on number two are eight millimeters closer together."

Schneider had a sudden thought, but dismissed it as being too outrageous. Hanson had reported that Nathanson had a new girlfriend. Women had smaller mouths than men, didn't they?

But that was ridiculous. Henley had given them a very thorough rundown on 'vampire' killers, and the one thing they were all certain of was that something other than manual suction had to have been used in order to remove the blood from the victims so completely.

On the other hand, it couldn't hurt to look around. Maybe someone had seen something this time.

"So," he said. "Jane Doe number eight and nine for the year?"

"Ten and eleven," the doctor said. "You forgot the two drowning victims last week."

"And you think it might be the murderer they had sex with?"

"It's possible. Since they were both killed very shortly after having sex, the killer is the most likely source."

"Not like the Irwin girl?"

"No. Our murderer was the one who killed her, but the semen came from Smith, who was probably also killed by the same man."

Schneider nodded. They had found Smith's rented apartment within a couple hours of discovering his body in the Tropical Breeze parking lot. The rented TV/VCR combination on the dresser in his bedroom was loaded with a porno loop collection, consisting entirely of Asian women having sex with various men, and with each other. Ten more porno tapes were stacked up beside it.

There had been a pair of powerful 10x60 binoculars on the bed, along with a pile of slick-paper, hardcore porno magazines. With the binoculars, the front facing rooms in the Tropical Breeze seemed almost close enough to touch. And with the lights on in the room, it was possible to see into Gail Irwin's room on the seventh floor.

The cheap carpeting on the side of the bed facing the window was liberally spotted with semen stains. And the pages of a couple of the magazines were stuck together, where Smith had ejaculated across the photos. The man had been an absolute slob, and a perverted one at that, Schneider thought. There was no doubt he had seen Gail Irwin in her room, formed some sick fantasy about her, and attacked her in the parking lot.

The question was who had attacked *him*? Was it their serial killer, or someone else? And had their killer now started having sex with his victims? Or had he been doing so all along, and just not leaving any evidence?

Chapter Twenty-Four
Wednesday, September 15, 1993

Port Morrow Beach

Nathanson was getting slightly frustrated. Schneider had let him alone for a while, but now he seemed to be interested again. The F.B.I. was involved, too, so perhaps they had pointed up a pattern that the locals hadn't noticed before. Other deaths, and his own proximity at the time. He had always tried to be careful, but it wasn't always practical to do his hunting at a distance from where he lived. Or to spend all of his time in places where it was possible to conceal his actions. During the time he had lived in Las Vegas, he had killed nearly every week, hiding the bodies in the surrounding desert. They were all buried on what the locals called "BLM" property—land owned by the Federal Bureau of Land Management—which meant that it was unlikely to be developed, with the resultant risk that the bodies would be found during site preparation work.

Here, however, he had indulged his propensity for risk taking by leaving his victims on display. Behavior a psychologist would no doubt relate to a desire for the finality of true death, after centuries of undead existence. A belief no doubt fostered by the fact that psychologists, like other people, were prone to read popular fiction, in which angst ridden vampires poured out their hearts, wallowing in the agony of the pain and suffering their depredations had caused. Self-hatred at the spreading of their affliction to the innocent.

The truth was more prosaic. To become a vampire was a punishment and nothing more. A fitting punishment, in fact, for one who defied God's exclusive power to create and end human life. For his audacity to place his own momentary despair at his love life over the original plan for his lifetime, Nathanson had been punished by not only failing to die as he had wished, but by having his life extended long beyond that of his contemporaries.

But he felt no particular guilt over what he did. Did the *shoichet* feel guilt when his knife was drawn across the steer's throat? Normal humans lived on beef, and there were naturally those whose function it was to provide it for them. In the same way, a vampire could only live on human blood. To a vampire, living human beings were in the same relationship as were cattle to normal people. They were a source of nourishment.

As for pain—as far as he had ever been able to determine, death at the hands of a vampire wasn't in the least painful. If the physical reaction of most of his victims was a true indication, it was quite possibly a source of extreme physical pleasure.

But he was sure he was being watched, even if not all the time. So soon, he thought, it would be time to move on. Perhaps even time to become someone else for a while. He had used his "real" name for many years, but there had also been intervals when he'd adopted a different identity. That was harder to do now, with the ubiquity of computerized records and the need for certain documents, but by no means impossible.

Particularly for someone who could find ways of influencing government clerks to issue the documents without realizing they'd ever done so.

It might be better to just vanish. Kill off Isaac Nathanson and become another person. Perhaps arrange a convenient automobile accident. He could send the Mustang off a bridge and into the Gulf, so that his body could be reported washed out to sea, where it would probably be eaten by sharks. Then he could simply show up in a different community, with a different identity. Perhaps even try settling down in Las Vegas again, where the tourist industry provided a steady stream of victims, and the consequences of people's gambling habits were such that sometimes they never returned home.

He might even set up a household with Dinah, taking on the roles of husband and wife for a few years. Their physical hunger for each other often seemed to interfere with more basic things—such as eating—but the twins had shown that they *could* combine their lusts with the fundamentals. It had even opened up a new world of possibilities. He now knew that, with a little help from Dinah, he could function sexually even with a mortal woman.

So, he thought, perhaps he would, indeed, kill himself off. He had been Isaac Nathanson for far too long now. It wouldn't be that hard to become someone else.

Easier, to be sure, than the last time he had changed from one person into another.

Chapter Twenty-Five
Friday, November 6, 1891

Baltimore, Maryland

Karl Lager, as Itzak was now calling himself, was getting desperate. A chain of circumstances had frustrated him for nearly two weeks, preventing even a light feeding.

Now he had his chance. He'd found the girl walking along a main street less than ten minutes earlier. The location was fortuitous. His house was no more than five minutes away, and it was now 4:00 in the afternoon, which meant that the sun would be setting in exactly one hour. On a Friday afternoon, that meant he had only an hour until he would have to return to his coffin, hidden beneath the coal cellar of his house, for his Sabbath rest. It didn't give him a lot of time, but it gave him enough.

The girl was a prostitute. She'd made that more than obvious from the moment he first saw her. Lager had no moral qualms about her profession; to him, she was just a source of nourishment. If she presented a public health threat, it was only to her "living" customers. The diseases of the living didn't pass with the blood—or, if they did, they didn't affect him.

She was a plain-looking girl, probably no more than 20, garbed in a plum velvet dress that, on someone of better quality, would have been striking. On her it merely looked cheap. He had long ago come to recognize that it wasn't so much what someone wore, as it was the *way* they wore it. This girl carried herself like a prostitute, and her expression was that of a wanton. At least, it contrived to be. Lager had no doubt that her actual feeling for her profession was one of disgust.

The doctors and clergymen all said that prostitutes were driven to their trade by their personalities. That they were all nymphomaniacs. Lager, who had much more experience of prostitutes than even the most profligate physician or vicar—and who also had the advantage of being able to read their thoughts as he drained their blood—recognized that the main impetus toward that profession was nothing more than simple poverty. They didn't seek constant sexual release because of some pathological inability to take any real pleasure in the sex act. It was simply a way to make money.

In the society of 1891 America—and most other places—there was little honest work available to an illiterate girl, and if she didn't quickly find a husband, about all that was left for her was to sell her body on the street, or in one of the many houses the city fathers were so careful to pretend didn't exist, even as they pocketed the bribes of the madams and pimps.

But just now, Lager thought, there was no time to take the girl back to his house. With the sun going down in an hour, he wouldn't have time to drain her and dispose of her body before the Sabbath arrived and he lapsed into his weekly stasis. If he killed her at home, it was possible that her body would begin to smell before he could wake up and get rid of it. And that sort of thing invited official attention.

He noticed a narrow alley and guided her into it. She was smiling. Why not? He had offered her five dollars to go with him—a fortune to a girl like this, who could live for a week or more on that sum. And she had no reason to suspect that he wanted anything different from her usual clients. He was dressed like a gentleman, and the girl presumed that gentlemen were simply more willing to pay a proper fee for their pleasure than the working-class clientele who usually made up her trade.

They went back into the alley about 30 feet. "This will do fine," Lager said.

"What?" the girl asked, with a slight laugh. "You'll be havin' me up against the side o' the buildin', will you?"

"It's convenient."

"Well, sure, it is that."

"What do you call yourself, by the way?" he asked.

"Eileen Murphy."

Irish, he thought. Hardly a surprise in Baltimore, which had started as a Catholic colony in the first place, and continued to attract Catholic immigrants at a greater rate than any city south of New York.

"Well, Eileen," he said, "if you don't mind, I think we should get on with it, eh?"

"Sure." She leaned back against the brick wall of the building, letting him unbutton the front of her dress and pull it open, so that her breasts were exposed to his view. With a calculatingly wanton smile, she pulled up her skirt and petticoats. Except for her cotton stockings, she wore nothing underneath.

She had done the same sort of thing a hundred times before. Usually for other unfortunates, who didn't have the money to pay for her *and* a room. This would be the first time with an obvious gentleman, though.

At the moment he was just looking at her. Smiling. Then he laughed softly, and she was astonished to notice the length of the sharp, canine teeth. How had she failed to see those, she wondered. He'd smiled before and his teeth had seemed entirely normal.

Then she looked up at his eyes, and found herself unable to move. His head lowered, tilting to one side, and there was a momentary pain in her neck. Her hands opened, letting her skirt drop back into place. Her body, being rapidly drained of its blood, was moving involuntarily in the familiar sexual rhythms. There was no pain. Only the trembling warmth of the climax she had often simulated, but had never actually felt until now.

His hands were on her breasts, massaging them, the nipples tingling with released passions. Her mind was flashing on a scene from the book her friend Mary had been reading to her. The image of the Transylvanian Count, which she had found curiously erotic at the same time it horrified her.

But that was fiction, and this was reality. Intellectually, she knew that she was dying, yet her body was trembling with weird spasms of pleasure.

And was she now being doomed to roam the night as an undead creature, preying on the blood of the innocent, as the author of that book had suggested?

Creature of the *night*? It was still daylight. And she had been standing in the full afternoon sunlight when this man approached her. Could that book have been wrong about that, she wondered?

There was a final spasm of supreme pleasure, and then she went limp in his arms.

Lager sucked out the final ounces of blood and let her body fall to the brick pavement. And as he turned to leave the alley he heard a shout, followed immediately by a gunshot and a stinging slap against his left arm.

And it was then that he realized he'd taken too long with the girl. In the Jewish section of Baltimore, housewives were beginning to light their Sabbath candles.

In another twenty minutes it would be sunset. Time enough to get home, he thought—if two cops weren't in the way.

He rushed at them, and the bigger one rapped him on the side of the head with his nightstick. Both of them fell on top of him, and in a moment there were handcuffs on his wrists. With the Sabbath about to begin, Lager lacked the strength to fight back.

At any other time, he could have simply brushed them aside like insects. The gunshot in his arm was meaningless. With a vampire's exaggerated healing capacities, the wound would close up completely in only a few hours. But now his strength was draining away as the sun neared the horizon. The alley was already in deep shadow.

• • •

"What have you got?" the desk sergeant asked.

"A lunatic, I think," the cop said. "Killed a girl in the alley around the corner. Ripped her throat out with his teeth, from the look of her."

"In there." The sergeant pointed to an iron cage in the corner of the room, which served as a holding cell until a prisoner could be interrogated, or until they could think of what to do with him. This one, the sergeant thought, would probably go to the asylum. From what the arresting officers were telling him, the man was clearly insane.

Lager, already weak with the approaching sunset, was thrust into the holding cell and staggered to the bunk, flopping onto the horsehair stuffed mattress.

And that was where the Sabbath found him, on the metal-framed bunk in the holding cell. At precisely 5:00 pm, as the sun vanished to the west of the city, the link between body and spirit was severed. His spirit would rise to its Sabbath rest and its longed-for—yet curiously terrifying—taste of the world to come. His body would seem, to any who encountered it, to be exactly what it had been since 1684.

Dead.

Vaguely, he had looked on, watching what was happening in a detached way. His spirit, which on the Sabbath was vividly conscious of the horror Itzak had become, actually felt a stirring of hope as the desk sergeant summoned a doctor. Perhaps they would find a way to destroy his body and thus release his spirit to return to its maker?

"He's dead," the doctor said. "No heartbeat and no respiration." Had he encountered Lager when he was up and walking about, there would *also* have been no heartbeat or respiration, unless Lager consciously willed it, but the doctor had no way of knowing that. Even if he'd been told, he wouldn't have believed it. You simply expected that anyone who was moving about was breathing, which meant that when they weren't you would put it down to an illusion of some sort—perhaps created by loosefitting clothing.

Dracula had been published only three years earlier, and the doctor had read it. But the doctor was a modern, up-to-date scientist. The fact that he knew less about medicine that a First Class Boy Scout would know a hundred years later didn't bother him at all; his medical knowledge was state-ofthe-art for his own time.

And he was certainly knowledgeable enough to know that people who didn't breath, and whose hearts were no longer beating, were obviously dead. Vampires were a Central European myth. So even the description of this man's crime wasn't sufficient to alert him to the truth.

Besides, he suffered from the same prejudices as Eileen Murphy. His knowledge of vampires was limited to fiction, and fictional vampires didn't walk around in the daylight, or drop dead in jail cells.

"He's been shot," the doctor added.

"Ryan did that," the sergeant said. "Couldn't have killed him, though. Look at the wound—it didn't even bleed."

The doctor nodded. "So I see. Something killed him, though. Send him around to the morgue. And see if you can find out who he was—he may have a family."

•   •   •

Autopsy procedures in 1891 were essentially the same as those in 1993. Lager's body was laid out on a steel table—this one coated with white porcelain—and the doctor took his measurements. These were different from those that would be taken a few years later, since the Baltimore police were still using the Bertillion system, which employed precise measurements to identify individuals. They were also taken in inches, pounds, and ounces, instead of millimeters, kilos, and grams.

Bertillion, a Frenchman, had decided that, if you took enough measurements, in a sufficiently precise manner, no two people would have exactly the same set of measurements. He was proven wrong within a few years, but by then Scotland Yard's fingerprint identification system had come into general use, and the old system passed with little notice, except by writers, who continued to use Bertillion's system of "types"—criminals had more prominent brow ridges than honest people, and smaller eyes, according to the good professor—in their character descriptions.

Once the body had been measured, it was washed down, and the doctor took a large scalpel and made the standard "Y" incision. The whole process took less than an hour, and when he was finished the doctor still had no idea what had killed the prisoner.

Having arrived at that non-conclusion, the doctor replaced the internal organs in the body cavity, paying absolutely no attention to their original location, and sewed up the long incisions with coarse, running stitches.

About the only conclusion he had drawn was that the man had probably been Jewish, and he'd figured that out before he ever picked up his scalpel. Clinical circumcision was still extremely rare at that time, so if you found someone who had been circumcised, he was probably a Jew.

Chapter Twenty-Six
Wednesday, September 15, 1993

Port Morrow Beach

The healing process, Nathanson remembered, had taken five weeks. All of those jumbled-up organs to be sorted out and put back in their proper place; the gross tissue damage inflicted during the course of the autopsy to heal. It all complicated and slowed the healing.

One of his neighbors had identified his body, and he had been buried in a small Jewish cemetery. When he finally rose from his coffin at the end of the fifth week, he made a fast kill to build up his strength and then put in an appearance at the police station, where he informed the desk sergeant that he was Emil Lager, Karl's twin brother, who had just learned what had happened and come down from New York to claim his brother's effects.

The sergeant took one look at him and turned him over to the captain. Since it never occurred to either of them that the "twins" were actually the same man, the formalities were observed and the property released.

"Will you be staying in Baltimore, Mr. Lager?" the captain asked, after the papers were duly signed and witnessed.

"I don't believe so. My brother was killed here, after all."

"Your brother, I'm afraid, wasn't quite a model citizen. He was captured in the act of murdering a young woman, and we have reason to believe he may have killed five others in the same way."

"Worse than I thought," Lager said, smiling inwardly. They were still unaware of the other two, it seemed. "We always did have problems with Karl," he went on. "He would do things to animals—no one ever understood why. But no one in the family ever expected it to end *this* way."

The captain nodded. He'd heard the same sort of thing said by parents, siblings, spouses, and even friends of countless other criminals. No one *ever* expected them to turn out that way—but they did. "So, you'll be going back to New York, then?"

"That's right," Lager said. "New York."

A day later, after making the arrangements to have his property packed up and shipped to a warehouse in New York, Lager boarded the train and left Baltimore.

He would return, but not before the 1930s.

But he wasn't about to let that sort of thing happen to him today. It wasn't that he really feared "dropping dead" in a jail cell when the Sabbath arrived. Or even the mutilation of another autopsy. They could chop him into little pieces, and as long as they all wound up in the same box his body would reassemble itself. Probably, he thought, it would even regenerate a few missing pieces.

But today, he feared, whatever was left after the autopsy would probably be cremated. And he wasn't sure that even *he* could recover from that. Even worse, he was just a little afraid that he *would.* If God could restore the bodies of those who had been buried for centuries to their normal condition—and Nathanson, better than most, knew that this was not only possible, but would eventually happen—what was to stop Him from reconstituting Nathanson's cremated body for further earthly punishment?

Chapter Twenty-Seven
Thursday, September 16, 1993

Cape Marl

Schneider was having a difficult time putting the beach murders out of his mind, which he knew he should do. The total was now up to six, and they were no closer to finding the murderer than they'd been when they started.

But this wasn't the right time to be thinking about death. At least, not the deaths of other people. For it was the first day of Rosh HaShanah, the beginning of the year 5754 according to the Jewish calendar, which numbered the years from the traditional date of the creation of the first human being. It was a day for looking back on your life, taking note of what you had done that was wrong, and making a conscious, earnest effort to change.

It wasn't a matter of feeling sorry for what you'd done. That was never more than a beginning. The important thing was the change. The Hebrew word usually translated as 'repentance' was *t'shuvah*, which actually meant 'to turn.' Turning from the wrong path onto the right path, Rabbi Hershkovitz had explained during the morning service.

Now, as he sat in his recliner following the delicious lunch Chayah had prepared, Schneider found himself thinking about the wrong lives. Not about his own. Not about the mistakes he had made, or about how to live his life in closer harmony with the divine, which was found in all things since all things came from God, but about where the investigation had gone wrong.

So far, the only suspect they had was Nathanson. And there was no real evidence to connect him with the case except for the probably mistaken statement of a single witness. A witness whose statement was contradicted by several others who actually *knew* Nathanson by name, and not just as a familiar-looking stranger seen in a parking lot. Otherwise, all they had was his general proximity to some of the older murders. And proximity could be nothing more than coincidence.

There was a soft rap on the door. Chayah put down the new copy of *The Jewish Homemaker* she was reading and went to answer it. This would be the first visitor of the afternoon, Schneider thought, though probably not the last.

Chayah returned to the living room with Rabbi Hershkovitz and his wife, and Schneider got up from his chair and went to greet them. He shook hands with the rabbi, and indicated the sofa. The rebbetzin didn't offer her hand; she came from a tradition where there was never any physical contact between unrelated men and women. Schneider, whose Orthodoxy was of the sort called "modern," was accustomed to shaking hands with everyone, but was quite willing to accommodate the wishes of those who followed the stricter practice.

In any case, even Emily Post had decreed that a man wasn't supposed to shake a woman's hand unless she offered it first.

"*L'shanah tovah tikateivu*—be inscribed for a good year," the Rabbi said, by way of greeting.

"And may you also be inscribed for a good year," Schneider responded. The traditional Rosh HaShanah greetings were based on an ancient tradition, which said that on Rosh HaShanah God opened three books in Heaven. In the first were written down all the evil people, who would die in the next year. In the second were the names of those good people who would certainly see the next Rosh HaShanah. And the third, which tradition said was the largest, contained the names of everyone whose fate was to remain undecided until Yom Kippur, ten days later. It was a further incentive to change for the better, since you never knew for sure in which book your name was written.

"So, you're having a good *Yom Tov*?" the rabbi asked.

The Alukam

"If I could just keep my mind where it belongs," Schneider said.

"And where is it instead?"

"Back at the office, I'm afraid. On a serial killer."

"So, Chayah," the rebbetzin said, "You'll show me the kitchen?" She had been a rabbi's wife for 52 years, and knew when it was time to leave her husband alone with someone.

After the women had left the room, Hershkovitz turned back to Schneider. "So, tell me about these murders."

"It doesn't seem an appropriate topic for *Yom Tov*," Schneider objected. Which was why it had been bothering him before the rabbi arrived.

"On Rosh HaShanah, you should be thinking about *t'shuva*, my friend. If there's something that keeps you from doing so, then you should maybe talk about it and try to resolve it. Then you can put your thoughts where they really belong, right?"

"I hadn't thought of it that way."

"So, you'll tell me?"

"I'm sure you've read about the killings. The papers have been calling them the 'beach vampire murders.'"

"Those. Yes, I've seen the stories. I haven't read them, though."

"So far, there have been six young women, all of them with dark hair, all of them tall and athletic, found dead on the beach. The two most recent victims were twin sisters, found together. All of the victims were dressed in bikinis. None of them had been raped, thought the twins had apparently had sex shortly before they were killed. And none of them had more than a couple of ounces of blood left in their bodies. That's about all we know to this point, except that the F.B.I. thinks these murders are connected with a large number of others, all over the country, going back to the late 1970s."

"And you haven't been able to figure out who is doing this. Is that the problem?"

"Exactly. I'm a cop—a detective. I'm supposed to be able to figure out why these things happen, who's doing them, and how to stop them."

"In the old country," the rabbi said, "the peasants would have seen this and said '*Upior*'—vampire. In America, of course, no one believes in such things."

"No. But the idea seems to work pretty well in newspaper headlines."

"You have no suspects?"

"We had one. But he was definitely at home when one of the murders was committed. I'm actually a little relieved, though I still can't help but think he's our best suspect, even with his alibi."

"This was a friend?"

"A relative. Some sort of cousin, though I'm not sure how close. Our families came from the same town in Poland, a couple of generations back. The man even looks like me."

The rabbi frowned. "Very much?"

"Like a twin, only younger. He's only 24, and I'm 38."

"Do you mind telling me his name?"

"Isaac Nathanson."

"Not a Schneider, then?"

"No. But he's sure we're related. The truth is, I only know my family history as far back as my grand-father. He was the first to leave Kapelskof and come to this country. Nathanson seems to have a lot more of the details at his fingertips. I'm not sure *why* I don't know these things. Maybe because none of my ancestors were particularly distinguished in learning. Or in anything else, for that matter. The family name is entirely appropriate—as far as I know my father was the first Schneider who didn't make his living with a needle and thread."

The rabbi was trying to think of something. A legend his wife, who had grown up in Kapelskof, had once mentioned.

"Have you ever heard of any cousins named Nathanson before?" he asked.

"Not that I remember. For that matter, no one in the family was ever called Isaac, either. I'm not sure why, but there is a definite family tradition that we *never* give that name to a son. Probably only in our own branch, though."

"And you don't know why?"

"No. If I had to guess, I imagine there was once an Isaac who did something the family disapproved of. Married a *shiksa*, something like that. So they just stopped using the name."

"Have you ever invited this cousin of yours for *shabbos*?"

"A couple of times. He hasn't come, though. Says he doesn't really believe in anything now."

"This is interesting, Reb Dovid." He smiled. "You've never studied Kabala, have you?"

"Not directly. I did some learning in *Tanya* once, but I'm not *chassidic*, and didn't find it overly compelling. Besides, I'm only 38, as I said, so it's still a couple of years until I'm really *allowed* to get into the mystical things." There was an old Jewish tradition which taught that a man was not to study Kabala—Jewish mysticism—until he was at least 40-years-old. The Sages believed that delving into those areas at too young an age could lead to madness.

The *Tanya* was a *chassidic* text, written by the first Rebbe of Lubavitch, which combined mysticism with a systematic study of traditional Jewish texts, and a concept for living in concord with the divine plan for the world. It was, literally, the only fully developed, written *chassidic* philosophy, since the *Alter Rebbe*, as he was called, was the only founder of a *chassidic* dynasty to write down his personal teachings.

"So," Rabbi Hershkovitz continued, "You know nothing of the *alukam*?"

Schneider vaguely remembered a passage in one of the Psalms that referred to such a creature. "Some sort of leech, isn't it?"

"That's how it's translated. As a horseleech, one of those parasites that fastens onto an animal's lips as it drinks. And sometimes it's translated as a beggar, which our *goyishe* friends also seem to think of as a leech of some sort. They've never quite come to the full recognition that, if *giving* charity is a divine commandment, then so is *receiving* it, otherwise how could anyone give? But the Kabala teaches that the *alukam* is a sort of demon, one that sucks blood, *like* a leech, but not a leech. But perhaps a vampire."

"That I'd never heard."

"Did you also know that, in our tradition, all vampires have red hair?"

"All?"

Rabbi Hershkovitz smiled. "That doesn't mean that all people with red hair are vampires, of course. King David had red hair, and he wasn't a vampire. You aren't one either. But a Jewish vampire will always have red hair. It has even been said that, if a suicide who was destined to become a vampire had dark hair when he died, it would turn red before he began to search for his victims."

Schneider, who was above all things a practical man, and didn't believe in monsters, still found the whole concept fascinating. "Any other characteristics?"

"There's the red hair. They would avoid the obviously holy, so they would not enter a synagogue, or touch a Torah scroll. I believe they might handle a *printed* Bible without harm, though. And the things the *goyim* think of as preventives, such as crosses, or holy water, wouldn't bother him. If the vampire lives in a house, he will place a *mezuzah* on the doorframe, like any other Jew, but the case will be empty. He sleeps in his coffin on *shabbos*, but otherwise he never rests."

"He could be out in the daylight?"

"He could."

"But how would someone become a vampire?"

"Suicide. He must be a red-haired man who commits deliberate suicide, and is buried without any ritual. If the appropriate prayers are recited over his grave, he will be bound in it, and cannot emerge. Also, exactly as in the *goyishe* vampire legends, he drinks the blood of his victims, and casts no reflection in a mirror."

"And his victims also become vampires?"

"No. That part *is* a myth. What has the victim done, except to be a victim? To become a vampire is a punishment for a grave sin. Tell me, which of the dietary laws do you suppose carries the gravest punishment?"

"Eating *trefe*, I suppose."

"So would most. But there are those who declare that it is eating meat with the blood still in it. Jews don't eat blood. The Torah forbids it. The blood of animals was reserved for the altar in sacrifices, and in ordinary food must be eliminated before the meat may be consumed. So what is the punishment for the total renunciation of all that is holy? This thing that we call suicide? It is to subsist *only* on blood. To be forced to drink blood in order to live. And to take other lives in the process."

Benjamin County Medical Examiner's Office

Margie Calloway frowned as she typed the report into her computer. This would be the seventh, she thought. And according to the newspapers, they were no closer to solving the case than they had been when they started.

Someone had evidently suspected Zack at one time, but she had been with him the whole night when the third victim was killed, so she knew better. Besides, he wasn't the sort. He was too gentle to harm anyone.

It never once occurred to her that her entire affair existed only in her mind. That the nights of passionate lovemaking had been hypnoti-cally-induced dreams. It certainly never occurred to her that her last session of "lovemaking" had not only been imaginary, but actually con-sisted of the details of something he had done with his *real* lover. Or that her mind was now linked to Nathanson's, so that he could discern her thoughts even at a considerable distance. She had never consciously re-vealed anything about the investigation to him—not that she knew all that much—but whatever she knew he learned as well.

Lockwood Acres

Sheriff Bill Mitchell was relaxing at home, after attending services at Temple El Emeth until about 1:00 o'clock. His wife, Tina, had put a chicken in the oven before they went to Temple, and they'd eaten it when they got home. None of this kosher nonsense for the Mitchells, of course; just a chicken from the Publix around the corner. Mitchell con-sidered the whole area of Jewish dietary law just another superstitious remnant of an ancient health code that had been made obsolete in light of modern science.

Besides, his wife's full name was Christina, and while she was content to attend services with him on the holidays and festivals, she had been raised as a Baptist and still was. It had surprised him, when he met her in college, just how dedicated a lot of Baptists seemed to be to the safety of Israel, and how much they cared for the Jewish people.

His brother-in-law, in fact, was a Baptist minister whose job at the moment involved running a center for Russian Jews in New York's Brighton Beach section. That the primary function of Jim Lindquist's center was actually to complete the work of the Soviet government by killing the Jewish souls of his refugees, then turning them into funda-mentalist Christians like himself, had somehow never dawned on his brother-in-law. Perhaps, because Mitchell was so thoroughly assimilated that he no longer thought like a Jew.

Mitchell was presently thinking about the beach murders. The desk had called him at home just before he left for the Temple to tell him a seventh body had been discovered. They couldn't reach Schneider, they told him. That didn't surprise him; the man was a fanatic and shut off his phones on the Sabbath and holidays.

And, unlike Mitchell, Schneider would also be out of touch tomorrow. Like many Reform congregations, El Emeth observed only a single day of Rosh HaShanah; the Orthodox, including Schneider, observed two days.

He was tempted to send a car over to Schneider's house and roust him out, but suspected that there would be no point. The killer had left no clues in the first six cases, so why should he suddenly get careless on the seventh? And if there was no vital need, beyond appeasing the County Commission, Schneider would certainly argue that his civil rights were being violated and would probably be able to convince a hearing examiner. Sheriff Reilly had screwed things up forever by accommodating the duty schedule to Schneider's archaic religious beliefs.

Port Morrow Beach

Nathanson was on the phone with a real estate broker in Toledo. He had very good instincts, and something was telling him that it was just about time to move on. Time, also, to become someone else for a while. The days when he could move every few years, becoming his own son in a new community, were probably ending with modern technology.

He had recently found himself somewhat envying the character in that Christopher Lambert movie, who also lived forever, but wasn't forced to kill people on a regular basis—at least, not anyone who wasn't trying to kill *him*—and so could remain essentially anonymous. Nathanson didn't have that option.

Nor could he take the television route of the tortured vampire, yearning to live a normal life and subsisting on the bottled blood of cattle. The reality was that there was no nourishment for him in anything but human blood. His condition was a *punishment*, not a disease. When God decided to inflict a punishment, there were no loopholes once you passed the border. He would remain as he was until the Messiah came, or until someone was able to confine his body to the grave and release his spirit from its prison.

The Messiah, he was sure, would come first. It seemed unlikely that anyone today even possessed the knowledge that would be required to release him. And, except on the Sabbath, he had no particular desire to be released.

He felt Dinah's hands resting on his shoulders. Smiling, he reached up with his left hand, placing it over her right. She laced her fingers through his.

"Yes," he said. "That sounds very nice. I like the idea of acreage and woods. My wife and I prefer a degree of seclusion."

Dinah squeezed his hand.

"Yes, everything seems to be correct. My attorney, Mr. Nathanson, has gone over the contract and tells me everything is perfectly in order. Just send the final details to him, and he'll have the checks drawn up for the closing."

A few minutes later he hung up the phone. "We have a house," he announced. "Fifteen acres, with the house in the middle of the property, completely surrounded by woodland. The house was built in 1850, but the agent assures me that the last owners had the amenities brought up to date. New wiring and plumbing, an updated heating system, but all, he says, installed so that the appearance of the interior remains true to the period of the house. Five bedrooms, a formal dining room, a large study, and three bathrooms. And since I assured him that I have no intention of developing the property, he was able to talk the owner down to $800,000. Apparently this is an important factor for the current owners. There's been a lot of development going on in the area, and they want to preserve the estate in its present condition."

"I like old things, too," Dinah said. "I'd be perfectly comfortable in an old manor house."

"Well, I think we can reassure the sellers we won't be subdividing the property. Considering what we are, having an isolated house should be an advantage." He laughed. "And as for the price—it's not like it's going to hurt my cash situation, is it?"

"He probably thinks you're some sort of drug dealer, paying cash for a house," Dinah said.

"He *thinks* I'm a very canny investor. I've built up a rather nice port-folio for young James Aston over the last few years, and all he had to do to confirm it was to run a normal credit check. Isaac Nathanson will just sort of vanish for a while, except as a signature on the odd document, and Jim and Deena Aston will slowly take over his holdings."

Chapter Twenty-Eight
Friday, September 17, 1993

Cape Marl

Rebbetzin Sarah Hershkovitz carried the newspaper into her husband's study and placed it in the middle of his desk. He looked up, somewhat annoyed. It was the afternoon of the second day of Rosh HaShanah, and he normally did not allow the outside world to intrude on his study.

More so, it was also a Friday, which meant that as soon as Rosh HaShanah ended, the Sabbath would begin. At this time of day, it was unusual to find his wife outside the kitchen.

"Are you sure we picked the right place to retire, Dov?" she asked. "You see—another woman murdered on the Beach!"

The rabbi glanced at the headline. **BEACH VAMPIRE KILLS AGAIN**, it read.

"So is he killing elderly women, Sarah? Why do you worry about this? It's a sad thing, to be sure, but I don't think we are personally in any danger."

"And what about Elisheva? She's been talking about coming over from Miami for a visit. Would she be in danger?" Elisheva was their grand-daughter, a beautiful young woman of 23. She was very much the physical type the killer seemed to prefer. Tall, fit, and with shoulder-length black hair.

"I tell you, Dov," Sarah went on, "I don't like this. It reminds me too much of the stories my *bubbeh* used to tell us when we were children in Kapelskof. *Gevalt! Itzak Rottkup, dem Schnaydersohn bist hier!*'

Hershkovitz nodded. He'd been trying to think of that before and couldn't. It was a legend confined to his wife's little town, with its picturesque castle and ancient ghetto wall. Itzak *Rottkup, dem Schnayderssohn* – Redheaded Itzak, the tailor's son. A story to frighten children, he'd always thought. Pure *bubbeh meiseh*—old wive's tales, they'd say in English. An appropriate name, for it was Sarah's *bubbeh* her grandmother—who had taught her the stories.

But it was the nature of the stories that disturbed him. *Dem Schnayderssohn vill dein Blut antrinken.* The tailor's son will drink your blood. The stories were the remnants of a vampire legend unique to that town.

"What was the story, Sarah?"

"Another girl killed on the Beach," she began.

"No. No, not that story. The old one—Itzak *Rottkup.*"

"Nonsense, Dov. A legend."

"Indulge me."

His wife shrugged, "It was just a story to frighten children, Dov. A tailor's son killed himself by jumping from the old synagogue, and shortly after that it was said that a vampire killed a number of the *goyim* in Kapelskof. And then the deaths stopped. According to the stories, the dead *goyim* were the men who had murdered the rabbi and a number of other Jews in a pogrom on the day that Itzak died."

"But he was long gone, wasn't he? When you heard the stories, I mean."

"They say he vanished before the beginning of the 18th Century. Or, at least, the murders had stopped by then."

Hershkovitz nodded. Was there any basis to fact in the story? The suicide was almost certainly factual. After all, even the grave of a suicide was marked, and since the graves were set apart from the rest of the burials in the cemetery, you always knew who the suicides had been.

"Did your *bubbeh* offer any proof for these tales?"

"What proof? It's a legend. Oh, I saw his grave in the old cemetery, but what does that mean? Besides, read the paper—the police say this 'beach vampire' is clearly a lunatic, not a real vampire."

The Alukam

So there really *was* a grave, Hershkovitz thought. But you'd hardly build up a legend of a vampire without a real suicide to attach it to, would you? As for the rest of the story, it could have been nothing more than a coincidence. If several murderers were, themselves, murdered shortly after a suicide, even the *goyim* would think of a vampire. Probably they would be the first to think of one. Such things were more common in *their* folklore. The kabalistic references to such creatures were obscure even for students of that difficult subject.

But then the murders had stopped. The rabbi knew that most of the Christian legends were nonsense. You couldn't kill a vampire by driving a stake through his heart. Only certain prayers would bind him in his grave.

Had someone known those prayers? Had Red-headed Itzak been destroyed in the late 17th Century? Or was there another possible explanation? Had he simply taken the same route as so many other Polish Jews over the years, and emigrated to the west? To America, perhaps? Hershkovitz didn't believe in disturbing the dead under any circumstances, but he found himself thinking it would be very interesting to see if there was still a body in that Polish grave.

What was it Schneider had told him? Their only suspect had been a redhaired Jew called Isaac—which was nothing more than the English form of the Yiddish Itzak. And that this Isaac was Schneider's cousin. A distant cousin, whose family came from the same town in Poland. The same town, the rabbi had already noticed, where his own wife had been born.

There was also, it seemed, a tradition in Schneider's family that male children were never to be named Isaac. Was there a connection to this story? Schneider was Yiddish for 'tailor,' and Itzak had been called *Schnayderssohn*—tailor's son. Was Itzak *Rottkup* the reason for that peculiar family tradition? And, more importantly, was it possible that the same Itzak was now residing on Port Morrow Beach?

"Sarah, are you already prepared for the Sabbath?"

The rebbetzin frowned. "All you can think about is food?"

"I can think about other things as well, my dear. But there are things I need to study now. Who knows—perhaps I'll find something that will settle your fears, eh?"

Chapter Twenty-Nine
Saturday, September 18, 1993

Cape Marl

Two of the men recited the final mourner's *Kaddish,* and the entire congregation chanted the *Adon Olam,* concluding the service for this Sabbath of Repentance. The special *haftarah* from Hosea was a reminder that God would always accept a sincerely repentant sinner back into the fold.

The rabbi walked out with Schneider. "I need to speak with you," he told the detective.

"What do you need, Rabbi?"

"I need you to take me for a ride this afternoon."

"On *shabbos?*" Schneider asked. With the exception of once during a hurricane, he had never, in his life, driven a car on the Sabbath, and he was pretty sure that the rabbi had never ridden in one on that day.

"When human life is at stake, we may ride on *shabbos,*" the rabbi said. It was a rule that was usually traced to the time of the Maccabees. At the beginning of that rebellion, the Syrian-Greek forces of the tyrant Antiochus Epiphanes had learned to attack on the Sabbath, knowing that the Jews would not violate the sanctity of the day by taking up arms. Before long, a rule was instituted that the saving of a life took precedence over the observance of a particular Sabbath. But the principle upon which that ruling was based was ancient, having been brought down from Sinai by Moses.

"Where are we going?"

"To your cousin's house."

"Why?"

"You saw the newspaper yesterday?"

"Sure."

"Then you know that your killer has struck again. I read the article, this time. I can't be positive, but I believe your first instinct about this man was right."

"He had an alibi for the third killing. A very good alibi."

"And what about the others? For these he also had proof of being somewhere else? We will go to see him, and if he is waiting to greet us at the door, then we will smile, say we have come to visit, and wait for *shabbos* to end and go home. But if he is not there, we will also wait, eh?"

"If you say so."

Port Morrow Beach

Nathanson could hear the voices in his house. Two men. The first he recognized as his grand-nephew, the detective. The other was a stranger; an elderly man, by the sound of his voice, who spoke with a slight accent.

They were moving about in the house, probably searching it. He didn't think they would find anything, though. The kitchen island was securely fastened from below. Unless you released the latches from the bottom—or knew where the remote switch was concealed in the bedroom—you would never be able to tell that the island wasn't nailed securely to the floor.

•   •   •

"There's no one here," Schneider said.

"His car is in the garage, though, isn't it?"

"Yes." Only Nathanson's Mustang was there, Schneider had noticed. Not the rental that had been driven by the Gehritty woman, who was obviously out for the day.

Schneider was looking at a notepad by the telephone. It was blank, but there was an impression from the previous page. Holding it up to the light at an oblique angle, he could read a phone number, and what looked like the description of a house and property. The area code was for northern Ohio.

"Looks as if he might be getting ready to move," Schneider said.

The rabbi had unscrewed the plug from the bottom of the *mezuza* case on the back doorpost and looked inside. "Empty," he said.

He opened the door. "Come, Dovid. We will look outside."

They walked completely around the house. There were shrubs planted close to the building, but if you got down on your knees you could see under it. Only sand, as far as Schneider could tell.

"You feel like crawling under a house?" Rabbi Hershkovitz asked. For an elderly man whose entire life seemed to revolve around the hundreds of religious books in his library, he had so far shown himself to be remarkably fit.

"There could be snakes," Schneider pointed out.

"So we pay attention to what we're doing, and if we see one we don't annoy him."

"What are we looking for, Rabbi?"

"If I see it, I'll know it."

Schneider found a place where the plantings were spaced sufficiently to crawl between them. The area beneath the house would have been just high enough to duck walk, if he'd been so inclined, but it was easier to crawl.

"Here!" the rabbi called, pointing up.

Schneider crawled over to join him. Above them, the floorboards were missing from a space about three feet long between the exposed floor joists. Heavy bolts secured something to the space. They could be operated manually, he noticed, but there also seemed to be a provision for opening the bolts electrically, with wires stapled to the bottom of the floor joists and running off toward the front corner of the house. The general area of the master bedroom, he thought.

"What's this?" he asked.

"Open it and see," the rabbi suggested.

Schneider reached up and retracted the bolts. There was a handle at one side and he pulled on it, swinging the island away from the access hole. He was back in the kitchen.

"Now what?" he asked.

The rabbi smiled. "Now," he said, "I think we have to violate a few more *shabbos* laws. See if you can find a shovel."

•   •   •

Nathanson could hear the sounds of a shovel digging into the sand above his coffin. Now what? he wondered. The sun was still well up in the afternoon sky, and he would remain utterly incapable of any movement until it had sunk below the horizon. That would not happen until 7:29 pm. Even then, his movements would be limited for another 45 minutes, for the Sabbath always lingered a while after sunset.

He should have dug the grave deeper. But the house was too close to the Gulf of Mexico, and the water table was too high for a deep grave. None of the homes in Benjamin County had basements, and the high water table was the reason for that stricture. The water was never more than about seven feet down, even during the dry season, and it frequently rose higher. High enough that empty swimming pools had been known to float out of the ground.

In another community he might have dug the grave so deep that no one would ever think to dig down that far in searching for it. He could, after all, pass through 30 *feet* of earth as easily as through a few inches. Or perhaps he should have covered his coffin with several feet of heavy rock. Here, the top of his coffin was only about three feet beneath the surface, buried in nothing more resistant than sand.

Yet there was also that within him that hoped they *would* find the coffin, and somehow manage to destroy his body. If that could be done, his spirit would be released at last, and the term of his earthly punishment would end.

But only if the ones digging knew what to do. He hoped they hadn't been influenced by too many vampire movies. The only thing driving a stake through his heart would accomplish was to inflict a great deal of pain, and hold him temporarily in his grave, until his body could heal itself and force the stake back out. Even cutting off his head wouldn't suffice. His body would simply reassemble itself, and he would arise after a time, hungrier than ever.

And what would Dinah be thinking? With her coffin separated from his by a mere two feet, she would hear the digging just as clearly as he did. She would know that they believed her to have gone somewhere, since her car wasn't in the garage. If they did something stupid with a wooden stake, would she then rise up at the end of the day and attack them in revenge? Or would she have the sense to go into hiding until he recovered, then continue as they had planned?

•   •   •

The shovel scraped on wood, and Schneider set about uncovering a wide, flat board. "I've found something," he said.

"Uncover it," the rabbi said. "We need to see if he's inside."

Schneider kept at it, wondering if he had somehow entered one of his own dreams. There wasn't the slightest chance they'd find Nathanson in this box—he couldn't think of it as a coffin yet. That sort of thing only happened in old movies of the sort he'd snuck off to watch when he was a teenager.

Finally, the lid was uncovered, and Schneider stepped out of the hole, using the edge of the shovel to pry up the lid. He moved it aside, and there was Nathanson, garbed in what looked like white pajamas with a long, white robe over them. But the legs were sewn shut at the ends, with strips of cloth around the ankles. These were the normal shrouds in which Jewish men were buried. He was absolutely motionless. Not even a slight movement of his chest to indicate that he was breathing.

"*Alukam*" the rabbi said quietly. "Vampire."

Schneider looked up at him. "Now what?"

"Now we have to hope we are very lucky, and the name he is using is his real name."

"What?"

"To keep a vampire in his grave requires that several prayers be said, including the *El Moleh Rachamim*, and that prayer, along with at least four others, requires the use of his Hebrew name. Isaac Nathanson sounds like a translation of Yitzchok ben Nosson. But what if either this man, or his father, had an additional name? We are praying for the repose of a particular person, and it will do no good if we pray for it in the name of a *different* person."

"How can you be sure you've got it right?"

"The sun will go down, *shabbos* will_end, and he will remain where he is. If we're wrong, of course, he will get up and very probably kill us." The rabbi found himself suddenly wishing that his wife had remembered the exact inscription on Itzak *Rottkup*'s tombstone. That would have been the name they needed.

Schneider looked at his watch. "We still have three hours before sunset," he said. "I think it's time we went through his personal papers."

They found the old prayer book in the back of a cabinet, about ten minutes before sunset. The leather cover was badly deteriorated, but the pages were in excellent condition. Books printed before the 1840s generally survived quite well, as long as they were stored under reasonable conditions, for the paper in those days was made of old rags, and lacked the high acid content of the wood pulp papers that came into use after 1840, guarantying that the majority of books printed after that date would self-destruct in a few years.

"Here," the rabbi said, "on the flyleaf. '*For my son, Itzak, from his poppa, Nosson Sh'muel ben Pinchas Chayim, for his bar mitzvah, Shabbos Parashas Shemini, 29 Nisan 5433.*' Your so-called 'cousin' had his bar mitzvah a little over 320 years ago." He smiled. "But now we know his name. And now I can say the prayers."

They walked back into the kitchen, and the rabbi took out a small notebook. He had written out the prayers for confining a vampire in his coffin, since they were not to be found in the standard *madrich*, or rabbi's manual, which he would normally read from at a funeral.

"*El moleh rachamim, shochein bam'romim...*" he began. "God, full of compassion who dwells on high..."

He could feel the light fading, the sun sinking beneath the straight horizon of the Gulf of Mexico. But his body wasn't responding as it should. The Sabbath stasis continued to grip his limbs. And as the prayers continued, the elderly rabbi reading from his notebook over his body, Nathanson could actually feel his spirit beginning to separate from the physical shell it had occupied since 1660.

•   •   •

Schneider and the rabbi watched intently as the first three stars appeared in the sky, and the Sabbath definitely ended. The body in the coffin remained inert. In the fading light, neither of them noticed a grey mist that rose from the sand alongside his grave, flowing rapidly away along the ground and out from under the house.

On the beach, at the rear of the house, Dinah resumed her solid form. She could see the two men in the kitchen. Nathanson's coffin had been buried directly beneath the access in the kitchen floor, and after building it he had placed hers directly beside his own.

It was frightening just how much like Itzak the detective looked. But Itzak was truly dead now. Even though the binding prayers had been read over *him*, and the rabbi had used *his* name, Dinah felt oddly weakened by them. No stronger than an ordinary mortal. She would have to feed very soon, she thought, and then it would definitely be time to move on and adopt another identity in a new city. Her only reason for remaining here was resting in that shallow grave, and would never rise again.

•   •   •

It was very much like the 'near death' experiences Nathanson had read about. With a curious feeling of relief, his spirit lifted out of his body, and he found himself hovering over the scene. The detective looking on nervously as the rabbi concluded the prayers. Both men looking at the kitchen clock as it ticked off the final minutes of the Sabbath. Probably wondering if their praying had accomplished its purpose, or if he would rise up to kill them in a few more minutes.

Even as he watched, his body began to dry out and crumble, the flesh falling from the bones in horrid chunks that turned to dust as they struck the wooden boards that made up the bottom of the coffin.

And then he was rising through the ceiling. Behind the house, standing naked on the beach—the burial shrouds remained in the coffin when a vampire became insubstantial, and at the moment there was no way for her to get back into the house and dress herself—he could see Dinah watching the house. She looked beautiful, and frightened, and angry, and he hoped that she would restrain herself. Schneider was only an ordinary cop, but this rabbi was clearly a kabalist of considerable skill and power.

Nor did Nathanson feel any anger toward the men. As his spirit floated upward, he could hear the sounds of the angels, singing their litany of praises to God, and shuttling back and forth between the physical and spiritual realms, conveying the prayers of the devout to the heavenly throne.

But there was another sound. Voices, each asking questions. And the first asked, "Did you set aside a time each day for Torah study?" And the answer came back, "Not since 5444," in his voice, but without his conscious response.

And another voice asked, "Did you kill Stanislaw the butcher?" And again his own voice, saying, "Yes." And on and on, each time the question, and each time the answer and he knew now, of course, never the *right* answer.

For in the few minutes it took his spirit to rise into the upper atmosphere, and there to pass the barrier between the physical and spiritual worlds, he realized the ultimate truth. That for a suicide, to become a vampire was *not* a punishment, but a final test. That if he had resisted the overpowering impulse to kill, to drink the blood of his fellow human beings, even to drink any blood at all, his sojourn in his resuscitated corpse would have ended at the turn of the year, and on the first Rosh HaShanah after his death his spirit would have been released to return to its maker.

Then he felt himself descending, knowing that he had failed. For a moment he thought he was to be placed back into his body another time. But then he realized he was passing through the broad, flat roof of Benjamin Memorial Hospital, and there was an operating room, with a doctor drawing a lifeless baby from the cut-open womb of a plain-looking young woman, while an anxious young man stood back, watching.

He could see into the opened womb, where a pure, white light was rapidly fading, and an angel, radiant and pure, rising up above the people in the room, while a spirit—the spirit that had been placed into the newborn infant 60 days after conception—rose up with the angel that had instructed it in the womb. One of those pure souls so attached to God that it couldn't bear to actually live in the physical world, and so would depart at birth to return to Him. The people in the room could see neither the light, nor the angel, nor the baby's spirit. Nathanson could.

And it was at that moment that he knew his fate. For his spirit to finally come to dwell in the next world, it would have to live the life of an observant Jew in *this* world. That was the sentence of the heavenly tribunal. And, because his was a *Jewish* soul, only living a proper *Jewish* life would bring eventual reunion with God.

As the baby's original spirit departed, his entered the tiny body, and with that act his consciousness of who he had been was annihilated. All that remained of Itzak ben Reb Nosson Sh'muel was a tiny spark that would one day remind him that his was a Jewish spirit, and that for redemption to come he would have to pass that final test and live as a Jew *should* live.

•   •   •

Schneider filled in the hole beneath the house and replaced the shovel in the garage. Then he had to go back under the house, pull the island back into place, secure the bolts, and crawl out the way he had originally entered.

The rabbi was waiting in the car.

"The murders are over," the rabbi said.

"How am I going to explain this?" Schneider asked.

"If I were you, I wouldn't even try. The man will disappear, and the murders will end when he does. After a time your investigation will conclude that you were wrong, that this Nathanson fellow really *was* the killer, and that he realized you were closing in on him and ran away."

"I feel like I've killed somebody."

"You haven't. He's been dead for centuries. All we did was confine his body to the grave, and release his spirit to go on to where it should have been gone in the 17th Century."

"You think he's at rest?"

"I think so. Yes."

•   •   •

As the car pulled out of the driveway, Dinah emerged from where she had been hiding in the bushes. The doors were bolted, but there was an unlocked window on the south side, and she was able to climb in through that. Her clothes and purse were still in the bedroom closet.

Benjamin Memorial Hospital, Port Morrow

For a moment the doctor had been worried. The emergency C-Section had got the baby out, but it had been unresponsive. The doctor was deathly afraid of a stillbirth. Like all obstetricians, he paid an enormous sum every year for malpractice insurance. People no longer accepted the idea that babies were sometimes born dead, and would sue when it happened.

But then the baby had started to move, and a moment later it began to cry. The doctor smiled and handed the child to the nurse. Now he just had to wait a minute until the body's mechanisms closed off the blood supply through the cord and began to draw oxygen from the air.

"Congratulations," he said. "You have a fine baby boy."

Reverend Harold Jones smiled through the surgical mask at his wife. "You hear that? A boy! Jesus be praised!"

"And he'll grow up just like his father," Carla Jones responded, rather weakly.

The last conscious thought Itzak's spirit had, before his personality completely vanished, was that if admission to the next world meant his spirit must live the life of an observant Jew, God was throwing him quite a curve with this family.

Port Morrow International Airport

Dinah Gehritty walked through the jetway and onto the plane. The flight to Atlanta would be the last time she would use that particular set of credit cards. Dinah Gehritty was about to vanish from the American scene.

In the airport parking lot, a young Marine corporal was sprawled across a mattress in the back of a van, his trousers down around his ankles. When his body was discovered, the Medical Examiner would eventually note that there were puncture marks in his shriveled organ, and that his body had been drained of all its blood. In his final orgasm, the Marine had ejaculated his entire life.

And Dinah, who was about to become Audrey Martin, was soon winging her way northward, her strength restored, thinking about the day when she would be able to return to Port Morrow for a few days and take her revenge.

9 781932 606027